MARI

Prologue: May 1986

Ned Braley gasped as he stared in horror at what lay at his feet. Not this. He'd not expected *this*...

It had seemed a simple job, and Ned liked those. A reliable tip-off and an easy way in. Easy? Blimey, that kitchen window left a lot to be desired, the catch faulty, the wood in no great shape; the sort of thing that made his work a doddle.

And the job was easy, the way she'd left all that stuff lying around.

Or should have been.

Because he didn't want any part of *this*...

It wasn't the way he'd worked all these years. He'd never laid a finger on anybody. Easy way in, easy pickings, easy way out. And nobody the wiser, the stuff passed on to one of his numerous anonymous contacts. Then, when Burge finally came calling: "Wasn't me, Des. Tucked up in bed and dead to the world, me. Can't do the late nights no more."

Not half he couldn't.

Ned tried to gather his wits. He had to get out of there quick. He'd picked up some decent-looking stash, filled his pockets, but now he had to put distance between himself and – *that.*

Just as he was straddling the window frame and wondering if he'd left any tell-tale traces – although he never slipped up there, always wore gloves, always ensured he hadn't left a footprint in a border – he heard a noise, a movement. Someone else present? He'd been warned about this. If someone was there, saw him, told Burge – blimey, it'd be all up with him then, for sure.

With sweat streaming down his face and his body uncomfortably sticky beneath his elderly, baggy suit in the warm spring night, Ned Braley panicked. He blundered down off the sill and landed in a heap, scrambled up and ran.

Running wasn't going to do much for him, at his age and in his condition. But he ran, panting, wheezing, his legs like lead. He was out on the drive. First base. Now to get up past the bend in the road, take a breather, light a fag and stroll back home as if nothing had happened.

As if nothing had happened? That was a laugh.

A bitter one.

Ned ran across the road, taking a hurried backward glance, in case someone had clocked him. He was only aware of the car as it rounded the bend. Not as if it was going fast, but he was rooted to the spot, gasped again as he stood transfixed in the inimical glare of its headlights…

1

August 1986

I was feeling pretty ordinary and rather useless, as I stood on the platform at Liverpool Street, awaiting the arrival of a Circle Line train.

As good a time as any, I suppose, to save a man's life.

I'd just come back from a three-month tour of drab north-west theatres, performing uninspiring supporting roles in several listless plays. I'd been in the acting profession for fifteen years and, at thirty-six, wondered where it was taking me. I'd embarked on the tour in possession of a steady girlfriend, Calista Payne, who'd just been signed up for a leading role in the West End. End of relationship.

And I'd lately come from a visit to the cramped office of my theatrical agent, Eric Di Mario, a kindly man, but almost as useless as I felt; actually, more so. He'd sat tilted back in his chair, studying me ruminatively, his horsey smile and affable voice designed to be encouraging.

"Nothing I can offer you just yet, Glen my friend." His tone suggested it might be a matter of minutes rather than months before he could. "But I'm working on something and, believe me, my lovely boy, it's going to be BIG."

We refer to him as Eric Dim in the trade: he's way out of touch with reality. I informed him that I'd be away for the next two weeks, visiting my sister. I left him her telephone number; not with much hope, I admit. He asked how Calista was. I told him: in the West End, implying that I could use a few weeks there myself. It didn't filter through. I hadn't expected it to.

Creaking into action, Eric roused himself from behind his desk, all five feet six of him, electric blue suit, swished-back hair (his own?) and ever-beaming smile. He accompanied me to the door, two whole yards away, a reassuring arm round my midriff. As so often, the brush-off. We exchanged the usual pleasantries and, holdall in hand, I set off for Liverpool Street station to save a man's life.

*

The platform heaved with humanity. It was August, and the football season had just kicked off, which, along with the cinemas and theatres disgorging their matinée audiences, went some way to explaining the throbbing press of bodies. There was a lot of jostling, as more people poured on to the platform, and I found myself hustled towards its edge, irrespective of the yellow line and 'Mind the Gap' exhortations, just as the train thundered out of the tunnel and into the station.

Suddenly, right beside me, a bulbous shape lurched forward. He teetered on the edge for a split-second, a blink away from toppling helplessly into the train's path. Without really knowing what I was doing, I flung out a hand, latched on to a shoulder and tugged hard. The train squealed in anguish, trundling to a halt, and, as the unseeing hordes piled through the peevishly flapping doors, a pale, pudgy face gazed up soulfully into mine.

I hauled him back from the edge, sat him on a seat on the now deserted platform, while the train groaned away to be swallowed into the black tunnel. I was still clinging to my new friend's arm, as I lowered myself on to the seat beside him. His eyes, wide and worried, were fixed on my face. He was wheezing horribly, and it took a few minutes before he was able to speak.

"M-my goodness," he stammered at last. "My dear young man. I – I am massively in your debt." He held out a hand, white and trembling. "Roland Pettifer, my good sir. At your service. Thank you so much for your prompt action. You saved my life."

I immediately recognised his reason for having stumbled. His breath was one hundred per cent proof. I shook the proffered hand. "Glen Preston," I replied. "My pleasure."

He was a tubby little man, probably well past sixty, with a face which reminded me of a dyspeptic toad. He wore a linen suit, baggy and creased with wear, and what might have been an MCC tie, somewhat twisted after his brush with death. I suspected that his grey hair, wispy and ruffled, might once have been covered by a panama hat, which had probably ended being mashed by the train.

He hadn't been far away from joining it.

Almost restored to life, Roland Pettifer nodded towards a train which was just rumbling in. "Better cut along," he said.

I helped him to his feet, and together we squeezed into a carriage. It was already crowded, and there was standing room only. He and I were crushed unwholesomely together, and even though I enjoyed the occasional scotch, I didn't much relish it this early in the evening or at second-hand. I asked him where he was heading.

"Paddington, young man. Your destination too?" He'd regained a voice, deep and confident.

I nodded stiffly. In that sardine tin, any movement was difficult.

"That's right. I'm heading for my sister's. A little place called Selsby-on-Thames."

He stared at me pop-eyed. "Lord save us! Coincidences abound. I've lived there for the last forty years, as well as before the war."

"Then you're bound to know her. She's been there almost ten years herself. Rosalind Blakeman."

"Ah, I know Rosalind. We're both good patrons of the Frobisher Arms; perhaps too good." He was smiling, displaying a mouth full of questionable teeth, which informed me that he was a smoker as well. "Still, we're both scribblers, and our excuse would be that we're driven to it."

"So, you're a writer too, Mr Pettifer?"

"Call me Roland, I insist." He was clearly back to form, his earlier, near-fatal mishap forgotten. "Oh, I work for the local rag, the *Selsby Bugle.* Done so for years. Chief Reporter." His expression clouded slightly. "S'pose I'd be considered a dinosaur these days. However, my dear Mr Prestwick…"

"Preston. Glen."

"My dear Prestwick, journalism's in my blood, and there's nothing which beats the thrill of a good story. For me, the old ways are the only ways."

The train squealed into Paddington and emptied within seconds. With Roland bustling along beside me, I made my way to the escalator, and we ascended to the main concourse. Roland thrust a finger at the destination boards.

"We'll catch the express to Reading and change there for Selsby," he said. "Otherwise, it'll take all evening."

Personally, I'd have settled for the stopping train over the express, so that I could get my thoughts in order. But it soon became clear that Roland preferred the express because it had a bar.

"Could do with a snifter." In my opinion, he'd been 'snifting' for most of the day. "Bit of a shock, you know. But it'd have been a whole lot worse, young Prestwick, if it hadn't been for you."

The train was packed and, despairing of finding a seat, I followed Roland along to the bar. On our way there, a man squeezed past us, heading in the opposite direction. He greeted Roland amiably.

"Ah, Morgan," Roland responded. "Good afternoon. Get you a drink?"

"Thanks, Roly, but must press on. Just seen someone I know."

He switched me a grin as he passed, and I got the impression of a sociable type, fortyish, with a thatch of fading blond hair and a thin moustache.

"That's Morgan Tambling," Roland explained. "Landlord of the Frobisher in Selsby." He shot me a twinkling glance. "He and I are well acquainted."

I didn't doubt it. Once at the bar, I succumbed to Roland's offer of a drink and asked for a small light ale. He ordered himself a double scotch, which came as no surprise.

He'd sunk two more by the time we blundered off the train at Reading. The connection to Selsby was waiting and, ahead of us, I noticed Tambling striding towards the front coach. I steered Roland to the rear one. The step almost defeated him, but I managed to bundle him in and install him in the nearest seat.

The journey to Selsby didn't take long, and Roland dozed for most of it. Once we were on the platform, I told him I ought to phone my sister, as I hadn't visited in a while and, in the gathering dusk, wasn't sure of the way to her bungalow.

"Oh, telephone from the Frobisher, old chap," he declared airily. "Indeed, I'll call in there with you. Why not ask her to join us?"

I pretended I hadn't heard the invitation, concentrating instead on persuading him to walk in something resembling a straight line. Morgan Tambling, who must have seen it all before, had skipped off the train before us and was walking at pace towards the lights of the village.

The Frobisher Arms stood a couple of hundred yards beyond the station on the main road. It was a former coaching inn with bright stonewashed walls, surrounded by a tall laurel hedge, which separated it from the road. A large car park lay at the front, while patio doors to the side opened on to a beer garden and children's play area.

The interior was well-lit, with plush leather seating around the walls. A restaurant area was situated to the side of the bar, with twenty or more tables. There was already a sprinkling of customers, giving the impression that the pub did a steady trade.

As we walked in, I took out my wallet, but Roland forestalled me. "Won't hear of it, old chap. You saved my life, and this is a small enough gesture of thanks."

We approached the bar, behind which stood a woman of thirty-something, attractive in a lacy white blouse which displayed her attributes. Her shoulder-length hair might have been a shade more auburn than originally. She met us with a wide smile and welcoming manner; but the gleam in her ice-blue eyes informed me that she missed very little.

Roland returned the greeting with a contented grin. "Ah, Lorna, my dear, what a welcome sight you are. A small light ale for this young man, and a double usual for yours truly, if you will."

"Certainly, Roly." Lorna paused to flick a smile in my direction, deftly summing me up, before she turned away to dispense the drinks.

At that moment, Tambling appeared through a door behind the bar. He was dressed in a crisp white polo shirt and blue jeans which seemed a little tight. I suspected that he'd changed his clothes; also, that he liked to appear younger than his age. He was tall, broad-shouldered and looked in reasonable shape, although I dared say that in time he might run to fat.

"Ah, Morgan, my boy," Roland greeted him. "We meet again. Dare say you went along to see the play, too? It was very well attended."

Tambling appeared a mite uneasy. "Er, no, Roly. I went to see it earlier in the run."

Lorna, meanwhile, had returned to place our drinks on the bar. She was smiling as she relieved Roland of some money, and I recognised its bitter edge. "Yes, dear Kirstie'll be back with us next week," she observed tartly. "No need then to be popping down to London quite so frequently."

Tambling missed the disdainful glance she threw him, but I imagined he sensed it, for he'd turned away to greet a couple who'd just entered and directed them through to the restaurant, which was where they'd been heading anyway.

Having succeeded in embarrassing her husband, Lorna turned to me, this time smiling fulsomely, as I picked up our drinks from the bar. She nodded towards Roland, who'd parked himself at a table close by.

"Not seen you in here before," she remarked. "You a friend of Roly's?"

"Er, I met him on the train," I replied. "I'm in Selsby visiting my sister, Roz Blakeman."

"Oh, I know Roz." Lorna's response was short on enthusiasm. I suspected she and Roz didn't get on particularly well, for whatever reason.

"Glen Preston," I added, including Morgan, who was hovering nearby, in the introduction.

"You're the actor, aren't you?" he cut in. "Roz mentioned it."

"That's right," I grinned back. "Just off tour and needing a couple of weeks holiday."

"Let's hope you have a good break, then," Morgan said, Lorna having moved along the bar to serve a new arrival while bequeathing me a smile which certainly didn't lack promise.

Roland was grinning mischievously as I joined him. "Oops! May have dropped poor old Morgan in it there." His voice was low and shameless. "But he *will* gallivant around. Surprised Lorna hasn't done something about it before now."

We sat and chatted for a while, long enough for him to need a refill. I gave him a few brief details of my not-so-illustrious acting career and asked him about his job with the local paper. Was he the editor as well as the chief reporter?

"Heavens, no." His tone was dismissive. "A newshound through and through, my dear fellow. Never known any different and never will."

I'd given him an open invitation, and he grasped it eagerly, his voice eloquent with scotch, his words tinged with bitterness.

"As for editing – pah! We've a woman editor now old Barnfleet's gone to glory. And it's no job for a woman! I've shored up that rag for years, gave up a career with the *Daily Post* to come back and bail 'em out. And what's more, *I* was the one who taught her all she knows."

He was beginning to get a little loud, but the Frobisher's customers seemed quite used to it. Only Morgan Tambling seemed to be listening, leaning on the bar five yards away and grinning. I happened to catch his eye, and he winked back: he'd heard it all before. He seemed quite relaxed: probably because his wife was serving in the restaurant.

Roland's mood was bordering on maudlin, and I guessed it was time to make a move. I excused myself to him and asked Tambling where I might find a public phone. He directed me to the main entrance, and I left Roland well into his second large scotch and nodding distractedly, staring out through the patio door at the far end of the lounge. I don't know what he saw, for darkness had fallen and there was no street lighting.

Roz answered on the first ring. "Glen – where have you been? I thought you'd got lost."

"I'm at the Frobisher Arms."

"Guessed you might end up there." The comment was unjustified. *She* was the expert at putting it away, not me. "I'll come and collect you."

"It's no bother. I can walk."

"And get lost. I'll be there in five minutes."

There was no point in arguing, so I thanked her and returned to the lounge.

Roland was still staring out through the patio doors, and I coughed to claim his attention.

He looked up, shaking his head, and I heard him mumble, "Must have been mistaken."

I waited for him to elaborate, but he didn't. "My sister's coming round to pick me up," I explained. "Can we offer you a lift?"

"Oh no, no thanks, dear boy. I only live across the road from here. In fact, I really ought to be toddling along."

He struggled to his feet, only making it with my support. He wobbled a bit, then managed to steady himself and flung out a chubby hand.

"Indebted to you, young man. You've been so kind." He faced the bar. "I'll bid you good evening, Morgan."

"Mind how you go, Roly."

Brow furrowed in concentration, Roland aimed himself at the open patio doors. I watched as he was swallowed by the night, then returned our glasses to the bar.

Tambling shook his head fondly. "He doesn't change." He deposited the empty glasses on a shelf below the bar. "Known him long?"

"Met him at the tube station this afternoon. He -er, had a bit of a fright."

"Let me guess. He tried to nosedive?" Tambling grinned at my startled expression. "Sounds like him, that's all. And hardly surprising, the amount he puts away."

I was about to reply, when we heard the anguished squeal of brakes, followed by a dull thud.

2

Tambling and I stared at one another in alarm. "That was out on the road," he gasped, nodding in the direction of the doors through which Roland had lately stumbled.

His words spurred me into action. I turned and hurried towards the exit, as he was extricating himself from behind the bar. Outside, a path led down to an open gate set in the laurel hedge. A car stood in the road, an elderly red Escort, although the make and colour didn't register with me right away.

What did register, however, was the body lying in the road in front of the car.

I went and crouched beside him. He lay on his back, his linen suit more rumpled than before, tie more twisted. His eyes stared vacantly up into the heavens, while blood pooled darkly beneath his head. I dithered, fearing to touch him, certain that he shouldn't be moved. But then his hand floated up and snatched importunately at my sleeve. He fought for words, his face grey, blood bubbling on his lips. I leaned close, couldn't be sure what I heard, for the words were indistinct, scarcely uttered.

"Warn -" His mouth gobbled feebly for a moment. "M-Marlow…" His hand fell to the ground.

I became aware of people around us. I felt dazed, as if they might be characters in a dream. A tall woman in a light-coloured windcheater, whom I hadn't noticed in the pub, bent down beside me, peering at the figure on the ground.

"Oh, dear Lord, it's Roly."

"I'll phone for an ambulance." I recognised Morgan's voice, firm and decisive, heard him running back towards the pub.

"We'll need the police too, Morg." Lorna Tambling was at my shoulder. Her voice softened. "Is – is he -?"

I flicked her a sideways glance, caught her stunned expression. "I think he's dead," my voice replied from somewhere far away. "Better not move him."

"What happened?" The tall woman spoke again.

The car door creaked open, and we swung round as the driver staggered out. Lorna had been joined by a short, pugnacious-looking woman in kitchen overalls; indeed, the whole pub looked to have turned out, for I was aware of a press and throb of bodies in the darkness around me. The unfortunate Escort driver had a decent audience.

"He dashed out in front of me." It was a voice I recognised, only feebler. "Seemed to trip. Suddenly he was just – just *there*."

I leapt startled to my feet, as I confronted the driver.

"Roz!"

She stared up into my face, all five feet three of her, my steely, unflappable, forthright sister.

"Glen! I might have known!"

Known what? She didn't explain. I darted forward and caught her, as she fainted away into my arms.

I picked her up and carried her into the pub, Lorna and the tall woman leading the way. Morgan had wasted no time contacting an ambulance, for a siren sounded from not far away, and a blue light winked in the distance.

I laid Roz down across one of the lounge bar's leather seats. Morgan had gone behind the bar and was pouring a brandy, which the tall woman collected from him and brought over.

"Morg, police and ambulance are both here." Lorna was at the patio door and waited for him to join her before going back outside.

The tall woman knelt beside my sister and began gently coaxing her awake. She glanced up at me and smiled. "I'm a friend of Roz," she said. "Shirley Newbury."

"Glen Preston," I replied. "Roz's brother."

"Oh, she talks about you a lot. Pleased to meet you." She lost the smile and frowned. "Pity it couldn't have been under different circumstances."

She was about my age, very tall and gangling, her brown hair cut short, smart-casual in windcheater and fawn-coloured slacks. I liked her immediately: there was an air of dependability about her.

"I'm with you entirely on that," I agreed. "You obviously know Roland."

"Work with him, for my sins." Shirley was intent on reviving Roz, patting her face and whispering her name, as she started to come round. "I edit the *Bugle*, for what it's worth."

"Ah. He did mention something."

"More than something, I'll bet. Roz – Roz, darling -?"

My sister's eyes flickered open. She saw me and groaned; saw Shirley and smiled weakly. Shirley held the glass to her lips, as I propped Roz up into a less supine position and draped a brotherly arm around her shoulders. She took a couple of sips, seemed slightly restored and brought her legs round so that she could sit up. She took the glass from Shirley, and we sat down either side of her. The last time I'd seen her in tears had been at Aunt Ava's funeral, and not often before that; but she was close to them now.

"Poor Roly," she mumbled, clutching my arm. "Oh, Glen, is he -?"

"I believe he's dead," I replied gently. "And I'm certain that what happened out there was no fault of yours. I'd been with him since before six this evening, travelled up from London with him." I caught Shirley Newbury's keen glance.

"Bet he was half seas over," she commented bluntly.

"More than half," I replied. "Could hardly stand. There wasn't any carelessness on your part, Roz. I'll bear witness to that."

"You may need to," she murmured.

A large, uniformed figure had appeared in the doorway. He rumbled towards us, removing his peaked cap to reveal a domed bald head, round the sides of which clung a few grey hairs. He pulled up a chair and lowered himself carefully on to it, facing us with what he intended to be a reassuring smile. Around us, the pub was resuming a semblance of normality, several customers drifting back in and the Tamblings bringing up the rear, with Lorna throwing us a long, inquisitive look.

"Sergeant Desmond Burge, sir." The officer addressed his remark to me. "I know Miss Newbury and Rosalind, but I'm not sure if we've met?"

I'd seen him on a previous visit, but we'd never spoken. "Glen Preston," I replied. "Rosalind's brother."

"Ah, yes, of course. This has been a most unfortunate accident, sir and ladies."

Burge was a burly, awkward man, achingly polite and irritatingly slow. He was unmarried and lived with his sister in a house adjoining the little police station in Selsby's main street. He'd been a fixture for years and, I was to learn, had a soft spot for my sister.

Roz knew what was coming, and I was glad to see the brisk, forthright side of her character starting to re-emerge. "Roly's dead?" It was almost not a question.

Burge nodded gloomily. "Dead at the scene, I'm afraid. I'm sorry."

"I'm sorry too, Desmond. More than I can say. But, well – he just suddenly appeared through the gateway there. I wasn't going fast – but I simply couldn't stop in time."

"I'm sure you couldn't, Rosalind. Now, please forgive me for this, but I must ask you to take a breathalyser test. It's a matter of protocol, you understand."

"Of course." I was confident the test would prove negative. Roz would never have got behind the wheel if it had been otherwise. "Although I've had a couple of sips of brandy." She indicated the glass which Shirley Newbury held.

Burge grinned. "Ah, I'm sure you'll be all right."

I helped her to her feet, and she pointedly removed my hand, a sure sign that she was getting back to being her own woman again. Burge led her off a little way and did what had to be done. When they returned, she took charge of the glass from Shirley. "I'll finish that off now. You and I can walk back, Glen. I dare say Desmond'll have to hang on to the car for forensic tests."

Burge was still looming in the background, notebook in hand, wanting to take our statements. Roz gave hers over a second brandy, and I followed it with mine. We promised to call in on him the next day to sign the typed documents.

Somewhere along the way, the local doctor, a dried-up, elderly little man, came in to report that he'd pronounced Roland dead at the scene and had arranged for his body to be taken to the nearest mortuary.

We thanked Burge, and Roz insisted on buying Shirley a drink before we left. At the bar, I deposited Roz's empty glass and my half-full one containing very flat beer. Lorna dispensed a gin and tonic for Shirley and switched a mischievous smile in my direction.

"Thought for a moment you had a new friend, Mrs Blakeman."

"My brother, Lorna," Roz replied equably. "Don't get excited."

"Oh, I might."

I'd been right about the hint of promise. I'd been involved with someone of Lorna's type a few years previously and didn't intend going there again.

"Spoken for," Roz whispered, to spare my blushes, and we wished the ladies a good evening, turned and left the way we'd come in, but less obtrusively.

3

It was quiet out on the road, and a light rain had set in. I slung a protective arm around Roz's shoulders, steering her away from a sight of her car, which Burge or his constable had parked at the side of the road. She walked with her head bowed, and I could tell she was reliving those awful moments of a couple of hours previously, for she kept silent, and I was content to wait until she was ready to speak.

I felt her pain. To an extent, it was mine too: a man I'd hardly known, but who'd been my companion for a few short hours; who'd laughed with and confided in me, who'd been thankful because I'd saved his life.

How I wished I'd been able to save him a second time.

With only the sound of our footsteps for company, we turned off the road into Burnage Lane. A long row of modest 1930s bungalows stretched down it beyond a sharp bend in the road, Roz's about two-thirds of the way along. She was proud of it, the only property she'd ever owned. There was a short gravel drive at the front and, as I recalled, a long, sloping garden at the back, part lawn, part vegetable patch. From the top of the garden, there was a good view across the rooftops of the main Oxford-Reading road to the right and, to the left beyond the village, the wide, gently rolling Thames.

Once in the hall, Roz switched on the light, turned and embraced me. For the second time that evening, she was in tears.

"Oh, Glen, this is a nightmare. Poor Roly. I've known him for years, drank with him scores of times in the FA. And now I've killed him…"

"Roz," I assured her firmly. "There was nothing you could have done. If anyone's, it's my fault for letting you come and meet me at the pub. And besides, Roland was in a heck of a state. I believe he'd been drinking for most of the day. I met him at Liverpool Street tube station, where he tripped and nearly ended up under a train. I'm afraid that he really was an accident waiting to happen."

I took her into the lounge and sat her down, sought out the drinks cabinet and poured her another large brandy. She took it from me, stared up soulfully.

"I shouldn't think you've eaten," she remarked, shaking her head. "This really wasn't the welcome I'd planned for my little brother."

I had to smile at the adjective: at over six feet, I was a foot taller than Roz. I told her I'd fix myself a sandwich and a cup of tea.

"You look worn out," I said. "Try to get some sleep, and we can catch up with one another in the morning."

She seemed to brighten a little, although I believed the large brandy – and it *was* large – was kicking in. "We'll do that, Glenny. It promises to be a nice day. Perhaps have a walk along the river through the woods?"

"And a spot of lunch somewhere," I concluded. "We can talk and talk. We've a lot to discuss."

Busy as ever, Roz insisted on showing me my room and unloaded various items from the fridge and pantry, so that I could sort out something to eat. Then she took herself off to bed. I looked in on her before retiring and was glad to see that she was fast asleep, the brandy glass empty on the bedside table.

Roz and I were actually half-brother and -sister, the issue of two different fathers, neither of whom we'd met, inquired or cared about. After all, neither of them had bothered about us.

Which, sadly, gave them much in common with our mother. Esme Preston, or Esmeralda, as she preferred to be known, had been a sometime dancer, actress and chorus girl, performing with repertory companies up and down the country. She'd just about managed to spare the time to give birth to two children, Rosalind, the fruit of a fleeting wartime liaison, and me some six years later, the result of yet one more brief coupling. Currently, Esmeralda (she would never allow us to call her 'mother') was shacked up on the Costa del Sol with someone else's husband. We'd correspond spasmodically, receive some utterly useless gift each Christmas, but hadn't set eyes on her for more than two years.

With Esmeralda perpetually absent ("Oh, darlings, I've another tour coming up. I shall miss you both *horribly*"), Roz and I were permanently billeted in a North London flat with her elder sister, Ava. It was the best thing that could have happened to us, because it brought much-needed stability into our lives.

Ava Trafford was the direct opposite of her sister. Widowed early in the war, she'd worked in various capacities as cook, charlady and home help, bringing in enough of a wage, along with Esmeralda's occasional subsidies, to ensure that we had clothes on our backs and food to eat. She was a short, tireless, breathless bundle of a woman, with grey permed hair and flower-patterned, ankle-length aprons, and we loved her to bits.

She kept us both in order – not that we were particularly unruly. Roz was six years my senior and, while Aunt Ava was out at work, she took charge of the flat, cooking, cleaning and sorting me out. It was done with such understated authority and, above all, love, that I couldn't help but respond. The result was that Roz and I were always very close and looking out for each other; more so, probably, on her part than mine.

We were poorly off but at least able, through Aunt Ava's gigantic efforts, to make ends meet. Roz left school at sixteen and got a job at a nearby branch of WH Smith. It proved a turning point. She'd always devoured the short stories in Ava's weekly women's magazine and, with the world at her feet on a wage of two pounds fifteen shillings per week, she began to indulge her literary tastes in the vast shoal of offerings from Mills & Boon and the like. Soon, she began writing stories of her own, and before long was placing them with popular journals such as *Woman's Weekly* and *People's Friend.* Full-length novels followed by the time she'd hit her mid-twenties, which enabled her to supplement our income and take some of the load off Aunt Ava's shoulders. By then, I'd left school and was working hard to pay my way through drama college. Aunt Ava, bless her, had seen some of my school plays – Esmeralda had even shown up for one – and both declared that I was the next Richard Burton, and that Hollywood was a shoo-in.

It didn't quite work out that way.

Through my own efforts and some financial help from Roz, I graduated from drama college and began picking up roles in TV and theatre, although the majority of these were no more than bit parts, and many TV roles were uncredited. I was working, however, and in between acting commitments lived with Aunt Ava. Roz, meanwhile, had earned enough to be able to afford her own place and surprised us both by deciding to move to the countryside.

However, the bungalow in Selsby-on-Thames proved a good move, and she was able to give Ava, in her declining years, something called holidays, which she'd never previously experienced.

Ava died four years ago, but I hoped that, between us, Roz and I had combined to make her last years happy ones, repaying part of the massive debt we owed for her care and devotion.

Between Roz's writing and my acting commitments, we hadn't had a lot of time to spend together in the intervening years, just the odd flying visit now and again. But, with the recent tour over and Eric hedging spectacularly over my next role, it was possible to find that time. I phoned Roz, and she invited me to Selsby for a couple of weeks, or however long it took until Eric Dim came good.

That could easily have meant a long stay.

4

We started off after breakfast the next day and walked as far as Pangbourne, an easy hike along by the Thames, giving on to an invigorating climb into Hartslock Wood, where we found ourselves high above the river on the edge of the Chilterns. The Thames glistened in the summer sunshine, busy with boats, while beyond it the main Oxford-Paddington railway line swished and rattled with passing trains.

Roz had slept well and regained a little colour, although I could tell she was making an effort on my behalf. What had happened the previous evening was very much on her mind, as it was on mine.

We shared the same mother but were different in temperament. Roz, short with spiky blonde hair, was feisty and combative, as anyone taken in by the snub nose and pretty, freckled face soon found out. She rarely stood on ceremony, favouring T-shirts, jeans and hiking boots, a pointer to her rough and ready approach to life. Beneath the scary exterior, however, beat a caring heart.

I, meanwhile, was an unobtrusive sort of chap, a character borne out in a plethora of acting roles. I was tall and dark, some distance short of handsome and quickly taken in by a pretty face. A gentleman to the last (I hoped), I was probably a good forty years behind the times.

"You're still with the same agent, I imagine?" my sister inquired, as we sat over Sunday lunch, accompanied by a foaming pint of lager (hers) and a small light ale.

"Eric Dim? Yes, he's promising great things."

"You do realise, dear Glen, that he's a waste of space?"

I considered this for a moment. "Hhmm. Close. But he's sure there's a decent role in the offing. A title role, no less."

She raised a doubting eyebrow. "Oh, right? And when did you last play a title role?"

"I'm sure there's been one in the last ten years." I paused for thought. "Well, fairly sure."

"'Nuff said. Still, it's something to hope for. From what you've told me, the tour was rather dire?"

"It nearly finished me off. The plays were boring, accommodation awful, and bad reviews to top it off." (*'Glen Preston played the part of Ronny with all the verve and enthusiasm of someone going to his own funeral.'*). "Still," I added glumly, "Calista did all right out of it."

"Calista would." Roz spat out the name as if it had a nasty taste. For my part, I'd forgiven her. In the acting profession, you go where the roles are. She'd been offered a plum in the West End and had snatched at it. I'd been excess baggage, abandoned by the wayside. I couldn't really blame her on either count.

"I should imagine she slept with the right producer." Roz had met Calista once, down in London, and the two hadn't hit it off. "Perhaps, dear brother, you should take a leaf out of her book. It could be the way forward."

"The producers are nearly always men," I pointed out.

"Well, spread your wings a little."

I almost choked on my roast beef, and the pair of us gave way to laughter, earning us stares, smiles and frowns from other diners. It was the cue for someone to come over and say, "Excuse me, aren't you Glen Preston, the actor?" Strangely, no-one did.

"And what about you, Roz?" I asked, once we'd recovered and were enjoying a dish of sticky toffee pudding. "All well with Rosa Peyton?" It was the name under which she wrote her tacky (her word) romances. The pseudonym afforded her a degree of privacy, which she welcomed. To most of her village acquaintances, she 'wrote for women's magazines'.

"There's a new title due out in the autumn." She frowned. "I'm sure I've used the plot before, but Fine Romance don't seem to mind. There are only so many plot lines, and I must have covered them all by now. The pay could be better, I suppose, but it's what I enjoy doing."

We shared the same motto: *if it ain't broke, don't fix it.* We were both earning steadily and able to maintain our undemanding lifestyles. Perhaps there should have been something more. In my case, I thought that might have been Calista. Back to the drawing board on that one.

Which brought me to the point…

"And do you see anything of Perry?"

"Not since he walked out."

I'd held my breath, because that question might have triggered an explosion but thankfully hadn't. Perry Blakeman was Roz's husband and antithesis: carefree, charming, one of life's innocents. They'd met four years ago, when Roz had visited me in London. Perry was a chef and had brought our meals to the table one evening, when we'd been dining out. He'd recognised me from some recent obscure television role, and the three of us had got talking.

I'd been able to tell, there and then, that Roz had been taken with him. That evening, unusually, she'd been wearing a full-length evening dress, as we'd just been to the theatre, and was looking, as she sometimes could, particularly attractive with a conservative application of make-up.

She was relaxed and positive, having been paid an exorbitant (to me) sum for a couple of stories, we'd each had a few glasses of wine, and the repartee was flowing. We invited Perry to meet us at a nearby club, once he came off duty, and before long he and Roz were dancing the night away. Things moved swiftly on from there, and in no time at all the pair of them were married and living in Selsby.

It didn't last long. Perry was unable to find more than temporary work in the Reading area and yearned for a return to London. Roz hated London: it had too many associations with her upbringing, and she was adamant about remaining in the countryside. Her bungalow wasn't a palace, but she'd worked for it, loved it and there she would stay. So, they agreed to part, which they'd done six months previously.

I'd liked Perry. There was never a hidden agenda with him, and I was always willing to fight his corner. "He was good for you," I said.

"You're the eternal optimist." She sighed. "And, yes, I know, I'm the eternal pessimist. He's a nice guy – none nicer – and he means well, but – oh, I was having a period of writer's block, and he couldn't find a job, and I was forever snapping at him…"

"Do you regret that?"

"Yes." She looked thoughtful, and I sensed the pain behind her expression. "Yes, I think I do." She picked up her glass, emptied and set it down. "Dare say he's found someone else by now."

I wasn't going there. Perhaps I could have postponed the subject of Perry Blakeman, but Roz and I had always been direct and honest with one another. She had enough grief as things stood, but strangely, as we began our walk back to Selsby, it was Roz who raised the subject of Roland Pettifer.

He'd been a local character, born and bred in Selsby. Unfit for active service in World War II, he'd worked as a correspondent for the *Daily Post.* With the war over, Roland had been surplus to requirements, although that wasn't the way he'd told it, and he'd returned to Selsby to work for the local weekly paper. He'd rubbed along well with the elderly editor, Fred Barnfleet, but when Fred had decided to retire – well past his sell-by date – the editorship had passed to the junior reporter, Shirley Newbury. In his heart of hearts, Roland must have understood that Shirley was far more capable of keeping the paper up together than he was. Pettifer was a loose cannon, never minding whom he upset in his quest for that 'big story', which always remained annoyingly out of reach.

He'd always been fond of the demon drink, but in later years it well and truly ensnared him, particularly as bitterness set in alongside a long-harboured resentment of Shirley Newbury. But to everyone else, Roland tried to be amenable, persuading himself that the scoop to end them all was just around the corner.

"He could be a pain in the butt, but he was a real character," Roz concluded. "It's a pity about what happened yesterday evening. He's the second Selsby character we've lost this year. You'll probably hear Ned Braley's name mentioned. That was a night-time road accident too." She smiled grimly. "But not down to me this time."

"Neither was Roland's," I replied spiritedly. "Roz, I told you about what happened at the tube station. He was well lubricated and unsteady on his feet. There was a real crush on the platform, but even so…" My voice tailed off, as a thought struck me.

Roz flung out a hand to halt me in my tracks. "Glen, you're not about to suggest that someone might have pushed him?"

I shrugged. "It crossed my mind for the first time, that's all. Nothing in it, of course. Why are you asking?"

"Last night, when he came out on the road. I wasn't doing any speed – less than 30mph? But, Glen, he seemed to come out of there so quickly, almost as if he tripped over his own feet. I mean, he didn't walk so much as blunder."

I decided I might as well tell her everything that was on my mind. I steered her off the path to a fallen tree trunk and sat down on it. Roz joined me, her expectant gaze on my face.

"In the pub last night, when I came back into the lounge bar after phoning you, I think Roland might have seen someone. He muttered something like 'must have been mistaken', and he was staring out into the darkness.

"But how much of that was down to the drink talking?" Roz asked.

"Well, maybe. Straight after, he got up, said his goodbyes and left."

"Might someone have just come in? Someone he wasn't expecting?"

"Not that I recall. And the only person I saw who arrived immediately after the accident was the newspaper editor, Shirley. She helped me get you inside."

"Might he have seen someone on the train?"

"Only the pub landlord, Morgan. And there was nothing odd or suspicious about their greeting."

Roz gave one of her cynical smiles. "So, Morgan had been gallivanting around in London again? Oh dear, Lorna won't be pleased."

"Roland wondered if they'd just come from the same matinée. But Morgan had seen the play in question earlier in the run."

"Wouldn't stop him seeing it again. There's a local girl in it, Kirstie Ryde. He's rather keen on her. She waitresses at the FA when she's not acting. Her mum, Barbara, is the cook."

"That fierce-looking woman?"

"Yes, she can be a bit fierce. But that won't stop Morgan. He's never been able to leave the ladies alone. Tried it on with me more than once."

"There's one more thing, Roz. When Roland was lying in the road, he grasped my arm. He spoke two words. Something like 'warn' and 'Marlow'."

"Warn Marlow about what?"

"That was it. Just those two words. Then he lost consciousness."

5

Whatever suspicions my sister and I might have had, they weren't shared by Sergeant Burge.

Soon after breakfast next morning, I answered the door to find his Panda car on the drive and the stolid, uniformed Burge passing the time of day with two of Roz's gossipy neighbours, about whom I'd been warned.

They both greeted me with fawning smiles, as Roz ducked past me, summoned Burge inside and glared at her neighbours. As I closed the door behind us, I heard snatches of their excited, stage-whispered conversation.

"'Xpect it's about the accident…That's her brother, I should think…Thought he'd be better looking for a famous actor…Well, *I've* never heard of him…"

With a shrug, I followed Roz and the sergeant into the living room.

An armchair squealed, as Burge lowered his bulk into it. Roz offered tea, he accepted, and I indicated that I'd make it. On my return, they were chatting away about all things Selsby, Burge's face illuminated with a delighted grin, my sister smiling on sufferance. I wondered idly if he'd polished the crown of his head especially for this visit: it gleamed magnificently in the morning sun streaming through the French windows behind him.

The tea dispensed and accompanying chocolate digestives sampled, Burge got down to business. His manner was slow and rambling, but the man's good nature was always to the fore. I could tell that Roz was well and truly off the hook, even if she still wasn't convinced of it.

"I've had the result of the post-mortem on Roland this morning," he rumbled. "You've nothing to worry about, Rosalind my dear. Your car, which, by the way, my constable will run back later, was travelling within the speed limit and, according to Dr Spence, it was the shock rather than the impact which did for the poor old chap.

"The doc's put it down to heart failure. He'd warned Roland on numerous occasions that his heart and liver were in a sorry state. In Spence's opinion, he could have gone at any time. So, my dear, if the fault was anyone's at all, it certainly wasn't yours."

Burge took the opportunity to reach across and place his meaty paw consolingly over Roz's hand. Relief had left her struggling for words, and she succeeded in putting up with it, as she burbled her thanks.

I'd decided I ought to let Burge know about the incident at the tube station.

"He was gasping for breath after that," I added, "and I persuaded him to sit for a while to recover. But I have to say, Sergeant, it did leave me wondering whether someone might have pushed him."

Sergeant Burge nodded sagely, as he considered this between huge slurps of tea. A few chocolate digestive crumbs sparkled on his otherwise spotless uniform.

"And remember, Desmond," Roz put in, "I did say at the time of the accident that Roly seemed to trip as he appeared in the road. Might he have been pushed, do you think?"

Burge pursed his lips and gave a ponderous shake of the head. I believe he'd have reacted in the same way if we'd announced that his trousers were on fire.

"Oh no, I'd not go quite that far, Rosalind. He'd been drinking most of the day, I'd imagine, and likely tripped over his own feet. As for the business at the tube station, Mr Preston, well, as you say, sir, a busy Saturday afternoon, people jostling for position to board the train, everyone a bit impatient... Ah, doubtless he was shoved, but I'd put that down as inevitable, given the crowd. And yes, as you say, the shock of nearly ending up under the train wouldn't have done his old ticker much good..."

Roz switched me a swift glance. We weren't likely to get anywhere with Dismal Desmond.

But I could tell he'd done nothing to allay our suspicions.

*

By the following day, the result of the post-mortem on Roland Pettifer was known throughout the village, and Morgan Tambling phoned Roz to invite us down to the Frobisher Arms that lunchtime. The pub would sorely miss Roly's custom and, as a tribute to him, Morgan proposed a gathering to raise a glass to his late patron. He and Lorna would provide a free buffet and a glass of something bubbly as a toast.

I had to congratulate the Tamblings on their business acumen. They were generous hosts, as Morgan's parents had been before them, but in return for their magnanimous gesture, they'd have a pub full of people, the vast majority of whom wouldn't stop at one glass of bubbly.

In fact, most of the village turned out, and the till was soon ringing. Lorna and Barbara Ryde had been busy in the kitchen and had produced a stunning selection of sandwiches and vol-au-vents. Morgan proposed a toast to Roland, and everyone pitched in.

Roz and I found ourselves at a corner of the bar along with Shirley Newbury and a slim, pretty girl with short dark hair and elfin features, who turned out to be Kirstie Ryde, the actress-cum-waitress. She'd returned from London only the previous day and so had been spared kitchen duties. I suspected Lorna's hand in that, because it kept Kirstie out of Morgan's reach, if what Roz had told me was the case.

Lorna had worked her way along to our end of the bar and chatted away with us between customers. I don't know if I was the intended beneficiary of her cleavage, but I certainly had an ample view that lunchtime. As Roz had said before we left, Lorna often tried to play Morgan at his own game, and I was a new face as far as the village was concerned. "So, be afraid," she'd warned in a sepulchral voice. "Be *very* afraid."

Naturally, the talk revolved around the subject of Roland Pettifer, and Shirley regaled us with some amusing anecdotes. My sister then steered the conversation round to the accident on Saturday night, and her relief at the result of the post-mortem. Both Lorna and Shirley declared that there was no way it could have been her fault.

"I could tell he'd already had a skinful," Lorna said. "Perhaps I didn't ought to have served him with those two doubles. Anyway," she turned to me with a gleaming smile and patted my hand intimately, "it must have been a shock for you as well, Glen? After all, you got to Roly first."

It hadn't been Lorna's intention, but she'd played nicely into my dear sister's hands. I caught the cunning glint in Roz's eye, as she flicked me the briefest glance.

"Yes. He mumbled something, didn't he, Glen? And you couldn't be sure what it was?"

Roz was determined not to let it go. And I was on the spot. I'd not mentioned it to Burge, but he probably wouldn't have seen it as important anyway.

"Well," I said, realising that several pairs of eyes were trained on me. "It sounded like 'Marlow'. I think he said 'Warn' and then 'Marlow'."

"Anyone know a Marlow?" Roz trilled.

By now, the pub was thinning out a little, and the general buzz of conversation had subsided. We had the attention of several more people, including Morgan, who'd made his way along the bar towards us, and Barbara Ryde, who'd started to clear away some of the empty sandwich trays.

"Perhaps I didn't hear it correctly," I put in limply.

Everyone was looking blank, although Shirley Newbury had been giving the name concentrated thought.

"I wrote an article back in the spring," she said. "That was about a man named Marlow. I can't remember which village he's from, but, as I recall, he was a retired vicar, celebrating his ninetieth birthday, so I really wouldn't have thought it could be him."

Lorna stole a brief, wicked glance at her husband. If she'd known what she was about to set in motion, I look back and wonder if she'd have dared open her mouth.

"Might it have been 'Marla'?" she asked sweetly.

*

Someone gasped. In one of those moments when everything seemed to freeze, I glanced around at their faces. Lorna looked smug, Morgan startled. Kirstie was frowning at Morgan, Shirley seemed thoughtful and my sister watchful, her gaze, like mine, taking in everyone's expression.

Barbara Ryde reacted first, slamming down a tray she'd picked up to clear away. Her pasty features had flooded with colour. "Well, I for one would be happy never to hear *her* name again."

"Oh, Mum," Kirstie protested. "It was *sixteen* years ago."

"And even now," her mother raged, "that name hangs over us like a curse."

Lorna squeezed out from behind the bar to wind an arm round the older woman's shoulders. "Barbara, I'm sorry. I didn't mean to upset you."

But Barbara wouldn't be appeased. She mumbled something, then strode bad-temperedly back to the kitchen, clutching her empty tray.

Roz picked up her drink and indicated that we'd head outside to sit on the patio. Shirley caught us up.

"This may be nothing at all." She kept her voice deliberately low, and we had to strain forward to hear. "Those words you heard Roly utter, Glen. They brought it all back. I was walking down here on Saturday night, straight after it happened, and saw you and Morgan bending over him. I'm almost sure I glimpsed someone – no more than a silhouette in the dark – hurrying off the patio and round to the front of the pub. I thought I ought to share that with you, although it's no more than a suspicion. I may not actually have seen anyone at all."

It was, however, food for thought. We thanked Shirley, and she went back to the bar to join Lorna. Morgan had returned to its far end, where he was in conversation with a bunch of locals.

"Hi! Mind if I join you?" A cheerful voice sounded behind us, and we turned to find Kirstie Ryde, Diet Coke in hand and a bright smile on her face.

"Be our guest," Roz replied expansively, knowing for sure that I'd have no objection. We went outside, to find we had the patio to ourselves.

Kirstie was dressed simply in a white halter top and short denim skirt. She'd applied a little make-up but didn't really need it, her features unblemished if a little pale, her brown eyes doe-like and appealing. She was studying me with something amazingly like awe, a reaction I certainly wasn't used to.

"When Lorna told me your name, I simply couldn't believe it!" she enthused. "You've been in tons of things – television and everything."

Roz's cruel little smirk seemed to ask if she should leave us alone now, but I felt it'd be best to come down to earth from the outset.

"And there's me just finished an uninspiring tour of theatres in the north-west," I countered, "while I hear you're fresh from a run in the West End?"

She laughed. "You make it sound so grand. The Burlington must be London's smallest theatre, and I've only been playing bit parts like waitresses – although I'm good at those – and police officers. Still, it was a step up from my last role. I was an understudy and spent more days off the set than on."

"Then you've made progress," I complimented her.

"S'pose you're right. But I'm sure I remember you in a dashing TV role a few years back. D'Artagnan in *The Three Musketeers*, wasn't it? I watched every episode."

"Then you'll have seen me. But I wasn't D'Artagnan. I was one of the palace guards, and D'Artagnan did for me with a rapier thrust."

"That sounds about right," Roz commented, and we shared another round of laughter.

Another round of drinks too, after a few more reminiscences. I noticed that Morgan was watching me a little warily, as I arrived at the bar and was obligingly served by Lorna. I didn't think that his wife's flirtatious remarks were the problem.

"So, who was Marla?" I asked, on re-joining Roz and Kirstie outside.

"It was before my time here," Roz replied. "But she seems to have passed into Selsby folklore. Not so good for you or your mum, though, was it, Kirstie?"

Kirstie looked pensive. We were into serious stuff now. "Poor Marla. It wasn't her fault, despite what Mum and the others say. Sixteen years ago. I was eleven at the time and had a real crush on her. She must have been about eighteen. She was gorgeous. I thought she was sure to be a film star or model. And she caused a real stir in Selsby. In more ways than one…"

6

July 1970

It was a bit early yet for some people, that Saturday evening in the Frobisher Arms, but the hardened bar-hangers were already there. Roly Pettifer and Ned Braley stood at the far end, with a convenient table and two chairs right behind them, brushing against their backsides, so that no-one else would want to sit there, and they could lower themselves down once they were tired or incapable of standing.

Marj Tambling was in the kitchen, preparing the evening's first round of chicken-in-the-basket; and Tony was down in the cellar, changing a barrel. Ned had complained about his first pint of best – called it 'worst', even though he'd downed more than half of it – and since he was likely for at least six more, Tony reckoned he ought to keep him on-side.

Then the two local hell-raisers tumbled in; well, that's how *they* described themselves. Morgan Tambling and Jamie Ryde, both in their twenties, although there were five years between Morgan and his pal, decked out in denims and flashy white trainers, hair brushing their shoulders, both full of exuberance and their own immortality. They'd just got back from a ton-up along the M4 to Swindon and back in Morgan's bright yellow Lotus Elan, a birthday gift from his parents.

Morgan had got it made, and he knew it. Tony and Marj were already, in their early fifties, discussing retirement. They were planning to head off to Spain in the next two or three years and maybe open a bar, if they felt so inclined. Morgan would take over the Frobisher Arms, the FA as the locals termed it, and at present he was learning the ropes. To be fair to them, his mum and dad weren't soft on him, where that was concerned. They'd worked their socks off, these last twenty years, building a successful business, and they didn't intend that it should be frittered away.

"What you having, J?" Morgan asked, as they fetched up at the bar.

"Pint of Skol, mate. Ta."

Morgan ducked under the flap, reached for two glasses and started pulling pints. As he did so, the kitchen door swung open, and Marj's head appeared. She grinned the moment she saw her son there. She never liked leaving the bar unattended, because Ned was crafty and not above helping himself to drinks, if the chance arose.

"Serve Roly and Ned while you're there, Morg," she called out in her smoky voice.

"Will do, Mum. Hi, Roly. Sorry, mate, didn't see you there."

"Don't see how you could have missed him," Jamie quipped.

"Probably 'cos he's part of the furniture." Morgan chuckled. "Hey! What about he's working undercover on that big scoop?"

"Yeah, right. The life and crimes of Uncle Ned."

"You watch your big mouth, our Jamie," Ned Braley growled. He was short, bald beneath his battered trilby and dressed in a scruffy dark suit, which, people joked, he'd been given on demob. He had sharp, darting eyes and quick fingers, honed from a life on the take. "C'mon, Morgan, look lively there, boy. Dying of thirst here. Pint of best, and your dad better have changed that barrel. Real gut-rot, that first 'un."

"And respect your elders and betters, young Morgan," Roly Pettifer chided him. "It's our money bought you that flash sports job, so that you could spin around charming the birds from the trees. Make it same as Ned's, if you will. And allow me to stand you this, my friend."

"That's very civil of you, Roland." Ned was always willing to be bought a drink.

Roland looked dapper in his trademark linen suit, panama hat parked proprietorially on the table behind him. After a long session, which it usually was, the tie would work slightly askew, the suit become slightly rumpled, and the voice louder and hectoring.

Having dispensed the drinks and relieved Roly of some money, although he'd 'forgotten' (again) to pay for his and Jamie's, Morgan returned to the customer side of the bar and perched on a stool alongside his mate. Tony Tambling had returned from the cellar and was chatting away to a customer at the far end.

"Hey, Roly," Morgan called out. "You're friendly with the Hartmans, aren't you? J and I been wondering about this bird we seen up there. She's a knockout – long blonde hair and legs up to her shoulder blades. We know old Leo likes 'em young. Got a new *au pair*, has he?"

"*She's* got a nice pair, for definite," Jamie glugged into his beer.

"That's his *daughter*, you prize buffoons," Roly replied scornfully. "Just back from her posh Parisian finishing school."

"She's certainly a bit of all right," Morgan enthused.

"And way out of your country-bumpkin league, Master Tambling. Anyway," he added, as a colourful splash in the doorway caught his eye," here comes your *amour*. And what a sight to warm the heart you are, lovely Lorna."

Ned's lips parted in a lascivious brown grin. "Goin' to pull a few pints in that outfit, are you, sweetheart? Here, come and pull something for me."

Lorna Pascoe threw him a tired smile and turned away, conscious that the eyes of both men were trained on her. She'd dressed to impress, so took it in her stride: shortest possible blue dress, auburn tresses swishing over her shoulders, glittery tights, platform sandals, glammy eyes, and her mouth a slash of red. Her gaze was for one person only.

"Hi, Morg. How's things?"

"Hi, babe. You look great." Without leaving his stool, he slung a possessive arm around her and pulled her into a kiss.

"Got her on tap as well as the beer," Ned wheezed.

"Everything's going for him," Roly grumbled. "Talk about a ruddy silver spoon."

"Hey, J," Morgan called out in mid-snog. "Shirl's here."

"Oh, great," Jamie groaned.

Shirley Newbury had followed her friend in. She and Lorna had been best friends since infants' school but were poles apart in all else. Shirley's face was fairly plain but pleasant. She wore her brown hair short, embraced fashion with a nod to short skirts and halter tops, but was gawky and angular and knew it wasn't really her. A serious girl, she was junior reporter for the local rag, and in idle moments she wished Jamie Ryde might be serious about her.

She peeped shyly round the entwined lovers. "Hi, Jamie."

"Hi, Shirl. You okay?"

"Yes, thanks. Been slaving away at magistrates' court reports all afternoon."

She didn't hear Jamie's *"Whoopee!"* He added, loud enough for everyone to hear: "Soon be leaving old Roly for dead."

"Not much hope of that," came the stinging retort from along the bar. Roly hadn't acknowledged Shirley's presence; only did so when he couldn't avoid it. Women reporters, indeed! But neither had Ned, too busy in a long, salacious appraisal of Lorna's legs.

Jamie flashed Shirley one of his winning smiles, and she felt her heart racing. He was a handsome devil, long dark hair and wearing that vest top with a silver medallion dead centre of his hairy chest. He worked at the local garage, and Shirley always made a point of driving her dad's car round there for petrol or a service in the hope of seeing him or, even better, having a chat. Not that he was really her type: a bit loud and flashy, always with big ideas and not quite honest. His name cropped up from time to time in the weekly court reports she wrestled with.

"So, what are we doing tonight?" Lorna and Morgan finally had to come up for air. Dolled up to the nines, Lorna didn't intend staying in the FA all evening for those sad old perverts to look up her skirt.

"Thought we'd try that disco in Wallingford again," Morgan replied. "Everyone up for it?"

"Yeah, let's go," they chorused.

"Bet he'll try to trap you on that back seat, young Lorna." Ned's face wore a wicked grin, as he emerged from the depths of his glass. "I know I would."

The mind boggled at that. Lorna's smile was pure saccharine. "Why don't you get lost?" She flounced outside, the others following.

They piled into Morgan's Lotus and careered out of the car park. Fifty yards down the road, Jamie yelled for him to stop. As soon as he saw why, Morgan squealed to a spectacular halt, jolting the girls, who were in the back seat.

The emergency stop had been imperative. Because a vision was walking towards them.

The vision was a girl in a long, clinging white dress, a gold necklace draped round her neck, gold lame sandals on her feet. Her long blonde mane swished alluringly in the light breeze, and her breasts bubbled invitingly over the dress's low neckline. Her pretty face wore an informed smile, the lips twitching cruelly, as if she knew she was the centre of attention and everything in trousers would fall mewling at her feet.

There were two such in the front of the yellow Lotus currently slewed wantonly across Selsby's main street.

"Hi there." Jamie had the advantage of being closest to the pavement, although he was never slow in coming forward when confronted by a nubile female. "You look as if you're on your way down to the FA?"

She drew to a halt with a bright smile: a toothpaste advertiser's dream. "I suppose that's the pub. Nowhere else, is there?"

"And all that's down the pub are a couple of lecherous old farts holding up the bar. We're Selsby's young generation, on our way to a real groovy disco. Wanna come along?"

"If you're sure you don't mind?"

Jamie didn't, and neither did Morgan, grinning stupidly while maintaining a diplomatic silence. The two in the back had no choice but would have objected strenuously if they'd had.

The vision squeezed her breath-taking frame into the back seat alongside Lorna and Shirley, who scrunched up huffily.

Jamie had donned some shades, reckoning they made him look like Barry Gibb (they didn't) and leaned back confidentially.

"I'm Jamie, by the way. This here's Morgan."

"And I'm Marla. Hi."

"That's Lorna and Shirley alongside you," Morgan cut in, as he drove off. "This Lotus is all mine. Did a ton on the M4 this afternoon." He'd taken his eyes off the road to flash Marla a macho smile and had to swerve to miss a delivery van.

"Wow! That's cool."

Morgan winked at Jamie. *That was the way to impress a bird.*

Jamie dismissed it with a shrug. Morgan had to concentrate on the road, leaving him free to concentrate on Marla. "You must be Leo and Venetia's daughter," he resumed.

"Yah. S'right."

"Not seen you around before."

"Oh, I've been living in Paris. Daddy has a flat there. Paris was something else – full of life. This place is the pits."

"Disco'll be lively, though. *We're* going there," Morgan put in.

"God, let's hope it is."

"Do people really talk like that?" Lorna murmured, as the boys chatted away like over-excited schoolboys. "Or has she got a speech defect?"

"Mouth full of plums, if you ask me," Shirley replied.

"Pity she doesn't choke on them."

Morgan was right about the disco: it was lively, but only in the sense that Marla had to fend off numerous advances. She was good at the cold shoulder, obviously well-practised. Jamie tried to stay close to her, wishing she'd let him get closer. Marla danced with him for most of the evening, her languid movements mesmerising. Her necklace swayed along with her movements. He remarked that it looked expensive.

"Oh, it cost Daddy a mint. It's actually a locket – a present for my eighteenth last month."

"Don't you keep someone's photo in a locket?"

"I shall when I meet the right guy."

"Not met him yet?"

The big smile made Jamie go weak at the knees. "I'll know when I have."

Morgan would have liked to get closer too, but the stumbling block was Lorna. No way was she going to let that posh, swanky tart get her hands on him. However, Lorna had to work hard to rein him in, finally inviting him to accompany her 'outside'. At least that ensured she won the battle: the war might be a different matter. Privately, she wished Jamie the best of luck in his pursuit of Marla.

Shirley had long ago resigned herself to being a wallflower on these occasions. Jamie might have the odd dance with her if there was no-one else who took his fancy, but it didn't help that she was a few inches taller than him. Tonight, however, he was fully occupied. A bloke tried chatting her up while Lorna and Morgan were absent, but he was at least fifty and had beery breath. *No thanks.*

On the way home, Lorna made sure she sat in front, but Jamie didn't object to sitting so close to Marla. Shirley was rammed up against the door and could hardly breathe. Fortunately, they didn't have far to go.

They dropped Marla off at the big house by the bridge: Riverlands. Jamie insisted on seeing her to the door, although she told him there was no need. "Thanks for asking me. It was such fun to meet you all."

"Was it?" A disgruntled murmur from Lorna.

"Listen," Marla went on, "why don't you all come up to the house for drinks tomorrow evening? We've stacks of room and booze, and Mummy and Daddy won't mind."

The boys accepted readily. "Won't keep me away," Jamie said, as they called in at the darkened pub for a goodnight coffee.

Morgan glanced over at the girls, satisfied that they were deep in conversation. "Get anywhere?" he asked.

"Nah. Early days." Jamie's sounded like a true voice of experience. "She's no pushover, for certain. But I'm working on it."

Morgan wished he could work on it too. He'd have to find some way to deflect Lorna.

"You score?" Jamie asked.

"Yeah. No problem," Morgan answered complacently. "And I'll score again when we get back to her place."

Jamie nodded towards Lorna. "Bet she's nice to have around. She's a good-looker."

"Yeah, there's that."

Morgan sounded wistful, and Jamie read his mind. "Listen, pal, I saw Marla first. Gimme some space, huh? 'Sides, you've got your bird."

"So've you."

"Eh?"

"Shirl."

Jamie pulled a face. "Shirl? Mate, you've got to be joking."

In a badly timed break in their whispered (and amazingly bitchy) conversation, Shirley heard his comment but let it pass.

Another dream gone west.

7

Morgan was aiming to have a few drinks and maybe cadge a couple of roll-your-owns off Jamie when they went to Marla's place the following evening, so he insisted they'd walk rather than take the car. Lorna wasn't greatly chuffed about that, stumbling along in her platforms.

As they came out of the village and crossed the long stone bridge over the Thames, they had a good view of Riverlands, sprawling in a dip next to the river. None of them, other than Jamie, had seen the house except in passing.

"Took Mrs Leo's car back after she'd had a prang. She's no bad looker and seemed as if she might get a bit friendly. Nearly got invited in, but I was expected back at the garage."

The house was ugly, stuccoed walls and a flat roof, thirties style, and first-floor balconies with French windows; imposing, nonetheless. A driveway led down from the road and circled round an ornate marble fountain. As they approached, the long windows gave them a view of spacious rooms and modern, low-slung leather furniture, rosewood chairs and tables. Beyond the house, a manicured lawn swept down to the river and a small boathouse and jetty. A sun-lounger sat in the centre of the lawn and, in full view from the adjacent towpath and bridge, a lithe female form in a bright orange bikini and shades lay stretched out upon it. The folds of blonde hair told them it had to be Marla, and the boys' eyes were out on stalks. Lorna, walking behind them with Shirley, said something uncomplimentary.

Marla saw them, whipped off her shades and waved vigorously, directing them round to a wicket gate which gave on to the towpath. It was only when they stepped on to the lawn that they saw she wasn't alone. Skulking in the shadow of the hedge was a girl of eleven or so, in a skimpy dress which had begun the day white, long fawn socks and brown sandals. She peered up at them guiltily from beneath her fringe.

"Kirstie, what the *hell* are you doing here?" Jamie exclaimed.

"I just invited her in for a chat," Marla drawled. "She'd been playing on the towpath with some friends. We've had a lovely time, haven't we, Kirstie?"

"Mrs Hartman gave me some cake and lemonade," the girl piped up.

"Right. And Mum'll go spare because she'll have expected you back an hour ago," Jamie pointed out. "Go on, get home quick. Say you've been with me all the time."

"Thanks, Jamie. 'Bye, Marla. See you again soon, I hope?"

"Of course, sweetie. Call any time."

Kirstie scampered off, hoping her brother's suggestion might save her from another whack on the back of her legs. That stick her mum had used the time before had left an ugly red weal, which had taken an age to go away.

Once Kirstie had gone, the boys pitched down on the grass beside Marla, who sat pertly on the edge of her lounger. Lorna hung back, her face like thunder. She knew she looked pretty good but felt overdressed, next to that flashy bitch in her bikini.

As for Shirley, she knew she couldn't compete anyway and wasn't even going to try. She felt sorry for her friend, so hung up on Morgan, Lorna had only taken the job at the FA to get close to him, and Shirley had to wonder if he was worth it.

"Oh, look, here come the Hartmans," she remarked, happy for the distraction.

Leo Hartman came rumbling across the lawn, clad in a natty red waistcoat, jeans and boating shoes. He was wheezing a little, for he was a big man, his face jowly, nose prominent, dark hair slicked back over his skull. He was mega-rich, ran an estate agent's business with shops in Oxford, London and Winchester, and he owned property in London and Paris, besides Riverlands.

His wife tripped along after him, martini glass in hand. Venetia Hartman lived in a social whirl. She was tall and leggy, a former dancer and model now in her early forties, curly dark hair framing her still pretty face, majestic in a long, silky, strapless evening gown. Leo liked to have her beside him at the many dinners and functions with the rich clients he entertained.

"How lovely to be meeting two such handsome young men," she cooed, as she fetched up alongside the boys. "And my darling girl attracts them like moths around a candle flame. Just as I used to – not so very long ago."

Marla smiled indulgently. Mummy was well away, as usual. Still, it was good to have her around when Daddy was in one of his moods. Venetia was an expert in getting not only her own way, but her daughter's too.

"This is Jamie and Morgan, Mummy," she said. "I've invited them round for drinks. Do you mind if we use the River Lounge?"

"Not at all, darling. Now, why don't you pop indoors and put some clothes on, and I'll take Jamie and – Morgan? -yes – over there. That's all right, isn't it, Leo, dear?"

"Oh yes, yes, darling. And perhaps I'll bring the ladies along. Now, it's Lorna, isn't it? Hhmm, yes, you've served me several times at the village inn. Must be their greatest asset."

Two of Lorna's greatest assets were peeking above her tight vest top, and Leo was practically salivating. In fact, Shirley reckoned, her friend's outfit covered such a small percentage of her body, she wasn't far off being in direct competition to Marla in her bikini.

Leo finally succeeded in tearing his attention away from Lorna's cleavage. "And you, my dear? I know your face, but…?"

"Shirley Newbury, Mr Hartman. I'm junior reporter for the *Bugle*."

"Oh, ah, yes. Didn't you do a feature on Riverlands not so long ago?"

"That would most likely have been Mr Pettifer."

"Oh, Roland. Yes, of course. Know him well. Right, let me escort you lovely ladies over to the house."

Lorna was teetering in her platforms, so Leo felt the need to take her arm to guide her to the safety of the path. Shirley followed on behind. Leo had called her 'lovely'. Last time that had happened had been a comment from her dad, when he'd seen her in her party dress. She must have been all of six years old at the time. Oh well, progress. She grinned at Leo's and Lorna's backs. She supposed it was in her nature to be a bit standoffish, but at least she didn't have some overweight, middle-aged, boozy lech drooling over her.

The River Lounge was a large upstairs room at the rear of the house. White leather sofas were ranged along two walls, with a number of oak coffee tables sprinkled around; while an impressive stereo system and small bar stood against the third wall. Beyond them, sliding doors opened out to a wide balcony overlooking the Thames.

Venetia escorted the boys over to the bar. She'd eventually recognised Jamie from the garage and Morgan from the pub. Morgan took confident charge of the bar and made sure his first task was to refresh Venetia's martini. She expressed her delight. "I really ought to employ you as my personal cocktail shaker," she exclaimed coquettishly, a beringed hand lingering on his wrist, as she sampled her drink.

By now, Leo had arrived with the girls and deposited Lorna lovingly on one of the sofas, examining her legs with the eyes of a connoisseur. Shirley found her own seat.

Once Marla had joined them, in a simple dark blue dress and the gold lamé sandals, the expensive locket dangling from her neck, the Hartmans withdrew, Venetia having to coax her husband away. "I think we should leave the young people to enjoy themselves." Shirley felt the words, for all their sugary sweetness, held a scarcely veiled threat. Anyway, Leo went.

Marla sashayed across the room and perched on a stool at the bar, crossing her legs so that her already short skirt rode up even further.

"We'll have Bacardi and Coke," she announced. Morgan opened a bottle from behind the bar and poured them each a generous measure in tall glasses. "And some music," she commanded. "Jamie, sort out something we can dance to."

"Perhaps I can have the pleasure of the first dance?" Morgan suggested smoothly, as he leaned over the bar to hand Marla her glass.

She cast a wicked glance over her shoulder. "Doubt if your girlfriend would approve," she said with a smirk.

That was a massive understatement. If the look on Lorna's face was anything to go by, Marla was about to be stretchered away to the nearest mortuary. "I think you ought to dance with her," she added in a stage whisper.

Morgan felt trapped. Enticed by Marla's nearness, even though the bar stood between them, and breathing in a waft of her heavenly perfume, he realised he had no choice. It was a pity this couldn't have been one of Lorna's nights on duty at the pub. Marla's twinkling gaze dared him to rebel, egged him on. There was no way, with all his advantages, that he was prepared to lose out to Jamie, who was just a garage hand, and the Rydes without two ha'pennies to rub together. But he knew he had to bide his time.

Jamie hauled out some LPs, and the music kicked in. Up-to-the-minute stuff: Chicago, Deep Purple, Elton John and, of course, the Bee Gees, so that he could prat around pretending he was Barry Gibb. Morgan partly redeemed himself by hauling the sullen Lorna from her seat and on to the patch of carpet in front of the bar.

Sadly, that left Jamie with Marla, and he soon cunningly switched the music over to something slow and smoochy. Lorna pulled Morgan closer, at the same time throwing Marla a vicious look. Marla, ignoring the fact that Jamie was nuzzling her neck, raised a laconic eyebrow and grinned back wickedly. She gave the impression of somehow being above it all, letting the simple village children have their fun.

Shirley, meanwhile, didn't leave her seat, studying the far wall and wondering how she might put a new spin on next week's WI reports, which had endured the same format for the last twenty-five years.

As they took a break from dancing and sat around over more drinks, Jamie with a possessive arm around Marla's shoulders, Lorna holding Morgan so close that he was having to fight for breath, Marla asked what they did for fun?

"Saturday night disco in Reading can be pretty cool," Morgan reckoned.

"Reading?" Marla's voice rang with contempt. "Ever heard of London? That's where it's at, and where we should be heading."

"Your wish is my command," Jamie promised expansively, before starting work on her neck again. Morgan was pleased to see that she was looking rather bored. *It was a job for a professional anyway, and he knew only one of those.*

Then a bright idea struck him. "Why not try our disco first?" he suggested.

"Oh, come *on*! Surely you don't mean that place we went to last night? Wasn't even a proper disco in my opinion."

"No, *our* disco. Actually, *mine*. Down at the FA, here in Selsby." He'd organised one last Christmas, knew a DJ who hung out in the next village.

"Oh, so you reckon you can run a disco, do you?" Marla had successfully escaped Jamie's embrace. She was staring at Morgan boldly, and he recognised the challenge in her voice. An invitation, too, if he was interpreting it right. Well, he probably was, 'cause he could tell he'd impressed her.

"Yeah, sure. Done it before. Piece of cake." He was oozing confidence now, knew too that he'd put one over on Jamie, who was eyeing him dispiritedly.

"All right, then, you're on. When?"

"Why not this coming weekend?"

"I'll certainly look forward to it." He caught the hint of promise, couldn't miss the naughty smile. *Great!* Pick that one out, Jamie. As for Lorna – *whoops!* It was getting late, and Marla wanted them gone. Jamie told Morgan he'd follow on. Had some stuff on him that he'd got from one of his mates at the garage, thought Marla might like a snort.

Morgan wasn't troubled. It was Jamie's way of trying to get somewhere with her, and he doubted he'd cut much ice. Once they were all gone, he reckoned Marla would be quick to give Jamie the brush-off.

So, Morgan, full of himself and his cleverness, walked the girls home. Dropped off Shirley first, then took Lorna along to her mum and dad's at the far end of the village. He was looking forward to some fun on the sofa in their front room, as Mr and Mrs Pascoe would have gone to bed ages ago.

Lorna didn't even invite him in and, to cap it all, it started to rain the moment he left her. He was soaked to the skin by the time he reached home.

8

The Frobisher Arms had a back room, complete with bar, which they let out for functions, beating the village hall hands down. Morgan knew it hadn't been booked for the coming Saturday, so he had a word with his dad. He promised he'd fork out for the disco from his own pocket. Tony was all right with that, provided everyone was charged the going rate for drinks, and Morgan cleared up any mess afterwards.

"Me and Lorna'll run the bar," he suggested cheerfully, not that he'd said anything to Lorna about it. He wasn't sure if they were still speaking, but he knew he'd talk her round. He always did – she couldn't resist his animal magnetism (his phrase).

Morgan set to work. His first task was to stick an ad in the *Bugle* about a disco at the FA on Saturday night, admission free. Shirley promised to do that but warned him that old Barnfleet would be sure to charge him for it.

Then he booked the disco. This guy, they called him Fuzzy, on account of his Afro hairstyle, who lived in a village down the road: he fancied himself as a DJ heading for the big-time. They agreed a price and a time for him to rattle along in his ancient Morris van and set it up.

He popped into the garage to see Jamie during the week. His mate slid out from beneath an old Standard Vanguard, hair in his eyes and overalls stiff with grease. Morgan wondered what Marla might make of that, compared to his own eye-catching appearance: new flared Levis, flower-power shirt and face splashed all over with *Brut. No contest.*

He told Jamie about the disco, and Jamie said he'd put the word around. Morgan could read his mind: it was his big opportunity to impress Marla. Well, he wasn't going to get it all his own way.

Then Morgan was jarred out of his complacency, when Jamie added that he'd give Marla the news, as he was going round to see her that night. Morgan's jaw dropped: *surely* Jamie couldn't be…? Not already? But no. His mind flicked back to the previous occasion and the disdainful look on Marla's face, when Jamie was trying to crawl all over her. *No chance.*

Jamie added that he'd let some of his mates know. They didn't read the *Bugle* – he called it by the name the locals had long adopted, which was far from complimentary.

Morgan's final and most daunting task was Lorna. When he walked her home from the pub that night, he told her how Jamie had been pestering him to put on a disco at the FA on Saturday night, so that he could impress Marla, and Morgan had given in to him. Would Lorna mind helping him run the bar? His dad would pay the usual rates and, as a bonus, they'd be together that evening.

She fell for it, as he'd hoped she might. She'd forgiven him for last night, said she'd stomped off in a huff to make her point. "Yeah, yeah, sure, sweetness, that's cool," he assured her. "I was being a bit of a prick, and I'm sorry. Will you forgive me – *please?*"

She did, twenty-four hours later than he'd expected, in her mum and dad's front room.

*

The disco attracted a decent crowd. Morgan reckoned there must have been close to forty of them, all told. Fuzzy did them proud. "Here we go, man, let's hear it for the *groo-viest* sounds of 1970." Before long, bodies were gyrating to the strains of Mungo Jerry, Christie and Edison Lighthouse.

The beer flowed too, and Morgan, working alongside Lorna, guessed that Tony and Marj would approve of the way his initiative was bringing money in. It was business as usual in the pub itself, although one or two regulars, Roly and Ned among them, looked in to see what was happening. The two old soaks only showed up so that they could leer at the talent, although Ned was, as ever, on the watch in case some bird had carelessly left a handbag open.

Lorna was feeling carefree, wearing her skimpiest mini and revelling in the attention she was getting from the male customers. As time went on, she was beginning to think that snobby Marla had stood them up. Mummy and Daddy wouldn't be keen on her hob-nobbing *too* freely with the local yokels. And there was pathetic Jamie, hanging about in the doorway, waiting for her, all poshed up in pink shirt and bell bottom jeans, thinking he looked really special, when he was just a common little garage-hand without ten bob to his name. Time had been when he'd *begged* her to go out with him – he hadn't been alone there – but she'd set her sights on Morgan, particularly when Marj had offered her the barmaid's job. Okay, pay wasn't great, but she'd got her hooks into him, and he was going to *own* the flipping Frobisher one day. So, she didn't intend letting go of him in a hurry.

Then, typically last to arrive so that everyone was looking at her, came Marla flaming Hartman in a short, loose, red and blue tunic and knee-high white boots, her blonde hair swishing around in a long ponytail, which Lorna desperately wanted to tug – hard. Jamie was all over her in an instant – *look, boys, this is my bird* – and brought her over to the bar, got her a Bacardi and Coke – where did he get the money for that? – and led her triumphantly over to a seat near the disco. Every male gaze was on her, including Morgan's – oh, she could have slapped him! – and then, to cap it all, he decided, because it was his disco, that he ought to 'mingle'. Lorna felt abandoned, betrayed, as she watched him slip out from behind the bar, only too certain of the direction in which he was heading.

"They're not worth it, Lor," a sympathetic voice piped up at her elbow, and she turned to find Shirley perched on a bar stool. "Don't worry. He won't stray very far."

Lorna could see why Shirley was so confident about that. While Jamie was around, no-one else was going to get close to Marla. And Shirley felt she had to be there for her friend. She disliked the way Morgan took Lorna for granted, could see he'd ditch her in an instant, if something he reckoned was better – like Marla – happened along. And Lorna was so in love with him, worshipped him. Well, she supposed that must be what love was like; not that it had happened to her or was ever likely to. Shirley cast her mind back to that last school reunion dance. Andy Hannigan pressing himself against her, all booze, cheap aftershave and smelly breath. *Ugh!*

"Good evening, gorgeous. Where've you been all my life?"

Shirley turned in amazement and disbelief as a large shadow fell across her; but the guy – as she might have known – was addressing her friend. Lorna immediately buckled under the compliment, her glum features somersaulting into a smile and a hand reaching up to push the hair out of her eyes. "Hi, what can I get you?" she cooed breathlessly.

The guy was older than them, mid to late twenties, large, pasty-faced, square-jawed and with a superior smile which Shirley immediately distrusted. He wore a gold-coloured blazer, red-and-white striped loons, and his mousy-brown hair curled around his collar. But the appearance seemed contrived, and his measured drawl suggested a public-school education, his expensive cologne money.

"Just passing through. Thought I'd suss out where the action is." He nodded at Lorna's unmissable cleavage. "Rather glad I did. The name's Rupert, by the way. But call me Roop."

"I'm Lorna, and this is my friend Shirley."

"Oh, hi. Almost missed you there. I say, pull me off a pint of best, will you, Lorna darling?" He watched, mesmerised, as she drew then served his drink. "I'd hoped to meet up with a friend of mine. Called at her house but was told she was out at a disco. Suppose this must be it." He looked around doubtfully.

Lorna had suddenly lost the breathless voice. "If you're looking for Marla, she's over there in the far corner."

Roop looked impressed. "Wow! How did you know I was looking for Marla?" He picked up his drink and, with a parting leer, shouldered his way through the dancers.

"Because everybody bloody is," Lorna snarled at his departing back. "Ooohh!" She dashed a fist at empty air. "Give me five minutes with her, just five, that's all I'd need."

"Perhaps he's come to whisk her away?" Shirley suggested hopefully.

"North Pole wouldn't be far enough."

Shirley let her friend rant on. Her journalist's intuition made her wonder if Roop might be trouble, and her active mind began running around an idea for an article in next week's *Bugle:* 'SEX AND DRUGS IN SLEEPY SELSBY'. Well, it'd put one over on pompous Pettifer for certain, but she couldn't see Fred Barnfleet wearing it. Still, a bit more exciting than court reports and the Selsby WI's cake competition.

Meanwhile, the newcomer had reached the spot where Marla was holding court to two admirers. Other male eyes were hungrily turned on her, and several disenchanted girlfriends were agitating for those eyes to be redirected towards them.

Roop took in the two suitors at a glance: one quite short, a cocky-looking little devil, long tangled hair and cheap pink shirt, with an arm slung possessively around her waist. Roop grinned disdainfully: knowing Marla, she'd only tolerate *him* for so long. The other was tall, quite beefy, swept-back blond hair and moustache to match. He thought the world of himself too: definitely more her type, provided he had the bank balance to match it.

"Marla darling, hi!" he called out, his plummy voice earning him several amused stares.

Morgan and Jamie looked up, affronted; more so, when they took in the newcomer's appearance. Marla's look was cool and superior. "Oh, hi there"; her greeting a long way short of enthusiastic.

"It's Roop. Surely, you've not forgotten me? Monaco, last Easter? I've certainly not forgotten you."

"Oh, yah. Of course." Rupert Blount. How Marla wished she could have forgotten him: he'd been a heck of a nuisance. But she decided she'd tolerate him. Knowing Roop, he'd probably brought something along which might alleviate the crushing boredom of Selsby-on-Thames. "So, what brings you here?" she asked, trying to inject something which might be construed as enthusiasm into her tone.

"You, of course," Roop gushed with a lascivious grin. Shorty was starting to fidget, although Roop was big and ugly enough to see *him* off. Shorty's chum, however, was appraising him thoughtfully. "I'm over at the Hannons with my folks for the weekend," Roop went on. "It's their usual summer bash. Lady H and Ma are cousins, so I was forced to tag along. What a relief it is to see a friendly face, particularly one so beautiful."

Marla met the compliment with a bland smile. She wondered if she ought to compile a book of corny chat-up lines.

"Perhaps we might have a dance?" Roop pressed.

Before Marla could answer, Jamie had inserted himself between them. "She happens to be with me, pal," he growled. "In case you hadn't noticed."

Roop threw him an inquisitive stare, as if he'd only just clocked him. "I hadn't, actually."

"Well, perhaps I ought to make sure you do."

He took a step forward, fists bunched at his sides. Morgan sighed. Typical J, when he'd had a couple of drinks and there was a bird to impress. He slid deftly between them. The posh guy was almost a foot taller than Jamie, and Morgan sensed a mean streak in him. "Come on, J," he coaxed. "This is my show here. I don't want it wrecked."

Jamie reluctantly backed down, pretty sure that Marla was looking at him in awe.

"I've no quarrel with anyone, you see," Roop said expansively. "All I want is a word with Marla."

She knew what sort of word that'd be. Roop was trouble, and his parents despaired of him. They kept him short of money, but he'd found ways to counter that. She wasn't keen on being alone with him for long either, and if they'd known how much she valued their company at that moment, Jamie and Morgan would have felt chuffed beyond measure.

Marla smiled sweetly and saw her two guardians melt predictably. "Shan't be a moment, boys."

Roop led her over to a dark corner in the shadow of Fuzzy's thumping, flashing disco. Jamie lurched forward anxiously, but Morgan held him back. "He's not her type," he whispered. "Don't think she can stand him."

It was too dark to see Roop slip the small white envelope into Marla's handbag or pocket the crisp note she handed him. She returned as quickly as she'd implied, Roop hanging over her like a curse.

"Better jolly along," he announced. "Join the folks for after-dinner drinks or whatever. Hanging out in Selsby long, babe?"

No longer than she could help, she didn't say. "Down in London by the autumn," she replied. "I'm getting my own pad, though Daddy insists I have to get a job first."

"No doubt I'll see you around, then." Roop threw Jamie a look, as if he was something he'd just scraped off the bottom of his shoe. "And, I say, do lose the hanger-on in the meantime. You've no need to slum it, darling."

That set Jamie off again, but Morgan was ahead of him and, even better, Marla had laid a restraining hand on his arm. Roop, meanwhile, had turned and was already walking away. Morgan followed him, wanting to make sure he was off the premises. His mum and dad would go up the wall if he allowed any rough stuff.

"Sorry about that," Roop apologised smoothly, as Morgan caught him up at the door. "But your little friend's a mite touchy. Wasting his time with a smart chick like Marla, though. She's more yours or my type, I'd say. By the way, did you mention you ran the show here?"

Morgan was beginning to change his opinion of Roop. He was quite perceptive, not your usual public-school pillock. That remark about him and Marla, him being her type. Get Jamie out of the way, and he'd have a crack at her. Oh blimey, but what about Lorna? Have to do something about her too.

"Yeah, I do," he replied. "My folks own the pub, and I help run it. But they're talking of retiring to Spain soon, then the whole show'll be mine."

Roop nodded thoughtfully. "Hhmm. Dare say you and I could do some lucrative business." He fished a card from his blazer pocket, passed it across. "Give me a bell when you're next in London."

"I'll do that. I'm Morgan – Morgan Tambling."

"Rupert Blount." They exchanged a handshake. "See you around, Morgan."

Morgan watched as Roop went out to the car park, got into a gleaming white MG and sped away. He'd given him plenty of food for thought. A glance across the room informed him that Jamie was dancing with Marla, and that she was maintaining a respectful distance between them. He shrugged, smiled slyly and re-joined Lorna at the bar. She'd been bitching away with Shirley, but her face lit up the moment she saw him. That animal magnetism again.

Before too long, everything had wound down and Tony Tambling had ambled across to make sure all was as it should be. Fuzzy was packing his gear away, and Morgan had paid him out of the till. Apart from him, there were just the five of them left.

Jamie's arm was around Marla's shoulders. "I better walk you home, sugar. Never know who's about."

"Good disco?" Morgan asked her.

She stared back coolly. "Not bad. Better than wherever we went before. Listen, guys, I'm splitting soon. Need to get myself a pad in London. That's where it's all happening. Come up to my place in the week, and we'll have a farewell party – Mummy and Daddy are out at some dinner. Wednesday or Thursday, but I'll bell you in the week, Morgan. Oh, and don't drive up – we'll be drinking big-time."

With an airy farewell, she sashayed out of the door, Jamie scurrying after her.

"Back to London, eh?" Lorna drawled. "Bloody good riddance too."

"Let's clear up," Morgan suggested, and Shirley offered to lend a hand. She'd noticed he was in a good mood and didn't think it had much to do with the prospect of seeing Lorna home. Or that it concerned Lorna at all.

She was right. Morgan had been thinking London thoughts, of a whole new future beckoning. Sure, his mum and dad could tootle off to Spain. He'd sell the FA, get established down in the big city, become a wealthy man, surround himself with some gorgeous dolly birds.

And he'd be going it alone.

9

Marla, all sweetness and light, secured Venetia's permission to invite her friends round for drinks on the Thursday evening. Her parents would be dining at the Randolph in Oxford with a gathering of Leo's well-to-do estate agent cronies, so they'd be nicely out of the way.

She'd asked Jamie to get there an hour before the rest, which had put his expectations on red alert. He'd been preening himself all day and boring his workmates senseless with details of what 'me and my bird' would get up to.

Marla, as usual, looked as if she'd stepped out of a dream, mouth-wateringly glamorous in the shortest white dress ever invented. But, again as usual, Marla was in control. She had uses for Jamie, although not along the lines he'd been hoping.

He'd smoked a joint on his way there and felt amenable enough to lug bottles of champagne, a crate of beer and a box of Leo's favourite claret up to the River Lounge. He offered Marla one, which she waved away. He guessed she might already have had a snort of whatever that public-school ponce had passed her the other night. She was her customary flirtatious self: high on promise, but short on delivery. However, the night stretched ahead of them, and Jamie was determined to pull her into a dark, unpopulated corner before he went home; then give his mates a blow-by-blow account next morning.

They took some champagne down on to the lawn before the others arrived, arranged bottles and glasses on a picnic table and lounged around, drinking. Marla positioned herself near the wicket gate, suitably distanced from Jamie's wandering hands. It was with some relief that she waved, as she saw them bob into view on the bridge.

Morgan looked rather dashing in denim jacket and a black shirt with a red rose pattern. Lorna, as always, was trying to compete. She'd plastered on too much make-up, and you could practically see her knickers as she hobbled along in those daft platforms. *Sorry, sweetie, no contest.*

As for Shirley, well, she was tagging along. Ought to grow her hair out, cover her face. That'd be an improvement. And Marla was certain she had little interest in men. Heavens! A real live lesbo in sunny Selsby! That horrible, toad-faced little journalist, who camped out in the pub and leered freely at anything in a skirt, could probably make a scoop out of that.

Trailing along behind, and Marla could tell none of them had noticed her, came little Kirstie, hair in her eyes, grubby T-shirt and a hitched-up pleated skirt which yearned to be a mini, her skinny legs protruding like a couple of pipe-cleaners. Marla grinned. She liked Kirstie, and the kid absolutely adored her. "What sort of adventures do you have in London, Marla?... Oh, Marla, I wish one day I'll grow up to be as beautiful as you... My boyfriend will pick me up in his super-fast sports car and whisk me off to London. It sounds wonderful, I'd love to live there..."

Marla had invited Kirstie round a few times, given her crisps, chocolate, lemonade; let her try on a dress or two, slop around in her high heels. Just let her have some *fun*. It must be a hell of a life with no father, a dragon for a mother and a brainless oik for a brother...

She greeted them as they tumbled through the wicket gate, then peeped round and said "Hi" to Kirstie, who stood dithering on the towpath.

"Kirstie!" Jamie had suddenly come alive, scrambling up and squashing the remains of his latest joint under his foot. "Where the hell did you spring from? Mum'll go spare if you're still out when she gets back."

"Oh, give her a break," Marla protested, as she strode over to the gate, took the girl by the hand and brought her on to the lawn. She invited everyone to sit, got Jamie to pour them each a glass of champagne and settle Kirstie beside her. The girl was in seventh heaven, particularly when Marla offered her a couple of sips from her glass.

The drink went straight to Kirstie's head, and she began to act crazily, although her antics made everyone laugh, the best mood they'd been in collectively since Marla had arrived on the scene.

Then a shadow fell across them, short, aggressive and in no mood for fun. Barbara Ryde slammed the gate behind her and marched up to her daughter.

"Kirstie – I've told you time and time again. You're *not* to come here. Get up and get yourself home!"

"Oh, *Mum!* I'm having such a lovely time. *Please* let me stay. Jamie, tell Mum I can stay..."

Jamie wasn't telling Mum anything, and Barbara's response was to yank the girl upright by the ear. Kirstie screamed in pain.

Marla leapt up. "There's no need to treat her like that!" she stormed.

Barbara shoved Kirstie yowling to the grass and faced Marla squarely, hands on hips. She was a good six inches shorter but spoiling for a blazing row.

"You, Miss High-and-Mighty," she railed back, "don't tell *me* what to do with *my* child. It's a pity you don't buzz off back to where you came from. Kirstie!" she yelled. "I said get on home. Now! I'll be having words later."

"Sorry, Mum." Jamie had found a voice at last, and there wasn't much fight in it. "It's not Marla's fault. Kirstie was being silly."

A glare from his mother silenced him. She turned to confront Marla; although Marla wasn't about to buckle.

"You're a disgrace!" Barbara bawled. "You with your booze and drugs and London ways, you think you know it all. Go back to blinkin' London, why don't you, and leave us decent folks alone?"

With that, she turned and bustled off, slamming the gate again. She must have caught up with Kirstie, for there came the sound of a sharp slap, and the girl cried out.

Lorna was exulting in Marla's dressing-down, grinning hugely; something she hadn't done in a long time. But Marla wasn't fazed, simply stared frostily in the direction the Rydes had gone, then turned to the gathering and invited them upstairs to the River Lounge.

"I think we need some drinks and decent music," she suggested calmly. "Take the nasty taste away."

She led them up there, marched across to the stereo and put on some music. Soon, the Rolling Stones, Deep Purple and Manfred Mann were blasting out of the speakers at full volume. The booze flowed: beer, gin and tonic, whisky, rum and Coke, as well as Leo's claret.

Jamie turned the lights down and grabbed hold of Marla. Unlike him, however, she could hold her drink and had no difficulty evading his clumsy advances. He was so drunk – the only one of them who'd been mixing his drinks with abandon – that he accepted her repeated replies of "Later, perhaps," to his increasingly lewd suggestions.

Lorna was glad that Marla had her hands full with Jamie. It kept her away from Morgan. Oh, she could read the looks he was giving her. "You won't get anywhere with her, hon," she cooed in his ear, as they swayed, locked together in the middle of the floor. "Besides, you've got me. What more could you want?" He didn't answer that.

Before long, Marla became so tired of Jamie breathing all over her that she suggested a change of scene. Shirley gave a silent cheer. She'd traipsed around with them that evening with no expectations at all, and she hadn't been disappointed. Indeed, she'd found enlightenment, wondered what she'd been on when she'd kidded herself she fancied Jamie Ryde. He was loud, spectacularly drunk, high as a kite and had bored everyone stupid with his boast that "me and Marla are shooting off to London, forming a rock group – lead guitarist, me!" (He couldn't play a note, had never picked up a guitar in his life). If Jamie was what men were all about, Shirley was off them forever.

Marla decided that it was such a warm, moonlit night, that they'd take a punt out on the river. "The rest of you finish your drinks, and perhaps you'd help me get it out of the boathouse, Morgan?"

Morgan didn't need persuading. Lorna looked daggers at him, but he didn't take the hint, and she watched, helpless, as he trotted off slavishly in Marla's wake. Shirley was in the loo, so she felt she had to wait for her, but the minute she reappeared, Lorna would be hot on their heels. She didn't trust Marla as far as she could throw her (and wished that could be a very long distance). Lorna thought Jamie might have protested, but he looked spaced out. She wondered if he'd sampled the contents of the white envelope Marla had whisked from her handbag some minutes ago.

Morgan caught up with Marla at the bottom of the stairs. He wasn't drunk, far from it. Realising Lorna hadn't started out after him, he reached out, grasped her arm and drew her into a clinch. She didn't resist him. When their faces parted, she was smiling mischievously.

"Been longing to do that, haven't you?" she whispered, with a careless toss of her blonde mane.

"Since that first night." His throat was dry, and he had difficulty forcing out the words.

"You can always come and see me in London," she teased. "Or haven't you ever been to London?"

He reached for her again, but she was too quick for him, racing away in the direction of the boathouse. He followed her at a business-like walking pace, having heard Lorna's feet clumping on the stairs and certain that she wouldn't suspect a thing.

The others caught them up at the boathouse. It was locked, and Marla flew into a rage. "Oh, the bastard! I knew it, knew he'd lock it – he never lets me have any fun. What a complete and utter *shit!*"

She said a lot more besides. The boys seemed to be in shock. Lorna enjoyed the sight of spoiled brat Marla in an almighty snit, and everyone now seeing her in her true colours. While Shirley wondered what the *Bugle's* readers might make of Marla's extensive vocabulary. That word her mum had warned her never to utter: she'd never dreamed it could be made to rhyme with 'parking'.

Morgan played the role of peacemaker; and Lorna despised him for it.

"Let's get back to the FA, have a drink or three in the back room. Dad won't mind. It's a private party, and I'll pay for the booze." *As if!*

Everyone agreed, the girls grudgingly, Marla with resignation. "Well, I never want to see my father again. To hell with him! I'm splitting for London."

"Yeah, but not tonight, eh?" Jamie lurched forward, seizing the moment. "Hey! If you're pissed off with your old man, you can stay the night at my place."

"We'll see." Her response was offhand, with no hint of promise, although naturally, Jamie didn't see it that way. She'd never been near there but was sure it was a place she wouldn't want to be seen dead in. She flounced off across the lawn to the towpath, Jamie struggling to keep up with her, the others dawdling behind, because Lorna had reclaimed Morgan and was sticking to him.

Marla's devil-may-care mood had returned once they'd reached the bridge. "Hey!" she cried out. "I'm going to walk across."

"Well, we all will, if we're heading back to the pub," Lorna sneered. "Silly cow."

"Bet you won't do it like this," Marla trilled back. She whisked off her shoes and, with one in each hand, leapt on to the parapet and wiggled her way to the middle. She turned gracefully, grinning wickedly. "Coming, Lorna?"

Lorna turned away in a huff, her face like thunder.

"Lorna's a scaredy-cat, a scaredy-cat," Marla taunted her.

"And you're a first-class *bitch!*" Lorna spat back furiously.

"Well, at least I've *got* class."

"Now, now, girls." Morgan sought to defuse the situation, while Shirley slipped an arm through Lorna's, worried that she might go for Marla.

"I'm coming!" Jamie wasn't going to be outdone. "Wait for me!"

"No – shan't!"

"All right, I'm coming to get you."

Before anyone could react, he'd scrambled on to the parapet and somehow hauled himself upright.

"Jamie," Shirley warned. "Careful. Mind you don't fall."

"Ah, get lost, Shirl. You won't get a story out of me. Hey – hey, how about a picture of me and Marla in bed on the front of next week's *Bugrake*? That'll make old Roly puff and blow!"

He threw back his head, laughed, teetered and fell in the same moment. Marla and Lorna screamed, and water whooshed up as Jamie hit the river.

"Oh God, he can swim, can't he?" Shirley gasped, as they all rushed forward to lean over the parapet.

"Yes." Morgan was suddenly the sanest and soberest of them all. "But he's not coming up." He peeled off his jacket, which Lorna took from him. Dashed down the embankment at the side of the bridge, kicked off his shoes and waded in.

Marla had leapt down from the parapet, staring into the water for some sign of Jamie. "He's not coming up!" she cried, looking desperately from one shocked face to another. "Oh, please, dear God, let him be all right..."

"Morgan's got him!" Shirley called out. "He's bringing him to the bank. He – he's – *oh no!*"

"Wh-what's happened?" Marla stammered.

Shirley hauled her away from the parapet. "Get back home and phone for an ambulance," she said commandingly. "Quick! There's no time to lose!"

Marla gaped at her for a moment. Then, seeming to gather her wits, she turned and ran back towards Riverlands.

"Come on, Lor." Shirley turned to her friend. "We must go and help Morgan."

But Lorna was too busy glaring after the departing Marla. "This is all your fault, you bitch!" she yelled. "If you hadn't come here, none of this would have happened! Get back to London! Get the hell out of our lives!"

10

As soon as her mum had left to work her stint at the pub, Kirstie took the opportunity to sneak back to Riverlands. Her legs were still sore from where Barbara had walloped her, but she felt it was worth the risk of another whack (or three) just to spend a little time with Marla. Kirstie idolised her, but, apart from that, Marla was really kind in return, and the girl didn't get a lot in the way of kindness.

On reaching the bridge, she immediately saw that something was very wrong. An ambulance stood at the side of the road, and Sergeant Burge's blue and white Panda car was drawn up on the grass verge beyond the bridge. Kirstie peeped over the parapet. A man was laid out on the bank, two ambulancemen bending over him, and the sergeant standing to one side, looking grim. Beyond them, she could see Shirley and Lorna crouched down beside – yes, she recognised the fair hair and shirt of the sopping wet figure which had to be Morgan.

But she couldn't see Marla.

And where was Jamie…?

The moment it occurred to her where Jamie was, Kirstie pressed a hand to her mouth, stifling a cry; stared again, saucer-eyed, at the scene below the bridge, then turned and pelted back to the village with all the speed her spindly legs could muster.

She burst into the Frobisher, where Tony, Marj, Roland Pettifer and her Uncle Ned all looked at her in alarm.

"Mum – where's Mum?" Kirstie gabbled, tears streaming down her face. "I must see Mum!"

As Marj came out from behind the bar to ask whatever was the matter, Barbara slammed through the door from the kitchen. "What on earth are you doing here, our Kirstie? And why are you making such a row?"

"Oh, Mum, there's been an accident down at the bridge. Mum, it – it's Jamie. I – I think he's badly hurt. There's an ambulance there, and Mr Burge and everything…"

"I'll run you down there, Barbara," Tony Tambling offered, immediately alert to the fact that Morgan must somehow be involved.

They headed out to his Rover, while Roly, Ned and a couple of others followed on foot, leaving Marj to remain, worrying, behind the bar and hoping that someone might remember to come back or phone her from a call box with the news.

As Tony pulled up on the far side of the bridge, the ambulance drew away, heading towards the main road and the hospital. Kirstie noticed that the Hartmans were back, because Leo's Bentley stood outside the front door of Riverlands. Sergeant Burge was making his slow way across the lawn to the house's side entrance, and the figures of Morgan, Lorna and Shirley didn't seem to have moved from their previous position on the bank.

Tony leapt from the car and hurried down to join them. Barbara got out, staring white-faced and fixedly after the departing ambulance, her mouth working silently at words. As Kirstie tumbled out, Barbara grabbed her hand, locked it in an irresistible grip. Most of her mum's actions held some measure of ferocity, but Kirstie felt that, somehow, this was different from all those other times; that her grip was possessive, almost caring, certainly not intending to let go.

Proud tears glistened on Barbara Ryde's face, uncompromising, as she led her daughter down the embankment to where Tony was squatting beside his son.

Morgan looked up as mother and daughter approached. Tears coursed unashamedly down his cheeks. "B-Barbara, K-Kirstie, I'm so sorry. He – he fell in – bashed his head on the arch of the bridge. I – I tried to save him. But he's dead, and I'm so, so sorry –."

"You were really brave, my darling." Lorna had him enveloped in a tight embrace. No matter that her best dress was soaked in the process. "You did everything you could."

"What happened?" Barbara demanded. She turned to Shirley Newbury, who'd been looking on, tight-lipped and serious. She knew she'd get an unvarnished account from Shirley: always got her head screwed on, that one.

"We were on our way back to the pub," Shirley explained. "We'd all had a few drinks. Jamie jumped up on to the parapet – he – he was trying to show off to Marla. He fell in. Morgan waded in and pulled him on to the bank, while Marla ran home and phoned for an ambulance. But Jamie had hit his head – an awful gash. I'm sorry, Mrs Ryde. He never regained consciousness."

Barbara's expression hardened. "Marla." She scarcely breathed the name, but her tone dripped venom.

"It wasn't Marla's fault, Mrs Ryde," Shirley said firmly, looking to her friends for support. Morgan was too distressed to speak, shaking his head in agreement; while Lorna was too intent on Morgan and probably wouldn't have defended the other girl anyway.

Barbara still held fast to Kirstie's hand. Now she dragged her along behind her, striding up to the towpath, then across the lawn to the house. Shirley moved to go after her, but Tony Tambling advised her not to. "Des Burge is there," he said. "He'll look after her." He turned to Morgan. "Let's get you home and dried off, son. Come on, girls. I'll run you back to the pub."

As they trailed back to the car, they passed a clutch of onlookers on the bridge. Roly and Ned were among them, but there was nothing to see. And Tony didn't feel like telling them. They could work it out for themselves.

*

The epicentre of the drama was the wide, plush lounge of Riverlands. Marla sat crying on one of the sofas, virtually smothered by a sobbing Venetia, who clung to her tightly, alternately feeding them both sips of Leo's Armagnac. Leo stood behind them, looking glumly on, while Burge dithered by the French windows, awaiting the eventual ebb of tears.

"My poor darling," Venetia purred. "How *awful*. Such an ordeal for my sweet, gentle girl…"

Everyone looked up as Barbara Ryde burst in, bundling the bovine figure of Burge aside and yanking Kirstie's hand with such violence that the girl tripped over the threshold and landed on her knees, scrambling up desperately, as she realised all eyes were trained on her and her mother.

Barbara glared balefully at Marla's huddled frame. "My son is dead." She spoke in a flat, dangerous voice. "It's down to *you*." She jabbed an accusing finger at the girl. "You are guilty, miss, and the law must punish you."

Marla detached herself from her mother and faced Barbara. Her hair was tousled, mascara staining her face and mingling with her tears. She was clearly in some distress. "I'm sorry, Mrs Ryde. He – he just fell. I'm *so* sorry…"

"I'll take you home, Mrs Ryde," Burge offered staunchly.

Barbara turned indignantly towards him. "I demand to see my son."

"Then I'll drive you to the hospital, ma'am. I can drop your daughter off at my house. My sister will –."

"Kirstie stays with me."

"As you wish, Mrs Ryde." He turned to Leo. "I shall need your daughter's account of what happened, Mr Hartman," he said. "Perhaps I'll call in on my way back."

"She can't possibly do that tonight!" Venetia stormed. "What's the matter with you, Sergeant? Can't you see how upset she is? It's been a horrible experience for her!"

"Perhaps I could bring Marla along to you in the morning, Sergeant Burge?" Leo suggested reasonably.

Burge nodded, relieved. Venetia had looked to be on the point of going for him.

"A good idea, sir." He turned back to Barbara. "Come along then, Mrs Ryde."

Barbara ignored him. With Kirstie in tow, she stalked up to where mother and daughter sat. Marla cowered from her, but Venetia, her painted eyes blazing, looked poised to spring.

"She's upset, is she?" Barbara spat. "What about my son, then, Mrs bloody Hartman? My son is *dead* – thanks to *her!*" She pointed furiously at Marla. "I shan't forget what you've done, you disgusting little tart. I shan't *ever* forget. Don't you for one moment think I shall."

"How *dare* you speak to my daughter like that, you ignorant woman?" Venetia uncoiled herself from Marla and rose magnificently to tower above their accuser. "How *dare* you come into my home and insult us. We're sorry about your son, but what happened was *his* fault, not hers."

In all his years on the force, Desmond Burge had never felt as anxious as he did then. Both women were incandescent with rage, and neither was likely to give ground. As stealthily as he could for such a big man, he insinuated his frame between them, slipped a custodial hand beneath Barbara's arm and, almost apologetically, edged her away. "Come along now, Mrs Ryde. We should get along to the hospital."

Barbara crumpled then, all her stern grief gushing out, as she suffered Burge to escort her back across the lawn to the waiting Panda car. Wrapped in her misery, she finally released Kirstie's hand, and the girl, trailing behind the hunched form of her mother and the reassuring bulk of the policeman, happened to switch a recalcitrant glance back at Marla.

Their gazes met, registering their mutual tears and emptiness; and Kirstie felt for that moment that they were like sisters in the sadness they shared.

11

August 1986

"Mum was all for prosecuting Marla," Kirstie went on.

We were on our third round of drinks, and I was amazed at how my sister could put it away. The gathering had begun to wind down, people drifting past us as they left by the side entrance. I was aware of Morgan standing alone behind the bar, watching us. He was frowning, no doubt wondering what we'd been talking about all this time.

"Really?" Roz raised a questioning eyebrow, as she dipped into her latest pint.

"Precisely." Kirstie looked sceptical. "Quite where we'd have found the money for that, I haven't a clue. But Mr Hartman and Roly Pettifer talked her out of it. They were both very kind, although Roly, as ever, was angling for a story. Even so, he didn't want it to go any further. He was good friends with the Hartmans and was all set to write it up as a tragic accident."

"All set?" I seized on the phrase. "You mean he never wrote it?"

Kirstie looked amused. "When Shirley told Mr Barnfleet she'd actually been present, an eyewitness, he got her to write it. It was a big break for Shirley – she was only nineteen or twenty at the time. The *Oxford Mail* and *Reading Chronicle* ran the story, which meant that Roly was seriously miffed. I don't think he ever forgave Mr Barnfleet or Shirley. "Selsby's biggest story in years, and he hands it to a junior." Morgan said he went on like that night after night in the pub. But, after all, it *was* just a tragic accident. The inquest bore that out, although Mum would never accept it.

"Mr Hartman was a decent man," Kirstie continued wistfully. "He was truly sorry for all that had happened. Venetia was *so* protective of Marla, and I imagine he had a heck of a battle to get it past her, but eventually, a couple of days after the inquest, Marla came to our house to offer her condolences. Mum answered the door but wouldn't let her in. I remember cowering behind the settee, because Mum was shaking with rage and soon had Marla in tears. She simply refused to listen to her. "It's no good you coming here saying how sorry you are, Miss Hartman. You're sorry, I'm sorry, everyone's blinkin' sorry. But let me tell you this. I'm sick of the sight of you, sick of all the damage you've caused. This was a peaceful village until you came swanking back here with your fancy clothes and foreign ways. Now you hear this and hear good. If you show your face here *ever* again, I'll kill you. Are you listening to me? I'll *kill* you."

"Poor Marla. She ran off in tears, moved down to London soon after, and we've not set eyes on her since.

"I felt sorry for Leo. He was genuinely upset for us. In time, Mum forgave him, but not Venetia or Marla. Jamie, bless him, had always been wild. We'd never really known our father. Apparently, he wasn't a particularly nice character, and he went off and left us soon after I was born. I think that somehow Mum blamed me for that: an unwanted additional burden. She always kept me in check, but not so much Jamie. He got into all sorts of trouble, often under the influence of Uncle Ned, Mum's cousin, who he looked up to. Jamie was often drunk, dabbled in soft drugs, and that didn't help on the night he died. Okay, I'm sure Marla led him on a bit – she was capable of beguiling most men. And Jamie was always out to impress, always prone to doing something silly. I long ago accepted that it was an accident, although Mum's never been able to see it that way.

"Still, she was grateful to Leo for helping us out financially. All we'd had was Jamie's wage and the few pounds Mum earned from working at the pub. Tony and Marj were good to us, slipping her the odd bonus and letting her bring home whatever was left in the kitchen at the weekend. But Mum's always had it in for Venetia and Marla."

Both Roz and I had listened with interest to Kirstie's narrative. "So, Marla went to London and never returned to Selsby?" I remarked.

"Not even for Jamie's funeral," she replied. "Mum was adamant that none of the Hartmans should attend, although she was the only one blaming Marla. Even Lorna -" Kirstie stole a quick glance back inside, but neither Tambling was in evidence. "Even Lorna admitted it was an accident. Jamie was drunk, and he just *fell.* He struck his head on the side of the bridge, otherwise he'd have been capable of making it to the bank.

"Venetia never knew it, but Leo paid the funeral costs. He was embarrassed by the way his wife and daughter had behaved. I think he felt that Marla was in some way responsible; although she and Leo never hit it off. She was always the apple of her mother's eye and could do no wrong. So, London was Marla's best option. They set her up in a flat in Chelsea, I believe. She had her own money, which she'd inherited from Leo's parents."

"Have you any idea what happened to her after that?" Roz asked.

"I heard she got a job in some trendy boutique – *Lady Jane* or *Girl,* I think it was, although I don't know how long it lasted. I heard she hitched up with a pop group which flopped, and I should imagine that awful man Roop was still chasing her. Shirley told me about the time he gate-crashed a disco here at the FA. She reckoned he was pushing drugs, so it wouldn't surprise me if Marla had got into that scene. In any case, we heard that she and Leo had fallen out big-time over her excesses, and she was never seen again in Selsby."

"Did her mother keep in touch with her, do you think?" If Roland had been seeing Venetia from time to time, I wondered if he might also have been in contact with Marla.

"I'm sure she did," Kirstie replied. "But without Leo knowing." She grinned, casting another backward glance. "You might have a word with Morgan. You see, he went charging off to London a few weeks later. I think he was after Marla, but nothing could have come of it because, before long, he was back in Selsby working at the pub. I think Tony and Marj must have given him an ultimatum. Anyway, back he came, rolled up his sleeves and pitched in, married Lorna and took over the FA when his mum and dad retired to Spain about ten years ago."

"Leo and Venetia were still at Riverlands when I came here," Roz said. "But the London move was a permanent one."

"Not one Leo wanted to make. He was okay, well-respected in the village, but no-one was keen on Venetia with her airs and graces. Except Roly, of course. Leo was away a lot, and there were rumours about the two of them. She kept nagging away at Leo about moving, must have been worse than a dripping tap, and eventually he gave in. They relocated to a luxury flat in Knightsbridge at the end of the 70s."

"And that was the last you saw of them?"

Kirstie looked uneasy. "Well – no. I got into drama at school, joined an amateur company in Reading. Leo came along to see me, took an interest and helped sponsor me through college. I certainly couldn't have financed it myself."

"That was good of him." My sister was positively purring, but I didn't think Kirstie wanted to go into further detail.

"Leo was a decent man," she resumed a little hurriedly, the second time she'd said that. "Sadly, he died two years ago – a massive heart attack. I went to the Knightsbridge flat to offer Venetia my condolences. I didn't think she'd want to see me, given all that had happened in the past, but she was surprisingly gracious. Mind you, she was heavily into the martinis. I couldn't stop her talking. Marla was still on a pedestal, but I got the impression Venetia didn't see a lot of her. I asked if I could get in touch, and she gave me Marla's address. I was really looking forward to seeing her again, only to get there and find she'd moved out years before with her boyfriend. I asked around, but no-one had any idea where she'd gone."

"You mentioned that Roland was friendly with Venetia," I said. "Might he have visited her last Saturday?"

"Almost certainly," Kirstie replied. "He turned up at my matinée in the afternoon and called into my dressing room after the performance. I could tell he'd been drinking then, so it crossed my mind that he might have been to see her."

"I don't suppose he mentioned Marla at all?"

Kirstie looked blank. "No, he didn't. I can't understand why he said those words about warning her. Unless he'd been in touch and hadn't told anyone about it. That was another thing about Roly. When he wanted to, he could keep his cards very close to his chest." She smiled at us and pushed back her chair. "I'd better see if Mum needs a hand with the washing-up. Dare say I'll get an earful, because I've only just thought about it. Nice meeting you, Glen. You too, Roz."

"Perhaps we might meet up for lunch one day and review our brilliant careers?" I suggested with my accustomed smoothness. *('Preston's chat-up lines were delivered with the suavity and charm of a public hangman').*

Her face lit up. "Oh, I'd really like that. I'll look forward to it."

I promised to be in touch, as Kirstie picked up our glasses and, with a parting smile, went back inside. Roz and I called out our thanks to Morgan and Lorna and headed for home.

12

Roz threw me a wry look as we turned down Burnage Lane.

"Don't waste much time, do you?" she observed. "You only met the girl an hour ago."

"We're both actors," I replied, squirming a little under my 'big' sister's scrutiny. "It'll be useful to compare notes – theatres, roles, agents, that sort of thing."

"Of course. And it helps that she's easy on the eye. Well, dear brother, all I'd say is watch your back."

"Morgan, I take it?" I recalled that he'd been looking on a little despondently. "Why?" I lowered my voice, although there seemed to be no-one else around. "Are they an item?"

Roz shrugged. "Doubt it. My impression is that Kirstie's nobody's fool. But I know he's been making a nuisance of himself when Lorna's been absent."

"Why does Kirstie stay there?"

"Because when she's not acting, she needs the wage to help her mum keep the house up together. In any case, Morgan's got other fish to fry. He's popping along to London often enough."

"Oh? Playing away?"

"Almost certainly, I'd say. He probably thinks he's being discreet, but he's playing a dangerous game. Shirley's seen him there in a pub with some woman. He completely blanked her."

"Did she tell Lorna?"

"Only me. Lorna would kill him, and that'd just be for starters."

"Kirstie mentioned something about Morgan going off in pursuit of Marla when she left Selsby?"

"Yes. It was long before my time here, but I gather that he fancied his chances. Jamie Ryde was no longer a rival, although personally I don't think he ever was. But Morgan had got it bad with Marla – he was obsessed, to the point where he threw over Lorna and hopped off to London. However, it wasn't long before he was back, with his tail between his legs. I'd imagine the London scene got a bit heavy for him. He was suddenly a small fish in a big pond, the reverse of his situation in Selsby. Also, Marla would have had no trouble attracting other admirers. There soon would have been no place for country boy Morgan."

"I wonder if that chap who followed her to Selsby was among them? Roop, wasn't it? He sounded awful."

"Another one who was besotted with her. Who knows? Anyway, it didn't take long for Morgan to come slinking back and, knowing him, he wouldn't have told it the way it was. Lorna had been heartbroken when he'd left, although he soon patched it up with her – in Shirley's opinion, she gave in too easily – and they'd married within the year. Still, Lorna's no mug. She knew what she was getting into with Morgan. She had her eyes on a higher prize – the Frobisher. Tony and Marj had made no secret about taking early retirement and heading off to Spain. Once they were satisfied that Morgan and Lorna were able to run the business, off they went, never to return. I'm no great fan of Lorna's, but she's a hard worker, and it's mainly through her efforts that the Frobisher's successful. Morgan's technically the boss, because he employed Kirstie. There's no way Lorna would have put temptation so obviously in his path."

Once we were back at the bungalow and the kettle was blasting away, the conversation turned to other matters, continuing to catch up on old acquaintances and all that had happened since we'd last spent some time together.

It was a welcome distraction. Interesting though the account of Marla's time in Selsby had been, I was no closer to learning exactly what Roland Pettifer had wanted to warn her about. And yet I was certain now that 'warn Marla' had been the words he'd uttered.

Our conversation flagged; the three pints of lager Roz had sunk were beginning to take their toll. As she dozed, I went and busied myself in the kitchen. Basic culinary skills had become essential since I'd been living alone, and cooking was something I enjoyed. Roz's kitchen was well stocked, and I'd rustled up a passable *tagliatelle carbonara* by the time she resurfaced. She complemented this with a bottle of *chianti*, and my diversion from all things Marla was complete.

Roz was up and about the next morning by the time I wandered into breakfast. She set before me a couple of croissants fresh from Selsby's little bakery and a pot of coffee.

"Once you're ready, dear brother," she announced breezily, "we're going visiting."

"Oh?" I was still sluggish after the previous night's wine, while she, who'd sunk more than half the contents of the bottle, seemed amazingly chipper. "And where might we be going?"

"The *Bugle* offices, to see Shirley Newbury. This week's edition is out today, so she'll have time to see us."

"Do you think she'll be able to tell us more than we've already learned?"

There was a mischievous twinkle in my sister's eyes. "Oh, I think we may be about to learn something new." Typically, Roz wasn't about to tell me what that might be.

The *Bugle* offices were housed in a narrow, low-ceilinged building in Selsby's main street. Two homicidal stone steps took us into the reception area, where a short, bespectacled woman with a grey perm and thick Shetland cardigan met us with a toothy smile.

"Morning, Deirdre," Roz greeted her. "This is my brother, Glen. We're here to see Shirley."

"Oh, this is the actor, isn't it?" Deirdre cooed, examining me as if I was a prize exhibit at the local Flower Show. "Ooohh, I recognise you now. I do believe you were in *Kramer vs. Kramer*?"

Clearly Deirdre was due to upgrade her spectacles. I thanked her for the compliment and assured her I'd never been to America, let alone Hollywood. I named a couple of TV dramas I'd most recently been in, wondering if she'd been alert enough to register my fleeting appearances.

She looked blank but kept smiling. "Perhaps Shirley'll write a feature on you, like she did on Rosalind?"

At that moment, we heard the creak of castors from the floor above, followed by footsteps on the winding staircase beyond the reception desk. Shirley Newbury appeared, tall and smart in grey trouser suit and crisp white blouse.

"Roz – Glen," she greeted us warmly. "Come upstairs, and we'll chat there. Deirdre, would you mind -?"

"Oh, I'll sort it out and bring it up," came the cheerful response. "Tea or coffee, Mr Presterman?"

We all settled on coffee, and Shirley led us up to a surprisingly spacious office on the first floor, containing two desks, on each of which stood a word processor. She explained that the printing of the *Bugle* was done off-site, and that her junior, Penny, was out interviewing a retired Army major about his voluminous stamp collection. Deirdre dealt with the classifieds and looked after front of house. They were a contented little team and enjoyed their work.

I couldn't help wondering how a hardened journalist like Roland Pettifer might have gelled with an all-female staff; and doubted that he had.

As Shirley invited us to sit, she whisked a copy of the *Bugle* off her desk and handed it to Roz.

"Poor Roly," she said, and I caught the note of compassion in a voice low and pleasing on the ear. "His obit's inside, and I hope I've done him justice. He *was* the *Bugle* for many years and, all right, he could be contentious – don't I know it? – but he was committed to his work, and we all learned a great deal from him."

I stood and glanced over Roz's shoulder to scan what Shirley had written, during which time the smiling Deirdre supplied us with coffee and digestives.

Shirley hadn't gone big on the accident itself, which I knew would spare my sister's feelings. But she'd written a warm tribute to the man and his work, on which Roz complimented her. "I know what a difficult time you had with him," she concluded.   "Water under the bridge now," Shirley replied generously. "There was a lot to admire about Roland. He was born and brought up in the village. His father died early on, an accident on the railway, and Roly was very good to his mother, who was something of an invalid. He was war correspondent for the *Daily Post*, reporting from the battle zones; but he was out of a job once the war ended. He returned to Selsby, and Fred Barnfleet took him on. Roly worked his socks off, always looking for the big scoop, which never quite happened. I believe he tried to move on but gradually became stuck in a rut where the *Bugle* was concerned. He and Fred rubbed along well, until Fred took me on as junior reporter when I left school. Roland was unhappy about that, declared it was 'no job for a woman'. He went out of his way to make life difficult for me: all I got were the magistrates' court reports, WI reports, and the 'Among the Villages' round-up. Then, of course, came Jamie's accident. It was one of the biggest things to happen in Selsby for years, and Roly was all set to do it justice. Although as soon as Fred learned that I'd been an eyewitness, he opted for my version.

"Roly was apoplectic – wouldn't speak to me for weeks. He and Fred quarrelled, and Roly was determined to move on. But his mother was very ill by that time, and he couldn't leave her. He went cap in hand to several other papers, but no-one wanted him, so he stayed put and turned to drink with a vengeance.

When Fred decided to call it a day – well into his seventies by then – he put the paper in my hands. As you can imagine, that didn't go down at all well."

Roz switched me a crafty smile. "Roly got his revenge though, didn't he, Shirl?"

Shirley grinned ruefully. "Oh, you bet he did." She turned to me. "Back in May, he got in ahead of me on a much bigger story."

"Indeed, he did." I knew that my dear sister was baiting me. She'd known that what was – eventually – going to be revealed had some significance. And she could tell that my interest was fired.

Shirley was no better. "Er, I gather from what you said when you phoned earlier, Roz, that it's the story you thought might interest Glen?"

"That's right," Roz confirmed teasingly. "Because, Glen, there's a Marla connection to what happened in Selsby three months ago."

"Roz," I declared, "you're infuriating. *What* happened in Selsby three months ago?"

13

March-May 1986

Roz and Shirley Newbury had made a habit of meeting at the Frobisher Arms on a Saturday evening to relax over a meal and a few drinks. The two women got on well, their friendship blossoming after Shirley had interviewed Roz in her guise as the romantic novelist Rosa Peyton two or three years previously. It had given rise to a signing session at the village library and then an *Oxford Mail* literary lunch at the Randolph Hotel. Roz's publisher, Fine Romance, had been purring, and while Roz hadn't been keen on going public over her Rosa Peyton alter ego, it had put a healthy complexion on her bank balance. She'd taken Shirley out for a meal, a thank-you for starting the ball rolling with the interview, and their friendship had grown from there. It had happened at a good time for Roz, because things had already become difficult between her and Perry, and only a few weeks before, he'd returned to London in search of work.

Saturday night at the FA saw the same cast of characters: Lorna and Morgan holding court at the bar, Barbara Ryde buzzing back and forth from the kitchen and, when she was between acting engagements, her daughter Kirstie doing the waitressing and generally helping out.

Roland Pettifer and Ned Braley were at the bar: that was a given. Roz reckoned the world might have stopped turning if one or – heaven forbid! – both had been absent. There was the usual clutch of other locals too, some who came for a couple of drinks, some for a meal and, particularly in spring and summer, people who were visiting the area. Roz and Shirley, both observant, were quick to clock a new face in the FA, and that evening, they'd just settled to their first drink, when they noticed the stranger.

She was sitting alone in a corner of the lounge, somewhat isolated, although it was early evening and the pub by no means full. A tall woman, probably pushing forty, oddly dressed in a long, wraparound turquoise skirt, and with a well-worn fur stole around her shoulders. She was thin, almost gaunt, her cheeks sunken, long ash-blonde hair flowing down to her waist. Some sort of gold pendant dangled from her scrawny neck. Roz thought she must once have been quite beautiful, but those days were long gone. The woman toyed absently with what looked like a gin and tonic on the table before her.

Realising they'd observed the stranger, Kirstie Ryde came over. "Roz, Shirley, hi. Couldn't do me a favour and go and speak to that lady over there? Her name's Pamela, she's just moved into the village and doesn't know anyone. I'd spend some time with her but I'm a bit rushed helping in the kitchen at present."

They agreed to do so and took their drinks to the corner table. The woman looked up, smiling cautiously as their shadows fell across her. Roz introduced them and asked if they might join her? She seemed relieved that someone had actually noticed her.

"Kirstie says you're new to the village?" Shirley began.

"Oh, yes. Moved in two days ago to a bungalow in Burnage Lane. I'm Pamela, by the way. Pamela Segrave."

She spoke in a pleasant, cultured voice, but Roz felt she sounded a bit distant, as if she was wandering around in a dream and unable to properly focus on her surroundings.

"Why, I live in Burnage Lane too," she exclaimed. "Number eleven, about halfway down."

"Oh, I'm near the top. Number three."

"That's been empty a while," Shirley remarked. "Used to belong to old Mrs Fletcher. Are you staying long, Pamela?"

"I've rented for a year. Wanted to move out of London." There was a wistful look on Pamela's face. "Needed to make a clean break. My parents used to live near here, I suppose that's why it appealed to me."

Both women were too polite to inquire further, even though they'd dearly have liked to. But the opportunity would arise. They'd booked a table in the restaurant for eight o'clock and invited their new friend to join them.

Pamela seemed quite overcome. "That's *so* kind of you. But it's a terrible imposition…"

"Not at all," Roz asserted and straightaway sought out Kirstie to tell her they had a guest with them.

"Oh, that's really sweet of you. Thanks for stepping in there, Roz."

As soon as Kirstie approached to announce that their table was ready, Roz and Shirley led Pamela through to the restaurant, stopping on the way to introduce her to Lorna and Morgan, who welcomed her to the village and the Frobisher. They introduced Roly and Ned too. It was difficult not to, as they were both in place at the bar and listening to the exchange with great interest. Roly slipped down off his stool, at his most gracious, smiling sleekly and not seeming to notice that Pamela was at least a foot taller than him.

"May I add my welcome too, dear lady. Roland Pettifer at your service, long-standing and long-suffering servant to the once great *Selsby Bugle.*"

This was a nasty tilt at Shirley, and Roz flicked her a wary glance, although she'd been sure her friend wouldn't rise to the bait. "Let the little man have his fun," she'd once remarked airily to a similar taunt.

Pamela shook hands uncertainly, seeming overcome by Roly, who could have that effect. Ned Braley added his own sly, brown greeting, although Roz didn't like the way he was eyeing Pamela's gold pendant. "Pleased to make your acquaintance, ma'am, I'm sure," he mumbled.

"That's an expensive-looking pendant you're wearing, Pamela," Roz commented, once they were seated, and Kirstie had taken their order. "It's lovely. Some sort of family heirloom?"

"Solid gold." Pamela fondled it lovingly, affording her two companions a closer look. They were tucked away in an alcove, well out of range of Ned's raking scrutiny. Roz wasn't being nosy, at least that's what she told herself, but she was looking for an opportunity to warn Pamela to safeguard any valuables. "It's a locket," she went on. "It's precious to me far beyond its monetary value."

She flicked a catch, and the locket opened to reveal the head-and-shoulders photograph of a good-looking young man with a mane of fair hair.

"Oh!" Roz gasped. "Your -er, husband?"

Pamela smiled, and Roz mentally kicked herself as she registered the pain behind it. The tall woman shook her head, tears glistening in her eyes. "We were so much in love. I – I lost him…"

Roz placed a sympathetic hand over Pamela's. "Oh, Pamela. I'm so sorry. I really didn't mean to -"

"No, no, it's all right. It's been a few years now, and I should be used to it. He and I had such wonderful times together, and I shall always keep him with me." Between them, Roz and Shirley turned the conversation to other things, and they spent an enjoyable evening with Pamela. Shirley lived at the other end of the village, so, once the meal was over, Roz offered to walk back with Pamela. As they left the pub, she noticed that Roly, well away by that time, was regaling

Morgan with a long (and undoubtedly boring) episode from his journalistic exploits; but that Ned had gone.

In common with most of the villagers, if not all, Roz didn't trust Ned one jot. As they walked back along the road and turned down the hill into Burnage Lane, Roz stayed alert, half-convinced that Ned would be following, to learn where Pamela lived. She didn't see him, nor did she hear anything untoward. But that was just it with Ned: one never did.

He'd been a village character for years, like Roly Pettifer, but then, not like him at all. Ned inhabited a scruffy bungalow in Riverview Crescent, tucked away from the more salubrious areas of the village. He did odd jobs here and there, but no-one could recall him ever having been in proper employment. Poacher, pickpocket, burglar: such was Ned's reputation, but he always managed to stay a step ahead of the police; although that wasn't difficult where Sergeant Burge was concerned. Ned was reputed to have shady contacts in Oxford, Reading and London, useful for passing on any valuables he might 'acquire'. Barbara Ryde was his cousin and had been appalled at the way Jamie and Kirstie had idolised him when they'd been growing up. She ensured that he had a hot meal, other than rabbit stew, a couple of times a week, and Roly and several others often stood him a pint.

Ned was always polite and friendly enough, Roz decided; even helpful. But trusting him was another matter entirely.

That evening, Roz saw Pamela safely home, advising her to ensure that doors and windows were securely locked. Pamela looked startled. "Why – are there thieves? In a quiet village like this?"

If only she knew! "It's best to be careful," Roz suggested. "We're not far from London, after all."

Pamela thanked her for the advice and for the way she and Shirley had taken her under their collective wing that evening. "I haven't enjoyed myself so much for a long time."

They arranged to meet at the pub again early in the week, and from then on meeting there for a meal or simply for drinks became a regular occurrence. Pamela also made friends with Roland, amused and flattered by his bombastic language and old-fashioned gallantry. There were occasions, Roz suspected, when the two might be 'seeing' one another; although Pamela never alluded to it, and Roz and Shirley were too polite to ask.

They'd also meet at each other's houses for an evening meal or Sunday lunch, when conversation and wine flowed liberally. Roz thought there was about Pamela a faded majesty, as she drifted languidly around with her pale, even haunted face, her dreamy eyes, long, swishy skirts, moth-eaten stole and expensive jewellery. She favoured the gold locket above all else, but on occasions would wear gold and silver bracelets and an exquisite-looking diamond necklace. Pamela seemed oblivious to the envious looks her jewellery received; and at different times, Roz and Shirley would warn her to take care.

Pamela had rented the bungalow fully furnished: very little about it seemed to belong to her. She had a gift for art and told her two friends that she'd lived for a couple of years above a small London art gallery, where she'd helped out. Then her mother had died and left her a little money, which was when she'd decided to put London behind her and move to the country. Dotted around the bungalow were some framed sketches she'd made, one particularly good of her handsome former lover, along with items of pottery, beads and jewellery. The long sleeves of Pamela's blouses hid her arms from view, but on the odd occasion, when she was showing off her artwork, her sleeves would fall back to reveal numerous needle-marks. However, she never elaborated on her previous life in London.

Roz felt that she and Shirley had managed to get as close to Pamela as might be allowed. She confided in her about her marriage to Perry, and how they'd agreed to part earlier in the year. The wine had flowed freely that evening, and Roz had been feeling down. Pamela, unusually, for there still seemed to be that mysterious distance between her and the other two, wrapped a consoling arm around Roz's shoulder.

"I can tell you, Rosalind, because, like me, you know what it is to have loved and lost. But, you see, he was my whole world – everything to me. And *she* saw him, wanted him and took him. Oh, how I *hated* her. But he is *mine*. He always was. And she can never, never have him now."

It only occurred to Roz much later that, had she not overindulged in wine and spirits (nothing unusual there), she might have asked Pamela to elaborate. She determined to do so when they met at the FA in the middle of the following week. Only she and Pamela were present, as Shirley was visiting her parents at their retirement complex in Didcot. Pamela had wafted into the pub in a silky evening dress, the customary stole about her shoulders and the diamond necklace at her throat.

Roly almost fell off his stool, surveying her pop-eyed. "Pamela, my dear, you're looking especially regal this evening."

"Why, thank you, Roland," she gushed. "You're *such* a gentleman. You've really cheered me up."

Roz beckoned her over and sat her down, then went to the bar and got in their drinks.

And at that moment, Ned Braley walked in, his busy gaze immediately fastening on to Pamela's diamond necklace. At the same time, she took out from her handbag and lovingly examined the gold locket.

Roz experienced something like foreboding. She'd have to warn Pamela again.

14

August 1986

Roz shook her head despairingly as she set down her cup.

"I wish I'd been more on the ball that evening. I *saw* the way Ned was eyeing Pamela's necklace and, as luck would have it, she'd just started fiddling around with that ruddy gold locket. Ned didn't stay long – unusually. He had a drink with Roly, then left. That caused some raised eyebrows around the bar.

"Not long after, Pamela decided she'd make a move." She looked at me with an air of challenge. "We never hung around at the pub in the week. Usually left at around the same time."

"No, we only got smashed on Saturday nights," Shirley grinned.

"Well, I walked back with her," Roz resumed, slightly affronted. "Left her at the front door and continued on down the lane. I thought at one stage I heard footsteps behind us, but that's probably my imagination, being wise after the event."

"So, what happened?" I asked.

"Pamela must have disturbed Ned. He'd broken in round the back. He must have been expecting a haul in the same league as the necklace and locket, although as things turned out, there was nothing remotely close to their value. Anyway, it appears that he panicked and whacked her with a statuette. His suit had deep pockets, and he'd stuffed as much stash into them as they could hold, including the necklace, locket, and the statuette with traces of her blood on it. He must have been shocked at what he'd done, ran at full pelt out into the lane and ended up under the wheels of a passing car. He was killed outright."

"The driver was some poor girl from London," Shirley continued. "That put paid to the holiday she'd just set out on. She'd turned down the lane to get to the by-pass and was within the speed limit. Suddenly, he appeared right in front of her. She tried to brake, but he went under the wheels. Still, she kept her head, had noticed the phone box at the top of the lane and ran back to call police and ambulance. Then – and wouldn't you know it? – Roly Pettifer happened along."

"Do you know, I've never worked out what he was doing there," Roz remarked. "He lived over the other side of the village from the pub."

"My guess would be that he'd fuelled himself up for a nocturnal visit to Pamela," Shirley said. "His story was that he reckoned he glimpsed someone bending over Ned's body. By that time, the car driver had disappeared up the lane – Roly heard her running footsteps. He'd had a lot to drink – when hadn't he? – and naturally the mysterious figure had gone by the time he'd reached the car. Roly gallantly waited for the girl to return and stayed with her until the ambulance and Desmond Burge showed up.

"Anyway, the bottom line is that he beat me to the story: *'Double Tragedy in Burnage Lane'*. I'd been out for the day, and his copy landed on my desk first thing next morning. I looked up into his vapidly smirking face. "What do you think of that, then, Madam Editor? From our man on the spot." Ooohh, I could have *killed* him. Oops, sorry! He'd only just stopped twisting the knife over that when last Saturday happened."

Roz was watching me. It was past opening time, and she invited Shirley to join us at the pub. However, Shirley needed to be elsewhere, so we thanked her and took our leave, saying goodbye to the starry-eyed Deirdre on our way out.

"We'll pop along to the FA anyway, Glen," Roz decided briskly, as we made our way along the village street. "Pints and sandwiches on me."

"You're *so* generous." My tongue was firmly in cheek, because she knew I'd be drinking fruit juice. I had probably less than a quarter of her capacity for alcohol.

"You're not kidding," came the slick reply. Her eyes still gleamed.

"There's more, isn't there?" I guessed.

"You bet there is," she grinned.

Trade in the Frobisher was slack, as it was only just after midday. Kirstie wasn't present: it appeared she was only called in to wait on tables and help in the kitchen at busy times.

Lorna, however, was very much in evidence, in a blouse with a purposefully low neckline. Roz placed our order and whirled away with a wry grin, leaving me to bring the drinks and be accosted by the landlady.

"Nice to see a new face in here," she trilled. "Particularly such a handsome one." Not content with dazzling me with her smile, Lorna waggled her unmissable breasts directly beneath my chin. "Roz tells me you're staying for a couple of weeks?"

"That depends on my agent," I replied. "I'm hoping to be back in work before too long."

"Must be exciting. All the different parts on offer?"

"It can be," I said, realising that it probably was for some actors. "I've been more or less promised some TV work." I sincerely hoped that whatever Eric was 'working' on might this time amount to a little more than 'dad enjoying new breakfast cereal with family at kitchen table.'

Lorna patted the hand which I'd extended to pick up Roz's pint glass. "We must sit and have a cosy chat about it one day," she enthused. "I'm *ever* so interested in the acting profession."

This was accompanied by another winning smile and flutter of eyelashes, but I managed to make my escape. Lorna was an attractive woman, although I felt she overdid her efforts to play her errant husband at his own game.

Talking of whom, as I turned away from the adoring Lorna, I caught sight of Morgan tucked away in the far corner of the empty restaurant. Our eyes met briefly, and he raised a hand in acknowledgement, before turning back to his conversation with a thickset man in a dark blazer. The man had his back to me, but he was leaning forward in earnest discussion. I noticed a white fedora resting on the table beside him. Morgan seemed to be doing a lot of nodding and listening, and I put his visitor down as some sort of salesman.

I took our drinks out on to the patio, and within minutes Barbara Ryde had deposited two plates of sandwiches under our noses. Once she'd gone, Roz took a quick look around to ensure we were alone.

"I got to know Pamela Segrave as well as anyone in Selsby," she said. "Roland might have been closer, but the jury's out on that. I knew enough about her to realise that she was a former addict, who might not altogether have kicked the habit. She seemed spaced out a lot of the time and continually harked back to her lost love, the guy whose photograph she kept in the locket. Pamela never mentioned his name, but when she described him as 'lost', I was sure she meant 'dead'.

"When Dismal Desmond examined Ned's body at the scene, Ned's suit pockets were stuffed with jewellery: most were no more than trinkets, but there were some valuable pieces too. Among them, two stood out. The first was Pamela's diamond necklace. It had been stolen, more than fifteen years ago, in a burglary at Hannon Hall, which is about ten miles away. So, how did it come to be in Pamela Segrave's possession? Lady Hannon – she's in her seventies now, but with all her marbles – is adamant that she didn't know Pamela."

"And the second?" I asked.

"Was, of course, the gold locket containing the long-lost lover's photo. Now, dear brother, here's the sixty-four-thousand-dollar question: who was the locket's original owner? Because it wasn't Pamela Segrave."

"How about Marla Hartman?" I suggested.

Roz grinned triumphantly. "Spot on. Once the police had finished with it, the locket was returned to Venetia. She was delighted. It was worth thousands. An eighteenth birthday gift from Leo and Venetia to their darling little girl. Venetia declared she'd return it to Marla when she next saw her. Shirley said she'd never suspected anything when she'd seen Pamela wearing it. But when she'd examined a close-up photograph, she recalled it was the one Marla had worn all those years ago."

"Then how did Pamela get hold of it?"

"How about she filched it from Marla?"

A thought struck me. "Roz, there's no way Pamela might actually have *been* Marla?"

Roz shook her head. "Barbara Ryde thought so. In fact, she got quite worked up about it – this was sixteen years on, and there might have been some similarity. But no, forget it. Pamela was Pamela, no question. Then there'd been all that talk about 'she can never have him now'. Had *Marla* stolen Pamela's lover? And anyway, who was he? Had Pamela taken some sort of revenge on Marla? It may be, Glen, that we're shooting well wide of the mark. Although somehow, I don't think so. Somewhere there's a connection between Pamela Segrave and Marla Hartman. Come along, eat and drink up. We're off to see Desmond Burge. Honestly, the things I do for you."

"For me, Roz?" I held her gaze. I'd known her so long and so well: her sense of justice; her compassion.

She smiled ruefully. "You're right, of course. For me too. I feel that I owe poor Roly. I'm convinced that he was on to something, and you and I need to find out exactly what."

15

Sergeant Burge occupied a stone-built Victorian semi at the far end of Selsby's main street. It adjoined the village's police station, daunting with its traditional blue lamp prominent above the doorway.

The door was opened by Burge's sister, Flora, a round, rosy-cheeked woman of fifty who, when we asked if we might have a word with the sergeant, smilingly ushered us into a cosy sitting room with flower-patterned armchairs and a wide bay window looking out on to a neat little garden.

"I'll let Desmond know you're here," Flora exhaled. "He'll be delighted to see you. He's not too busy this morning."

My sister's expression, as she settled into a chair, seemed to wonder when was he ever? Flora bustled away, promising some tea, and was replaced by her brother, large and ponderous in a smart uniform and impeccably shiny shoes. He beamed down on us.

"Ah, Rosalind. What a pleasure it is to see you. And your brother too. Good afternoon, Mr Preston."

I stood to shake hands, my smile of welcome disguising my amusement. Roz threw me a vicious glare but, on turning back to Burge, who was in the act of wedging his generous frame into the armchair opposite, was all sweetness and light.

"Sergeant Burge, we wondered -?"

"Oh, Desmond, Rosalind, please. We know one another well enough, don't we?"

"Desmond. My brother wanted to have a word with you…"

She was interrupted by a buffeting noise on the other side of the door and, given that Burge had only just made it into his chair, I leapt up and swung open the door to admit Flora and her tea tray.

"Oh, thank you, Mr Preston, you're a gentleman," she beamed. "I was only saying to Desmond that I shall have to report to my Women's Bright Hour meeting that we've had a famous brother and sister visit us this week. Oh, they'll be *thrilled*."

The thought crossed my mind that if that was the way they got their kicks, I pitied them. But I held on to a benevolent smile, as Flora set down her tray, poured, handed the cups around and departed, her kind, round face wreathed in smiles.

"You were saying, Mr Preston?" Burge resumed, before taking a huge slurp of tea.

"I didn't mention this at the inquest, Sergeant," I said briskly, "as I didn't feel it was relevant. But the other night, as Roland lay in the road, he grabbed my sleeve and whispered two words. They sounded like "Warn Marla." Roz and I have discussed this, and we thought I ought to tell you."

"I see, Mr Preston. Warn Marla about what, sir?"

"He didn't say. It was just before he lost consciousness."

"Ah." Burge paid further homage to his tea and frowned thoughtfully. The process looked as painful as it must have felt. "Marla, you say?" he said at last. "Wouldn't that be the Hartmans' lass?"

"That's what we thought."

"Hhmm. Yes, good-looking piece as I remember, and didn't she know it? Caused a few hearts to flutter around here, I'll be bound. Yet I can't ever recall her coming back to Selsby before Leo and his good lady left. I believe she went to live in London, which'd be about right for Miss Marla, I'd say. Hhmm, after that unfortunate business with young Jamie Ryde, I reckon one or two people were gunning for her, so to speak. But that had been a tragic accident and nothing more. Oh, I dare say she led the boy on, but Mrs Ryde was wrong to have blamed her for *killing* him. And she didn't mind who she told that to, didn't Barbara." Burge glanced across at me. "'Course, Mr Preston, Roland often popped down to London to keep in touch with Mrs Hartman. Perhaps your answer lies there?"

"Maybe we'll have a word with Mrs Hartman, then?" My tone was speculative, although I was sure Burge wasn't about to set any obstacles in our path.

"Do that, sir, do that. Personally, I'd not read too much into it. Roland, God rest him, was always one for the booze. The pathologist reported that he'd had a right royal skinful. 'Course, he'd been off the leash these last three years, since his old mother passed on. She disapproved of his habits and, by crikey, she'd lay into him if he ever came back to the house the worse for wear – or maybe I should say 'when'."

"Sergeant -er, Desmond." Roz took up the baton, which was just as well, as I felt quite exhausted listening to Burge's peroration, which had been delivered in a sleepy, rumbling burr.

"Yes, my dear?" Burge's eyes had assumed an unnaturally ecstatic gleam. My sister had, in her early forties, retained her girlish figure, but I sometimes felt her T-shirts were a little tight in a certain area.

"I just wanted to add that when the -er, accident happened, Roly seemed to come out very quickly into the road. It was almost as if –"

"Ah. Dare say he tripped over his own feet, Rosalind. As we know, he'd certainly drunk enough."

"And before he left the pub," I weighed in, "he was staring out of the patio windows. I can't help wondering if he'd seen someone he'd recognised out there?"

"Indeed, sir. A valid point. But I'd imagine the drink might have also accounted for him being in that state."

Burge was untroubled: rather a good epitaph for him, I thought. Roz and I exchanged glances: case closed. However, as she still had all his attention, she decided to make the most of it.

"Desmond, do you remember Pamela Segrave?"

"Indeed, I do. Another tragic occurrence."

"Glen and I wondered if she might have known Marla Hartman when they were both in London? I don't suppose you'd be able to shed any light on that?"

Burge looked pained. "Nothing, my dear, I'm afraid. If it was the case, I wasn't aware of it." He shook his head sadly. "Ah, that poor woman. I still ponder over Miss Segrave's death. I simply can't credit, even now, what Ned Braley did. In all the years I knew him, I never thought there was a violent bone in his body. A knee-jerk reaction, I suppose you'd have to say." (I wondered if the good sergeant had ever experienced anything as cataclysmic as a knee-jerk).

"She came back earlier than he'd expected," he went on, "disturbed him, and he hit out in panic and couldn't get away quick enough. He was close on sixty and wouldn't have relished seeing the inside of a prison at his age. By crikey, though, he ought to have seen that car! Given it was dark, but the car was one of them light blue Fiats, and it's not as if the young lass was doing any speed. Still, the car went right over him and killed him outright. That poor girl, a young Miss Blenkinsop from London, oh, she was real cut up about it. Dear me, another tragic accident. But probably just as well for old Ned, given what he'd done."

Roz had one further request. "Desmond, I don't suppose you'd have Pamela's previous address? I believe she lived above an art gallery in London? I think she said it was in Bethnal Green?"

"Of course, my dear. Do you mind if I ask why?"

"Well, Pamela and Roly were very friendly. I'd like to contact any family and reassure them that she was among friends during the few months she lived here."

Burge nodded judiciously and heaved himself out of his armchair. We waited as he rumbled away to his office, reappearing a few minutes later with a slip of paper, which he presented to my sister with an air of reverence.

"Here it is. As you say, a small art gallery in Bethnal Green. I've noted the names of the two women who own it."

"Thank you, Desmond. You've been very kind."

"And you're very thoughtful, Rosalind, if I may say so. A heart of gold you have, my dear, a heart of gold."

I shook hands with the sergeant on our way out and thanked him for his time.

"Always glad to help," he replied, puffing out his chest. "And if there's anything more I can do, anything at all – well, you know where to find me…"

"He directed that last comment at you," I observed mischievously, as we made our way back to the bungalow. Roz was walking purposefully, and I was hard pressed to keep up with her. "Must be nice to have such an ardent admirer. How do you do it?"

My sister snorted. "I need a drink," was all she'd say.

16

I phoned Kirstie Ryde that evening and invited her to lunch the following day. Having secured Roz's gracious permission to borrow the car, I offered to drive round and pick her up, but she said she'd meet me at the bungalow. I suspected that she wasn't too proud of where she lived.

As it happened, I'd walked past there the other day, while taking an early morning constitutional. It was one of a clutch of ugly, pebble-dashed council houses in a far corner of the village. I was sure Kirstie preferred London but felt it necessary to contribute towards the housekeeping for her mum. However, I could understand her reasoning. Aunt Ava's flat, where I'd lived for my first twenty-three years, though impeccable inside, was part of a hideous high-rise block.

Kirstie showed up looking fresh and pretty in a lacy pink blouse, jeans and smart white trainers. She'd applied some lipstick and blusher, both which helped relieve her pallor. I guessed she'd realised we were unlikely to be lunching at the Ritz.

My sister was smiling creamily as she waved us off, always living in hope as far as I was concerned. I wasn't good with relationships, being the original soft centre who was always attracted to the heartless, ambitious types like Calista Payne.

However, nothing more than friendship was on my mind, as Kirstie and I drove away. We were two actors not exactly at the height of our profession, and the chance to trade stories and compare notes was likely to be useful to us both.

We headed to Henley-on-Thames, where I knew of a quiet, inexpensive Italian restaurant. Like me, Kirstie tended to abstain from alcohol during the day. With two jobs which were predominantly carried out during evening hours, she needed to keep awake. For my part, having understudied a notable actor such as Piers Harcourt, who had difficulty remaining sober at any hour and could become indisposed at the drop of a hat (or should it be the tilt of a bottle?), I needed to stay alert at all times, because I never knew when I might be called in to replace him.

We spent an enjoyable and refreshing couple of hours in Henley, firstly over lunch, and then strolling along the banks of the Thames on a beautiful August afternoon. We talked mostly shop: the latest issues covered in *The Stage*, the foibles of some of our fellow actors, plays we'd have loved to perform in but hadn't so far been given the chance. Kirstie was amused when I quoted some of my worst-ever reviews (I couldn't recall the best – doubted if there were any), and it was good to see her so relaxed.

'Unfortunately, Glen Preston had to stand in for Piers Harcourt, who'd been taken ill (!) shortly before the curtain went up. This reviewer wishes Mr Harcourt a speedy recovery…'

"I think I can go some way to matching that," she declared. "How about this: *'The diminutive Kirstie Ryde, as WPC Henderson, seemed intimidated by the hulking villain she'd presumably arrested and was clearly discomforted by the audience's obvious amusement.'"*

It turned out that her agent, Beverley Irvine, was a lot more on the ball than dear Eric Di Mario. "She's got a few of us on the books, all about the same age and ability. We may all have our resting periods, but Bev works hard to make sure none of us wait too long for the next role."

She knew about Eric Dim. "I've heard him described as a promising agent," she remarked.

"That's because he's always 'promising' to find his actors the ideal role. I suppose I've been with him too long to look for a change. It'd be nice to have a starring role for once, though. He's always promising that but so far hasn't delivered."

Moving the conversation away from the acting profession, I asked Kirstie if she'd been in Selsby on the night that Pamela Segrave and Ned Braley had died?

"No, I was down in London, at the Burlington. I heard all about it when I got back. That poor girl…"

"Yes. On holiday, I believe Shirley said."

"That's right. A Miss Blenkinsop, I think, although I never got to meet her. Apparently, she was terribly upset. Lorna and Morgan took her in overnight – they're really good like that – and didn't charge her a penny. She had to stick around for Sergeant Burge to take her statement, and I believe Roly interviewed her for the *Bugle*. It put paid to her holiday. Lorna said she felt so sorry for her."

"And I believe Ned was a distant relation of yours?"

"Yes, one we became increasingly less proud of as the years went by. He and Mum were cousins. You know, Glen, we simply can't get over what he did. He was a poacher, thief, you name it. 'Dishonesty' was his middle name. But I still can't believe he'd have *killed* someone, particularly a person as harmless as

Pamela. He could be such fun when we were kids, and I know Jamie idolised him, a sort of substitute dad, because ours took off soon after I was born. Must've guessed I'd be trouble."

She smiled up at me, but I sensed some hurt behind it. Her hand slipped effortlessly into mine as we walked.

"Glen?" The question sounded tentative. "When Roly came to see me after the matinée that afternoon, I think I told you that he seemed a bit preoccupied. Do you think there might have been anything in those two words he spoke to you: 'warn Marla'?"

I wondered how much I should tell her and quickly decided that I ought to get a bit farther down the road before answering her question. It seemed as if Marla had no wish to be found – perhaps couldn't be found; and any link between her and Pamela, such as the locket, was tenuous.

"There might well have been," I replied. "But if so, it's beyond me."

Kirstie seemed content to leave it at that, as we strolled back to the car and returned to Selsby. Once again, I was willing to drop her off at her mother's house, but she said she was happy to walk back.

"We ought to do this again." I suggested hopefully, as we got out of the car.

"Yes, I'd really like that. It's been fun." She came round the car, stood on tiptoe and brushed her lips against my cheek.

I placed my arms around her waist and started to pull her into a kiss. After all, there didn't appear to be a nosy neighbour in sight.

Except one.

The front door swung open to reveal my sister sporting an ear-to-ear grin.

"Hi, Roz," Kirstie greeted her cheerfully, giving a reasonable impression of someone who hadn't been too fazed about missing out on a kiss.

"Hi, Kirstie. You're looking remarkably well for someone Glen's tried to bore senseless with a list of all his acting successes."

I laughed. "That would have taken less than a minute."

"And mine not even that," Kirstie gave back, smiling. She glanced at her watch. "Heck, I'd better get ready for my shift at the FA. There's a party in for dinner tonight, and I promised Lorna I'd help Mum prepare. Thanks for a lovely time, Glen. Be in touch."

"Hhmm, sounds promising," Roz murmured, as we waved Kirstie off up the lane.

"Well, it might have been."

"Oh? By the way, sorry if I interrupted anything just now."

"No, you're not."

We exchanged grins and went inside. "However," Roz went on, "you should be pleased to know I've not been idle while you've been out enjoying yourself. Two things. Firstly, you might appreciate a look at this." She whisked a sheet of paper off the coffee table   and held it out to me. "Shirley made me a photocopy. It'll give you a bit of background."

I took it from her. It was a copy of the front page of the *Selsby Bugle,* dated June 1971.

DARING JEWEL THEFT AT HANNON HALL

By our Chief Reporter Roland Pettifer.

Over last weekend, a theft of jewellery worth an estimated £50,000 was carried out at Hannon Hall, near Wallingford.

Sir James and Lady Ursula Hannon were away, spending the weekend near Glyndebourne with their friends, the financier Roger Blount and his wife. The Hannon Hall staff had been given the weekend off, and only the butler, Albert Peake, remained on the premises.

It is thought to be in the early hours that the thieves gained entry at the rear of the house. A windowpane had been smashed, and the thieves had gained access to the kitchen. Mr Peake, whose quarters are two floors above and in the far wing of the house, heard nothing.

The jewellery had been taken from a wall safe in Sir James' study. Among the items was a diamond necklace, which has been in the Hannon family since the eighteenth century and is alone reckoned to be worth £25,000.

Mr Peake discovered the theft early that morning and immediately alerted Sir James and the police. Detective Inspector Cameron Harris of Thames Valley Police believes that the thieves parked their getaway car along a track a half-mile distant from Hannon Hall and walked the rest of the way. Tyre marks and footprints were relatively fresh, although partly obscured by overnight rain.

Sir James Hannon told our reporter, "This robbery was clearly carried out by someone who was aware that Lady Ursula, myself and the staff would be away. These jewels have been in my family for many years, and I am relying on the police to make every effort to retrieve them and punish those responsible for the theft."

A police spokesman confirmed that inquiries were in progress, and that several suspects were currently being interviewed.

———

I read the report with interest. "Were the thieves ever caught?" I asked.

Roz shook her head. "Several items popped up over the years, but the diamond necklace didn't resurface until it was found in Ned Braley's pocket."

"So, how did it arrive in Pamela Segrave's possession?" I wondered. "Along with Marla's locket?"

"That, dear brother, is what we're going to find out. Which brings me to the second item of interest."

"Oh?"

"We're travelling down to London tomorrow. Knightsbridge, to be exact. I phoned Venetia Hartman earlier and secured an invite to drop in on her for morning coffee. Thanks to my glowing description, she's longing to meet you. All you need do is create the impression that you're famous. That'll test your acting skills."

17

The next day, Roz and I took the train to Paddington and strolled through Kensington Gardens and Hyde Park to Cavanaugh Close in Knightsbridge, where Venetia Hartman occupied a luxury third-floor flat. The building boasted an underground garage, and I wondered if we might have brought the car, but my sister rightly argued that her elderly, battered Escort would look a little out of place among the Daimlers, Bentleys and BMW 7Series we glimpsed as we walked past the ramp.

In the foyer, with its marbled floor, orchids on windowsills and rosewood reception desk, a deferential, uniformed concierge rang through to Mrs Hartman to announce that Mrs Blakeman and Mr Preston had arrived.

He confirmed that Mrs Hartman was expecting us. "If you'd like to ascend in the lift, sir, madam? It's on its way down now. You'll want Floor Three."

We thanked him and approached the lift as it whistled to a halt. The doors flew open, and a large figure blasted out and past us, startling Roz and almost crushing my toes in the process. I frowned at his departing back. As he swept out into the street, he jammed a white fedora on his head.

"Charming," Roz exclaimed, then frowned at me as I took her arm and steered her back towards the reception desk.

"Excuse me?" I asked the concierge. "You wouldn't happen to know the name of the man who left just now?"

The concierge looked his disapproval. "He gave his name as Mr Smythe, sir," he replied. "Mrs Hartman didn't seem to recognise it but asked for him to be sent up to see her."

I thanked him and escorted Roz back to the lift. "What was all that about?" she asked.

"It may be a coincidence," I said. "But the other day in the Frobisher, there was a man in conversation with Morgan Tambling, a big chap with a white fedora parked on the table beside him. I'm wondering if this was the same man, although I didn't get a look at his face on either occasion."

"And here's white fedora man visiting Venetia today," said Roz. "As you say, a possible coincidence." She grinned up at me. "But somehow I doubt it."

The lift took us up and disgorged us on the third floor in about three seconds flat. In front of us, a set of double doors swung open, and a woman appeared.

She was tall, and from what Roz and Shirley had told me, now in her late fifties. She cut an elegant figure in some sort of emerald-green sari, with her unnaturally jet-black, shoulder-length hair, wide, red, smiling mouth and a wall of green eye shadow. Expensive silver earrings flirted with her shoulders and a silver necklace clung round her neck. She walked a little unsteadily, owing not so much, I guessed, to high heels as the contents in the half-full glass she carried.

"Mrs Blakeman – Rosemary," she gushed. "It's been *too* long." Roz had told me on the journey down that she'd met Venetia a few times in Selsby, before the Hartmans had moved to London. The woman saw herself as a socialite and had liked to gather what she saw as the cream of Berkshire society around her. Because Roz was a writer, that, in Venetia's eyes, placed her in the 'famous novelist' category. I'd been warned that her categorisation of me would be a definite upgrade: perhaps it wouldn't leave me far off our dear mother's Richard Burton comparison.

Venetia's face lit up, as Roz introduced me. In my opinion, a tumbler of gin and tonic at eleven o'clock in the morning did that sufficiently anyway.

"My goodness! Graham Pressman! Who'd have thought it? Do, *do* come in, both of you."

Her free arm snaked with deadly efficiency through mine, and the next I knew, I was being wheeled through the double doors and deposited lovingly on a white leather divan, which ran the length of one wall. It was a long room, opening out on to a balcony, which looked out across Hyde Park and the Serpentine. A burgundy carpet, punctuated by white sheepskin rugs, covered the floor, and in the far corner stood a well-stocked, horseshoe-shaped bar. Venetia plonked Roz down in an armchair which faced me across a glass-topped, aluminium coffee table and asked what we'd like to drink.

It was too early, even for Roz, and we both opted for coffee. There was a percolator gurgling away on the bar, and Venetia glided over to dispense our drinks. Roz fetched it for us, while our hostess replenished her own glass. Clearly, the sun was over the yard arm somewhere.

Despite being well-fuelled, which, I suspected, was an almost permanent state, there was a certain elegance and grace about Venetia Hartman. Shirley had told Roz that she'd been at various times a model, cabaret singer and dancer, before she'd caught Leo's industrious eye. Little was known of her background, but she'd married above her station and had lost no time adapting to a higher plane. Leo Hartman had been a rich businessman who'd become ridiculously richer, and the lifestyle he'd offered had suited Venetia's ambitions.

As a young woman, I thought she must have been very beautiful, and that Marla had inherited her mother's looks, for Roz informed me that Leo had been no oil painting. However, it seemed that at last a surfeit of alcohol was taking its toll, for her features were beginning to assume the slightly bloated look of the hardened drinker.

Venetia cruised back from the bar and, as I'd feared, plumped down beside me with a winning smile. I could tell that my sister was enjoying this.

"Now, Mr Pressman," our hostess crooned. "I'm Venetia. And I'm sure you won't mind if I call you Graham?"

"Of course not," I replied sweetly. "But my name's Glen. Glen Preston."

"Oh, silly me. But I recognised you the moment I opened the door. I thought you were marvellous as Jesus of Nazareth."

I suggested that she was confusing me with Robert Powell (he was certainly better-looking), but that I had indeed appeared in that epic. Had she been alert at the time, she might well have seen me, provided she hadn't blinked at the wrong moment.

I had all Venetia's attention and wasted no time using it. "Er, as Roz and I were about to enter the lift," I said, "your previous visitor stepped out. I felt I ought to know him. A Mr – Smythe?"

"I really couldn't place him, Glen, dear," she replied airily. "He was looking for Marla. One of her former *beaux*, I suspect. But I doubt if she'd wish to see him. He seemed a little seedy and quite impatient. My darling girl's moved on a long way from there."

I flicked a glance at Roz. This was going to be hard work. But Roz was intent on another tack.

"Venetia, we thought we ought to come and see you, because we understand you were a good friend of Roly Pettifer. You -er, *have* heard the news?"

"Oh, my dear Rosemary, yes. Morgan phoned me the day after. The poor lamb! I cried and cried. Do you know, Roly had been with me *that very morning?*

We'd had a few drinks together." Spurred by that memory, she took a deep glug from her glass. "He'd come to town for some insignificant matinée – apparently that awful Ryde girl was appearing in some wretched play. I'll never understand why Leo felt he had to help her so much."

My sister and I shared a quick grin, unnoticed by Venetia. Given Leo's roving eye, the reason seemed obvious. From what Roz had told me, Kirstie hadn't been the first aspiring actress in whom Leo Hartman had taken an avuncular interest.

Roz continued probing. "You never knew Pamela Segrave, did you, Venetia?"

"Who? Oh, that strange woman who came to Selsby and got herself murdered? No, my dear, not at all. But Roly told me all about her."

"So, you've no idea how she might have got hold of Marla's gold locket?"

"Oh, Roly asked about that. All I can think is that the unfortunate woman must have stolen it. Marla absolutely *treasured* it – can't think how she came to lose it. It was there one day and gone the next. She told me she remembered the woman vaguely from years ago, although they were never what you'd call friends."

My interest was aroused and, thoughtlessly, I wriggled in my seat, causing Venetia, sitting far too close for my comfort, to turn and smile at me bewitchingly. "Yes, Glen, darling?"

"Then you got the locket back?" Across from me, I sensed Roz hanging on Venetia's reply.

"Oh, Burge returned it to me, and I gave it back to Marla on her last visit here. She was thrilled! It was an eighteenth birthday gift from Leo and I, and she'd always treasured it and missed it horribly. And do you know -?" Venetia was in full flow, and my sister and I exchanged a grin, happy for her to gabble on. Sadly, she'd latched on to my arm, was squeezing it tight and then tighter, and it had gone numb.

"Do you know, the Segrave woman had somehow also got hold of Ursula Hannon's diamond necklace? It's worth *thousands!* Ursula telephoned me the other day. She'd given up all hope of ever seeing it again. It's been *years* since she was burgled, although several of the stolen items have resurfaced during that time."

"You obviously see Marla regularly," I remarked casually, aware again of Roz's avid interest.

Venetia crushed my arm viciously. "Oh, dear Glen, not perhaps as often as I'd like, but my darling girl leads such a *busy* life. I didn't see her for years, as she and Leo never got on. Indeed, he chased her away, felt she was irresponsible, demanded that she change her ways. I believe she's done that. Yes, she comes here, and we'll go out to a show or for a meal. She was due round at the weekend but had to cancel. A date with another of her *beaux,* I dare say. But that's my Marla, still dazzling men with her beauty." She smiled at me lovingly, mashed my arm a little more. I began to distrust the gin-fuelled glint in her eye. "A chip off the old block, wouldn't you say, Glen, dear?"

Although amused at my burbling discomfort, Roz hurried to my rescue. "Marla still works, doesn't she, Venetia? Wasn't she in a boutique?"

"Oh, good heavens, no!" Her tone was disparaging. "No, she moved on from there long ago. She's a fashion consultant to the rich and famous and travels to their homes, dispensing sage advice." She chuckled maliciously. "No doubt persuading these silly women that they can get to look like her. Oh, she's hardly ever in town. "Mummy," she told me. "I'm *forever* rushing around. Life's so *busy.*""

"Forgive me for asking, Mrs Hartman -," I began

"Oh, Venetia, Glen, my sweet, I *implore* you."

I honestly believed I'd lost the use of one arm, as the pressure she'd exerted upon it was immense. Across from me, my sister was convulsed and had to pretend it was a coughing spasm. She'd been amply recompensed for my jibes about Desmond Burge.

"Er, Venetia. But, you see, on the evening of his accident, Roly travelled with me to Selsby and, from what he said, I couldn't help wondering if perhaps Marla had – well, an enemy?"

"Marla?" The name flew out in a discordant screech, but at least the pressure on my arm was eased. "No, that's inconceivable. Why, my darling girl hasn't an enemy in the world. Well, except -?"

"Yes?"

"There was that terrible fuss when that boy died all those years ago. It was entirely his own fault, but some people, notably the boy's mother and that hussy who married dear Morgan, were vicious. That uncouth Ryde woman even threatened to *kill* her. It certainly wasn't Marla's fault, and the poor darling was so upset."

Venetia wound down and sought refuge in her glass. Roz seized the opportunity to nod at me meaningfully: we'd rehearsed this on the way down.

"We'd love to call in on Marla," I remarked unctuously. "I'd like to meet her: she sounds fascinating. Would you mind giving us her address?"

"Oh, I gave it to the Ryde girl a while ago. What was it now?"

"Kirstie mentioned it," Roz put in. "But Marla's moved on from there." *Ages ago,* she didn't add.

Venetia shrugged carelessly. "Well, she does move around with her work."

"Do you have a phone number for her?"

"Oh, *she* always phones me. Never gives out her number – says she's been on the wrong end of too many nuisance calls. But you gave me your number in Selsby, Rosemary. I'll have Marla contact you there, and you can arrange to meet up." She beamed at me. "I'm sure she'd *love* to meet Glen."

It was time for Venetia to have another top-up and for us to leave. As we walked to Hyde Park tube station, we agreed that there was an element of mystery surrounding Marla. Why was she so elusive? Venetia hadn't seemed to question that, although, having met her, I could understand why not. And was there a more tangible link between Marla and Pamela Segrave? Venetia had remarked that the two women had known one another, however briefly, some time ago.

Then there was Morgan. He'd kept in touch with Venetia. Did he know more about Marla than he'd admit? He'd abandoned Lorna and gone chasing to London after her. Was he in touch with Marla too?

And we were no nearer to knowing what Roland had meant when he'd uttered those dying words: *"Warn – Marla."*

18

The art gallery was in a quiet street in Bethnal Green, a late Victorian terraced house with steps up the door, which bore the prim notice: 'FRANTICITY: our little gallery.' Below were listed the names of the proprietors: Fran Branston and Felicity Potts, with the invitation 'Do Walk In'.

We walked into a tiled hallway to be greeted by a sculpture of two entwined nymphs with impossible-sounding Greek names. Beyond them, we entered a large parquet-floored room, which featured several forms of art. Paintings and sketches lined the walls, each with a neatly italicized label, bearing details and price, while the floor space and shelves were dotted with sculptures of all sizes, and a wide selection of necklaces, tiaras and bracelets housed in tall glass cases.

From behind a small desk in a corner, on which stood an antiquated till, a small woman bobbed up, smiling an effusive welcome.

"Hello! *Do* come in. I'm Felicity. Please feel free to look around and just let me know if anything catches your eye."

"Er, well, we actually came to ask about someone you must have known," I explained. "Pamela Segrave."

"Oh – *Pamela.*" Felicity's lovely smile stretched wider, then faded just as quickly. "Poor Pamela. Just a moment, I'll call my partner in here." She opened a door behind the desk, giving us a glimpse of a cluttered workroom. "Fran? Oh, Fran, dear? There are two people here asking about Pamela."

A large shape loomed in the doorway. Fran, in baggy jeans, a once-white shirt and braces, towered over Felicity. She dwarfed Roz too, as she stepped out into the gallery, wild-haired and scary, her hands and arms coated with a chalky substance. Her voice, however, though booming, was friendly enough.

"I don't believe I've had the pleasure?" She leered at Roz, amazingly demure in a dove-grey two piece and low-heeled shoes.

My sister, as so often, was unfazed; which had always been the form whenever I was scared witless.

"Roz Blakeman," she replied easily, offering a hand. "This is my brother, Glen Preston."

"Good morning to you both. I won't shake hands. No offence, but I've been mixing plaster of Paris, and it gets everywhere. Fliss, darling, pop along and do us all some tea, and let me find the two of you a seat."

Felicity squeezed out from behind the desk and Fran's hulking frame, still smiling sweetly. I wondered if she might have been a former librarian, in light-coloured blouse, grey skirt, sensible flat shoes and pink horn-rimmed spectacles. She had that abiding aura of self-possession and patience about her. In stark contrast to Fran's intimidating bulk, she was graceful and petite; and even shorter than Roz, which was saying something.

Fran galumphed about gathering chairs, which she scattered around a small oak table. "So," she demanded, as we lowered ourselves on to seats, "how do you come to know Pamela?"

"I became friendly with her when she came to live in Selsby-on-Thames," Roz explained. "Glen didn't know her – he's visiting me at present. But we're both trying to track down someone whom we believe Pamela knew."

"Well, Fliss and I certainly knew Pamela," Fran boomed. "She lived here with us for a while."

A door at the end of the room wheezed open, and Felicity appeared, bearing a tray with four huge mugs of garish flowery design. Fran paused to drag back a chair and allow her to set down the tray on the table.

"I was saying that Pamela was our house guest," Fran explained, and both women laughed, Fran with gusto, Felicity with tinselly decorum.

Felicity handed around the mugs, in which lurked some transparent concoction of herbal tea. "You must forgive our amusement," she begged. "We both liked Pamela, although she was a tiny bit eccentric."

"That's putting it mildly," Fran guffawed. "Bless her, she was a total fruitcake."

"How did you come to know her?" Roz asked.

"Must've been about four years back," Fran replied. "One of the craft fairs. Fliss?" She snapped her fingers, as she tried to remember.

Fliss supplied the answer readily, as I rather thought she might. "St Agnes church in Stepney, dear. It was their Festival of Art. We take a craft stall at most fairs in the vicinity," she added for our benefit. "Good publicity for us, and St

Agnes is one of the best, particularly since the new curate's wife has been organising it."

I'd been casting an admiring glance around the gallery. "Is this all your own work?" I asked. "It's most impressive."

"Oh, how kind. Thank you, Mr -?"

"Preston. But, please, call me Glen."

"Yes, most of its ours, Glen. The jewellery's mine, the sculptures are Fran's. Most of the paintings and sketches are from other local artists, on whose sales we receive a commission."

"That's how we got to know Pamela," Fran waded in. "She was wandering from stall to stall, and we fell into conversation. She'd done some sketches, asked if she could bring 'em along to the gallery."

"We gave her our card, and she turned up on our doorstep the next morning," Fliss continued, "a grotty-looking holdall over her shoulders and a pile of sketches under her arm. Poor soul, one had to pity her."

"You'd take pity on a serial axe murderer," Fran scolded cheerfully. "But, yes, dear, you were right to bring her in. She was in a bit of a lather. We could tell she'd been an addict by the state of her arms. Bloody hell, acupuncture for beginners, or what?"

"She'd been living in a squat," Fliss went on. "She seemed – well, not quite with it."

"Spaced out big-time, I'd say," Fran rumbled. "But that was Pamela all over. Forever drifting around in a daze."

"Yes," Roz agreed. "That was Pamela."

"But she fell in love with the gallery immediately," Fliss twittered. "'I could see myself helping out in a place like this,' she said."

"And you, of course, fell for it right away," Fran cut in. "Pamela had brought some sketches with her. They really weren't bad, and we agreed to put them on sale, so long as she paid us our usual commission. She was over the moon. Then, when it was time to go – and you'll know, my dear," she winked at Roz, "how Pamela had that languid way about her?" Roz smiled and nodded. "Well, she'd wandered as far as the door, before turning to ask if we knew of anyone in the area who had a room to let. "I've been living in Mile End," she said. "But it's time to move on now.""

"I looked at Fran, and she at me," Fliss trilled.

"And I thought, damn it all, I know what *she's* thinking. Kindness personified, aren't you, you daft old bat?" The women smiled at each other warmly. "So, we offered Pamela the garret. It's quite small, but clean and comfortable. Honestly, you'd have thought we'd offered her the moon. She absolutely leapt at the chance – I'd never have credited her with having so much energy."

"And it's not as if she was destitute," Fliss continued. "She had money left her by her mother, and she was able to pay her way. Not that we charged her a lot, of course, and she did help out in the gallery."

I'd been sipping my tea, as I'd listened to this. It was some sort of rose-hip concoction, which I desperately wanted to give up on without appearing rude. If only there'd been a convenient plughole within reach...

"When Pamela was here," I asked, "did she have a gold locket?"

"Oh, she wore the bally thing all the time!" Fran exclaimed. "Always fondling it. Had a picture of some guy in it – good-looking, I suppose, if you're into that sort of thing."

"I asked who he was," Fliss simpered, "and dear Pamela came over all misty-eyed. "He was my darling H," she replied. And then her expression hardened – goodness, I was quite shocked. "He's mine," she went on. "Always mine. *She* will never have him now." Fran will say it's typically feeble of me, but I thought I ought to change the subject, and Pamela quickly calmed down."

"It *was* typically feeble of you. I'd have asked the silly mare outright. But she never alluded to him again. Still wore the locket, though. It looked very valuable."

"It was." Roz had been fidgeting in her seat, perhaps due partly to the rose-hip tea; but now she took the initiative. "Fran, Fliss, did she ever mention the name Marla Hartman? You see, she's the person Glen and I are trying to track down. The locket was Marla's, and Pamela must have stolen it from her."

"Stolen, eh?" Fran thundered. "That figures. When Pamela left here, we felt one or two items had gone walkabout. Only footling bits of Fliss's home-made jewellery..."

"Which I'd gladly have given her, if I'd known she'd wanted them so badly." Fliss sounded hurt.

"But you got them back eventually," Fran soothed her. She faced Roz and I squarely. "Now. This woman Marla. No, Pamela never mentioned her by name, but she certainly had it in for her. Fliss, dear, pop into the workroom, will you, and fetch it from that box of junk Pamela left behind? You know what I mean. I dumped it over in the corner. I believe our visitors may find it interesting."

Fliss skipped away, and we heard her rummaging around, while Roz and I waited expectantly. She returned almost immediately and deposited a small cardboard box on the table before us.

"Nothing much of note," Fran declared. "Although you're welcome to go through it. But I'm sure you'll want to have a look at this." She handed out a creased LP sleeve to Roz, and I leaned over for a closer look. "The disc itself is jiggered," Fran went on. "She'd broken it into a dozen pieces, and we binned it. But the sleeve'll tell you what you want to know."

The psychedelic cover boasted the title *Journey to the Planet of the Free,* and the group's name, *Daze of Sorrow.* A photograph on the reverse named the members: Jem Stander, Marla Hartman, Hal Page and Jimmy Fritz. Roz and I shared a grin. Mine was wider than hers, and I knew she'd ask me why. I'd tell her later. The LP had been produced in 1971, and I'd never heard of the group. But there were two interesting points to remark upon.

"That's him!" Roz seized jubilantly on the first. "The photo in the locket: Hal Page, Pamela's lover."

"And no doubt," Fran added, "your Marla was the girl who stole him away."

That was the second point; and it hadn't needed much working out. Marla's features had been obliterated, I guessed with scissors and by Pamela Segrave.

"And wow! Didn't she make a job of that?" Fran gasped. "Which begs the question: did she make a job of Marla too?"

Roz and I had agreed in advance not to mention our conversation with Venetia. According to her, Marla was alive and well, living goodness knew where and popping in for the occasional visit.

Fran and Fliss were happy for us to hang on to the LP sleeve, but I declined, earning me a sharp glance from Roz. We thanked the ladies for their hospitality, although I'd only ever drink rose-hip tea again at gunpoint and got to our feet. Fran and Fliss escorted us to the door and wished us luck.

"A strange woman, Pamela," Fran remarked wistfully. "Often away with the fairies. I should imagine she'd never quite kicked the habit."

"Me neither," Roz replied. "But I liked her. One or two of us befriended her, and she was grateful for that."

"Same here. In fact, she left us a nice little bequest in her will. Quite floored us, didn't it, Fliss? Her parents had been dead for some time, and there were no siblings. The rest went to a young cousin, although, of course, the police took charge of the stolen items."

"Oh, the cousin, Georgia, was a lovely girl," Fliss cooed. "And I think Pamela's money came in useful. She visited the gallery once, you know, and she and Pamela got talking and found they were related through their mothers."

"Yes, we met Georgia again at the solicitor's last month," Fran said. "She lives not far away in Shoreditch, even invited us for tea a couple of weeks back. You know, she made the point of how strange Pamela was. They'd got on really well, but Pamela never informed her, when she left here and moved to Selsby. Mind you, she never told us she was going to Selsby either."

"I wonder if you'd be kind enough to let us have Georgia's address?" I asked. "As she got to know Pamela, possibly she might have learned more details about Marla."

"Good point, young man. Go and make a note of it for them, Fliss, there's a dear? It's in the diary on the desk."

Once this was done, we took our leave, with a gushing invitation to call again at any time. I felt this was directed at Roz rather than at me. However, I didn't feel put out: at least I'd steer clear of rose-hip tea.

"So why were you grinning like the cat that got all the cream?" Roz challenged me, as we made our way down the street. "Were you so amused by Marla-with-the-scratched-out-face? And that LP sleeve would have come in useful. I didn't get a proper glimpse at the names of those two other guys."

"Ah, but I did," I replied smarmily. "I happen to know Jem Stander, because I've worked with him. He's an actor-producer these days and doing quite well for himself. I'm sure I read in *Stage* the other week that he's got a new show coming up in the West End. I'll phone Eric and get him to track him down."

"Eric Dim?" Roz raised a dubious eyebrow. "Don't hold your breath."

19

We'd established a definite link between Pamela and Marla, and I was hopeful that Jem Stander would be able to fill in a few more details. I figured that he must have known Hal Page quite well and maybe, through him, both women. I'd never really connected with the music scene, but Page's name rang a distant bell. I had the feeling, from what we'd learned, that he might not still be alive. Roz was even less of a music buff, and this was a time when Perry Blakeman's knowledge would have come in useful. However, I wasn't going there: the mention of Perry's name these days prompted mixed reactions from my sister.

We parted company outside the nearest tube station. Roz intended to take advantage of being in London to drop in on her publisher, as there were a couple of issues to discuss concerning her latest manuscript. We'd agreed that I'd seek out Georgia Derry, Pamela's cousin, whose address in Shoreditch had been supplied by Fran and Fliss.

I walked the rest of the way to Georgia's flat, which was in a small square off Old Street, the ground floor apartment in a row of terraced houses converted into flats. A young woman of twenty-something, with short dark hair, a perfect smile and looking healthily bohemian in baggy T-shirt and stonewashed jeans, opened the door to me, once I'd explained my business and been buzzed in. The flat was small and cluttered, and Georgia asked me to excuse the mess. She specialised in home-made jewellery, evidence of which was scattered around on table, shelves and floor, as well as make-up and face painting.

She came across as pleasant and unassuming, quickly explaining that she'd been expecting me, as Fliss Potts had phoned ahead to say that a visitor was on his way, seeking information about their late mutual friend, Pamela.

"Fran and Fliss are my adopted maiden aunts," she laughed. "Fran might come across as fierce, but they're both really lovely."

"Have you known them a while?" I asked, as I sat, and Georgia brought me a mug of coffee from her tiny kitchen. It had to be an improvement on the rose-hip tea.

"Only since I visited their gallery and met Pamela there," she replied, plumping down opposite me to sit cross-legged on the floor. "She and I had met once before, you see. I'd never known Pamela or her family, but apparently my mum and Pamela's were first cousins. When Pamela's mother died, I was called along to the solicitor's office for the reading of the will. She'd left a small bequest to Mum, who'd sadly died a while before, and it passed to me.

"Well, then, months later, I met Pamela at Franticity. She couldn't place me at first and only remembered me when I mentioned our meeting at the solicitor's. She came across as rather vague, but, as you can see, we had a common interest in costume jewellery. She was wearing this fantastic necklace – Fliss was purring over it all the time I was there – it honestly looked the real deal. Anyway, I don't think Pamela had many friends, and when I invited her here for tea, she leapt at the chance."

"Did you see much of her after that?" I asked.

Georgia frowned. "She was difficult to get to know. Struck me as rather troubled. I expect you know she was an ex-heroin addict, and I'm not sure that she was entirely off it, made her seem older than her years – she couldn't have been more than forty – and her movements languid and laboured. She came here a couple of times, and I thought we might become friends, but suddenly she just upped and moved away. I went round to the gallery one day, and she'd gone. Fran and Fliss were as shocked as I was, and she'd not left a forwarding address or anything. It was as if she'd intended to make a clean break."

"That must have been earlier this year?"

"That's right. And then, a couple of months later, I heard from Fran that Pamela had died in a burglary gone wrong in Selsby. I really didn't expect her to leave me any money, but it's come in very useful, because my line of business is so hit-and-miss. And, of course, all that lovely jewellery – well, Fran told me most of it wasn't in fact hers. One of the pieces had been stolen more than fifteen years ago and was extremely valuable."

"You knew about her passion for jewellery," I said. "Did she ever show you a gold locket?"

Georgia smiled at the memory. "Oh, she wore that on the few occasions we met. Quite precious to her, if that's not an understatement?"

"Definitely, I'd say," I grinned. "But she never by any chance mentioned a girl named Marla?"

Georgia was already shaking her head. "The name's not familiar. But she did show me the photo of the guy in the locket - her darling H. And someone had wronged her years before, stolen him away. I caught her mumbling his name a lot

– she'd seemed obsessed, staring into space. But she never mentioned anyone named Marla. She'd always refer to this woman as 'her' – and with venom."

I thanked Georgia for her help and got up to leave. At the door, I gave her Roz's phone number, explaining that I was staying with my sister in Selsby for a while and asked her to get in touch if she had anything more to add concerning Pamela.

Roz and I met up at Paddington late that afternoon. We'd each managed to grab a sandwich along the way and agreed to eat at the Frobisher Arms that evening. It was bordering on the rush hour, and we were glad to get back to Roz's for a cup of tea and change of clothes before making our way to the pub.

As I'd hoped, Kirstie waited on us and, as the restaurant wasn't yet busy, stood and chatted for a while. I brought the conversation round to Morgan Tambling's visitor two days previously. Kirstie hadn't been present at the time, so I gave a brief description, mostly of the hat, but it rang no bells with her.

Morgan had welcomed us as we'd come in and had lately disappeared into the cellar. Somehow, I guessed that he wouldn't want to discuss his visitor. To me, there'd been something shady about their meeting.

Lorna had been leaning on the bar, probably in an attempt to overhear what we'd been discussing. Kirstie waved her over, and I asked the question again.

"You see, I'm sure I should know him," I lied. "I saw him down in London earlier today. Have you any idea who he is?"

"It'd put us out of our misery if you did," Roz added.

"Oh, I recognised him all right," Lorna replied darkly, "even though the years have taken their toll." She turned to me, perking up noticeably. "What you said the other day about Marla, Glen. He would have known her – some Hooray Henry who came here chasing after her all those years ago." She nodded at Kirstie. "About the time of your brother's accident."

That last struck me as an unnecessarily vicious comment, and I guessed there wasn't much love lost between Lorna and Kirstie. A bit of payback for Morgan's wandering attention, perhaps? Unless there was more to the Morgan-Kirstie relationship than I'd been led to believe.

Kirstie, however, seemed unfazed. "Oh, the one who Marla sent packing?"

"Probably hitched up with him again in London." Lorna's normally attractive features were suddenly bruised with scorn. Sixteen years had passed, and Marla's name still had the power to rile her. "Right, Kirstie," she resumed briskly. "Another four guests due in five minutes. Better get along and see if your mum needs a hand."

She must have witnessed the quirky grin Kirstie threw me as she turned away, for Lorna's expression became, if anything, more severe. The girl looked appealing in her tight-fitting waitress garb and, sadly for Morgan, it wasn't lost on him. He'd just emerged from the cellar, cast an admiring glance after her as she disappeared into the kitchen, and then realised that his wife had just witnessed it.

"Hi, Glen. Hi, Roz," he greeted us cheerily, although his expression looked hunted. "Good day in London?"

"You'd know all about London," Lorna sniffed. Then her tone became breezy, although the smile remained vicious. "Morgan, dear?"

"Yes, hon?" Morgan tried to look stoical, as he prepared to meet his fate.

"That guy who was sitting down with you at lunchtime a couple of days back? Glen thinks he ought to know him."

"A couple of days back?" Morgan gave a passable impression of someone racking his brains for a recollection, but it cut no ice with Lorna.

"Yes. You were deep in conversation with him." She sounded impatient now. "I remember him coming down years ago, the time your precious Marla was here."

"Oh, you mean Roop – Rupert Blount." He turned to me, hoping I'd be his escape hatch. "You know him too, then, Glen?"

"I think I've got him mixed up with someone else," I replied apologetically. "Thought he might have been an actor."

Roz had been enjoying this exchange. "Doubt if he was ever that, eh, Morgan?" she put in.

Morgan smiled weakly and was about to respond, when Lorna cut in, her tone dangerously conversational, as she asked the question I'd been edging towards. "So, what was he doing here, then?"

"I – um, knocked around with him those few weeks I spent in London," he admitted, suddenly unable to meet her gaze. It was as well he couldn't: Lorna's uncompromising expression barely withheld her anger. I recalled what Shirley Newbury had said: that Morgan had abandoned Lorna and torn off to London to try his luck with Marla. The wound had never healed, for it had gone too deep.

And she'd never forgiven him.

That truth hit me now, as I witnessed her standing, arms folded across her ample chest, awaiting his burbling explanation, enjoying his wriggling discomfort.

"Er, he knew I owned the FA. He – um, he'd had a spell inside – drug dealing. His family had cut him off, and he's not long been out, needed some money. I -er, I'm afraid I lent him a few quid – an old friend in need and all that…"

Lorna shook her head incredulously. "You utter fool. You'll never get rid of him now."

"Oh, but he won't be back. I told him straight it was a one-off, just to tide him over for a while."

Kirstie returned, bearing our meals. Lorna shrugged, turned and walked briskly back to the bar, while Morgan, after an embarrassed grin in our direction, trailed after her.

Before we left, well pleased with what we'd learned, I had a private word with Kirstie, asking if she'd heard of Jem Stander.

"Yes, Glen. I don't know him personally, but he's working on a revival of *Guys and Dolls.* It's opening soon at the Maybury, just off Leicester Square. A friend of mine's in the chorus. Why? Do you know him?"

"I've worked with him," I explained. "And there's something I need his advice on." Much as I liked Kirstie, I didn't feel I could take her into my confidence at that moment.

The next day, I rang Eric Di Mario's home number. It was Saturday, and Eric's weekend was sacrosanct, his rest cure after the rigours of the working week. But what did I care? I asked if he could get Jem Stander's phone number for me, as there was a matter I wanted to discuss with him?

Eric agreed to do it, but his tone was suspicious. "Not thinking of cutting out the middleman, are you, dear boy?" He sounded a little hurt.

"Not at all, Eric. You know me." *Spineless. Laid-back. Stick-in-the-mud.* "It's a personal matter. Er, no doubt you'll have some news for me before too long?"

"Working flat out on it, dear heart. My goodness, but you're going to be pleased with me!"

I ended the call, reflecting that there was a first time for everything.

20

To give Eric his due, however, he came back quickly with a contact number for Stander, one of the new-fangled, mobile phones, unwieldy and the size of a brick. I couldn't see the trend catching on.

I thanked Eric, phoned Jem and was invited to drop in on him at the Maybury Theatre on Monday, where he'd just started rehearsing his new take on *Guys and Dolls*.

I found him down in the stalls, watching a group of young actors being put through their paces on stage. Typically of Jem, an attractive young female assistant stood at his shoulder, looking studious in rimless spectacles, as she made notes on a clipboard.

He'd been his usual obliging self on the phone, but I'd got the impression he hadn't quite been able to place me. However, most of the TV- watching and theatre-going public were with him on that one; although the moment he glanced in my direction, he recognised me.

"Glen Preston!" He leapt to his feet and flung out a hand. "Yes – *now* I can put a face to the name. I have the feeling I might have killed you a couple of years back?" At this, the pretty assistant's eyes widened in alarm, almost displacing her spectacles. Jem's next utterance left her looking possibly more apprehensive.

"Let me guess – I stabbed you?"

I shook my head. "No, I'm sure that was Phil Jephcott. You shoved me out of a third-floor window. I'd come up from behind and tried to garotte you."

Stander grinned reassuringly at the girl. "Remember *MacGillivray, Gina?*"

Gina returned the smile uncertainly. "Oh! Yes – of course."

MacGillivray had been a short-lived private eye series of the early eighties, more a vehicle for Jem Stander, as he moved into acting towards the end of his pop music career. He'd always been pleasant and fun to work with and took pains to call everyone on the set by their name. I was amazed that he'd remembered me. I'd only worked with him twice, and they'd been my usual fleeting appearances.

"We must have shot that scene a dozen times," Jem recalled. "We managed to get in a real tangle between us."

I remembered it well: it had been my first and last appearance on the show. I remembered Stander well too, one of those fortunate beings who seemed to get younger as the rest of us got irretrievably older. He must have been in his early forties, looking fit and tanned, his long dark hair tied back in a ponytail and merry blue eyes sparkling. He wore a collarless white shirt, tight black jeans and gleaming white trainers and exuded an aura of laid-back authority and kindly good humour.

"How can I help you, then, Glen? If it's work you're after, I can fit you into this production, provided you can sing."

"The show wouldn't survive beyond the first night, Jem, but thanks all the same. I'm here because I need your help. It's about someone you worked with when you were in a group called *Daze of Sorrow*."

His response was to throw back his head and laugh. "Gina," he said, "you pop along for your lunch now, although you may not see me again. I could well have died laughing by the time you get back."

That brought another uncertain smile from Gina, who'd probably not yet got used to her boss's expansive sense of humour. She thanked Jem – exhaling his name adoringly – bade me goodbye and wandered off looking bemused.

Jem Stander pointed me to a seat, turned his attention to the group on the stage, clapped his hands and invited them to take a half-hour break.

"*Daze of Sorrow*," he said briskly, with a wicked grin. "Talk about a blast from the past. Thought they were dead and buried long ago. In fact, with hindsight, they should never have come into being. So, how can I help, Glen?"

"You played with them, didn't you? You see, Jem, I'm trying to track down someone who was in the group. Her name's Marla Hartman."

Stander let out a long whistle. "Whew! That takes me back. And I remember her, because she was so difficult to forget. If I hadn't been dating at the time, I'd have been sorely tempted. Wouldn't have stood much chance, however, 'cause she only had eyes for the lead guitarist, Hal Page. I'd just split from *Broken Promise* when Hal came to me and asked if I'd help him get a new group up and running. Don't know if rock's your scene, but he was a talented guy, who never quite made it to the top. And he'd picked up Jimmy Fritz on drums. Remember him? Bit of a rock legend, mainly because of his drug history. Marla just sort of drifted in and took up with us. Why would any of us have minded? Hal certainly didn't."

"But, as I've found out, there was someone who minded, wasn't there? Because didn't Hal already have a girlfriend?"

Stander pondered this for a moment. "Yes, Glen, you're right. There was a girl who was always following him around. Now, what was her name? Pat? Pam?"

"Pamela Segrave. She turned up in Selsby-on-Thames, where my sister lives, earlier this year. Roz got to know her quite well. But sadly, Pamela's dead: she was killed at her bungalow in a burglary that went wrong."

"I'm sorry to hear that – not that I knew her well. But, yes, it's all coming back. A tall girl, must have been in her mid-twenties then, quite good-looking, very flower-power. Guess she'd been around Hal a while. In fact, he'd intended bringing her in as our vocalist, but she was a long way off the mark. Marla stepped in to fill the breach. No brilliant singer by any stretch, but she had looks and energy on her side, while Pam was lethargic, to say the least. Marla made no secret of the fact that it was Hal she wanted. He was a bit embarrassed to begin with, because of Pam. But with Marla's encouragement, he soon shunted her aside."

"And I should imagine that didn't go down well?"

"You can say that again. The girls had a right set-to, with fur flying in all directions. I remember Jimmy Fritz enjoying that, and poor Hal trying to prise them apart. Pam flounced off – her language was an education, although Marla gave it back in spades. Pam kept turning up, time after time, threatening the other girl; but she had a habit, and it soon got the better of her. A case of good riddance, because she was wasting her time trying to get back with Hal."

"How long did the band stay together?"

Stander grimaced, pained by the memory. "Not long. We flopped totally. Three singles and one album amounted to scraping into the Top Fifty at best. The songs, the publicity, they were all crap, but they weren't the only reasons. See, Glen, what I hadn't reckoned with was the drug element. Sure, we've all done them from time to time, but once you move on from the soft stuff, there's no way back. The other three were off their faces most of the time – in fact, Jimmy OD'd the following year. It caused ill feeling, but I just had to split. The scene was getting too heavy. Luckily for me, Terry Black came along and signed me up for *Turning Vision*."

"Any idea what happened to Marla?"

"She and Hal were around for a while. But Pam was still a nuisance, and there was this posh guy dogging Marla's footsteps. He'd known her from way back and fancied the pants off her. I got the impression he was her and Hal's supplier. But suddenly, he wasn't there. Whether he'd OD'd or got arrested, I don't know. Hal tied up with a couple of bands after *Daze,* did okay with some Dutch group but never hit the heights he was capable of. I saw his obit in the NME a few years back. Drugs had got the better of him, and I can't help wondering if Marla went the same way."

We chatted on for a while longer, but Jem had nothing further to add on the Marla front. I thanked him for his time and, typically generous, he suggested my agent should contact him, if I needed work at any time.

"I'll light a fire under him," I replied darkly, as we shook hands.

"Do I know him?"

"Eric Dim."

"Oh." He grinned. "Better make it a big fire. Best of luck, Glen."

I left the auditorium and crossed the foyer on my way out. Two girls stood chatting near the main doors and, as I drew alongside them, a familiar voice called out, "Hi, Glen!"

It was Kirstie, looking summery and appealing in T-shirt, shorts and sandals, carrying a colourful canvas bag over her shoulder and smiling a greeting.

"Hi, Kirstie. What brings you here?" If the reason was that she couldn't bear to be away from me, I decided I could live with that.

"Oh, I'm up for an audition."

"What? Here? With Jem Stander? I've just been speaking with him. I could put in a word."

"No," she laughed. "Over on the South Bank." She indicated her friend, a petite, smiling blonde, with a nod. "I happened to have a little spare time beforehand and thought I'd catch up with Janie. She's in the chorus."

"How do you like working with Jem?" I asked.

"Oh," Janie breathed, "he's just *sublime.*" More adoration. How did he do it? I, a mere mortal, felt rather inadequate.

"I'm heading for the tube now," Kirstie resumed. "You too?"

"Calling on a friend in Stepney. Green Park station's close by. Let's walk there together."

"Suits me." Kirstie and Janie parted with a hug, and we waved her back into the auditorium. "How did you fare with Jem?" Kirstie asked, as we set off down the street. I'd mentioned at the pub on Friday that I'd be paying him a visit today.

"He remembered Marla," I replied. "Back in the early 70s, he played with a group called *Daze of Sorrow,* for which Marla happened to be the vocalist. They weren't around for long, but she and Hal Page, the lead guitarist, were an item. Jem lost track of them then, although he told me Page died a few years back."

Kirstie frowned. "Surely Venetia must have some idea where her daughter's living at the moment?"

"You'd think so, wouldn't you? Roz and I went to see her the other morning, and the address she gave us is the same she'd given you."

"But that was ages ago! And even then, Marla had been gone from there some time."

"And Venetia doesn't have a phone number for her. Marla's the one who always gets in touch."

Kirstie shook her head. "That's very odd. It's almost – well, as if she doesn't want to be found."

Privately, I thought there was something more sinister about it but didn't want to involve Kirstie just yet. For me, it wasn't so much *where* Marla was, as *who* she was.

By this time, we were entering the station. There was a press of people around, tourists, shoppers, as well as office workers heading for or returning from lunch. The escalators descended a long way into the bowels of the earth.

We'd reached the top of the second escalator, when I felt a sudden and violent shove in the back. Kirstie was in front of me and pitched forward with a cry, as I slammed into her. I heard a collective gasp around me, like air escaping from a balloon.

Time seemed to freeze and, for what seemed like crucial seconds but could only have been the briefest moment, it felt as if we were teetering on the edge of the top step before crashing down to the bottom. In that moment, I instinctively flung both arms around her, catching her before she collided with the people two or three steps farther down. Somehow, I succeeded in propelling us both to the side, jamming her against the escalator rail, before losing my balance.

Luckily, I fell backwards and pulled Kirstie down on top of me, ending up wedged across the escalator. By the time we'd got to the bottom, we'd succeeded in scrambling to our feet, drawing an anxious gaggle of onlookers around us.

"You okay, miss? And you, mate?"

"What happened there? Did one of you lose your footing?"

"No, they didn't," a man's voice piped up. "This gent was pushed, I saw it. Some creep in a blazer and white hat. He scarpered up the other escalator before anybody could nab him."

"Yeah, I saw him too. Didn't hang around, did he?"

"Anybody get a good look at him?"

"No, he was off like a shot. Clumsy sod."

"Clumsy? I reckon he did it deliberate. Hey, mate, you got a rival who fancies your bird?"

I thanked everyone for their concern, and they moved on, leaving us alone. I realised that I was still holding Kirstie, and rather tightly. I apologised and released her.

I could tell she was still shaken, as she gazed up at me misty-eyed. "Oh, Glen, there's nothing for you to be sorry about. It's quite possible you just saved my life. Thank you."

Ditching her shoulder bag on the floor, she stood on tiptoe, draped her arms around my neck and pulled me into a kiss.

"Perhaps I should make a habit of it," I gasped, when she finally let go of me. "Roz's theory is that ladies only kiss me because it's a good omen for their careers. Dare say you'll win an Oscar a couple of years from now."

She grinned back. "Can't wait that long. Let's make it a year." And she did the same again. This time I was able to savour it, the pair of us oblivious to the nods, winks and murmured comments of the crowd passing by.

Kirstie still clung to me, as we made our way to the platforms. We parted with another lingering kiss, before going our separate ways.

It was only as I was on the train, hurtling through the tunnels towards Stepney, that I wondered if that shove in the back had been meant for me?

Or for her?

21

St Agnes was a fine Gothic church a little way off Mile End Road. However, by the time I reached there, its only occupant was a smiling, elderly lady, who was polishing the brass candlesticks around the altar. I told her I was seeking information about someone who'd visited the Craft Fairs on the premises and was there anyone who might remember her? Pamela Segrave's name seemed to ring no bells, and the candlestick lady directed me across to the church hall, where I was to ask for Mrs Ainsley, the curate's wife, who she knew had been involved in organising the Craft Fairs in recent years.

The church hall, a large, echoing building, served as a soup kitchen, and now, with the afternoon drawing on, work was beginning on the preparation of that evening's meal. On the mention of her name, a woman emerged from the kitchen, looking warm and slightly flustered, and I guessed she'd been busy with culinary exploits.

"I'm Hannah Ainsley. How can I help?" She greeted me with a friendly, if tired, smile. She wore a long black cotton skirt and loose-fitting cardigan. Her dark hair, tied in a long ponytail, the rings beneath her eyes and almost total absence of make-up made her seem older than she probably was, which I guessed might be around forty. There was about her something I couldn't quite define. Despite her obvious fatigue, it was a look almost of serenity.

"My name's Glen Preston," I replied, as we shook hands, her grip frail and slightly moist. "I realise you're busy and don't want to get in your way, but if you could spare a few minutes? There's someone I'm looking for."

Her smile set me at ease. "Oh, we shan't be serving for a while yet, and the other helpers will make sure nothing boils over. Come and sit over here, and please, call me Hannah."

"And I'm Glen." I wondered if she thought I was a soul who needed saving. If so, she was probably right.

The hall was lined with benches and trestle tables, and Hannah Ainsley led me over to a seat farthest away from the kitchen. "So, who are you looking for, Glen?" she asked.

"Well, I have to say I'm not actually looking for her as trying to trace someone through her," I explained. "But I know she attended the Craft Fairs here a few years back. Her name was Pamela Segrave."

Hannah thought for a few moments. "Yes, I remember her from when I first arrived here. She came to St Agnes' Festival of Art. I can't say I really got to know her. A former heroin addict, wasn't she? She could be a bit -er, troublesome." She leaned forward confidentially. "But you said 'was', Glen. Do you mean that she's -?"

"She left London to live in Selsby-on-Thames, a few miles west of Reading," I replied. "My sister, who lives there, befriended her. Sadly, Pamela -er, died three months ago."

Hannah's face creased with concern. "Oh, I'm sorry. As I said, I didn't know her well, but, surely, she couldn't have been that old? Early forties?"

"There was a burglary at her bungalow," I said. "Pamela disturbed the burglar, and he lashed out in panic. I'm afraid she was killed."

She looked genuinely sad, her gaze cast down, and I saw her in that moment as a woman of some compassion; fitting for a curate's wife in the environment where she worked.

"Pamela's really the link to the person I'm trying to track down," I went on. "Years ago, Pamela met a girl whom she later accused of stealing her lover, and there was bad blood between them. The girl's name was Marla Hartman."

Hannah's gaze had just come up to meet mine, and I noticed in her eyes a flash of what I interpreted as recognition. I felt a sudden rush of elation.

"Did you know her, Hannah? Did you know Marla?"

"I remember her," she admitted cautiously. "And yes, I remember how Pamela reacted against her." She smiled wanly. "I can't say I knew Marla well. The last vicar, Hubert Melford, who retired up north more than a year ago, gave her a job in the little café and gift shop that we run in the church's east wing. She and her – I'm not sure if he was her boyfriend or husband, and I'm trying hard to remember his name…"

"It was Hal. Hal Page."

"Yes, of course, Hal. It's all coming back now. They lived nearby in a tiny flat a few streets away. He'd been heavily into drugs – I suspect they both had at some stage. They'd returned from Holland, where he'd played guitar in a rock group. I remember Reverend Melford saying that Marla had been through re-hab, but Hal hadn't been able to kick the habit and was in a bad way.

"I gathered there'd been some trouble before. Pamela had never forgiven Marla for taking Hal from her. That's partly why they'd moved abroad, to get away from her. But when they came back, it didn't take her long to catch up with them."

"What happened then?" I asked.

"I think their money was running out, because Marla worked here to supplement it. It was a measure of her devotion to Hal that she spent everything on his treatment. But it was no use. He was already very ill. And by then, Pamela was back, snapping at her heels, accusing her of being the cause of his illness, of allowing him to get beyond the point of no return. My take on it is that she made the girl's life a misery, and things reached the point where she simply upped and left."

"Have you any idea where she went?"

Hannah shook her head. "None. It was soon after Hal died. She was there one day and gone the next. Didn't even say anything about it to Reverend Melford, although he knew she was very unhappy."

"You don't think Pamela might have harmed her in any way?"

"I hope not. I don't think so. I believe Reverend Melford made some inquiries in the block of flats where she'd lived. She'd confided to one of the neighbours that she intended to move on, and her rent was paid up." She smiled wanly, suddenly seeming more tired than previously. "Pamela was calmer once Marla had gone, although she was still troubled. Her addiction had left its mark. She'd developed a bad habit of stealing things – trinkets, mainly. Quite frankly, I was relieved when she moved on."

"To Fran and Fliss?"

"Oh, you've met them?" Suddenly her face was alive, her eyes sparkling.

"Only the other day."

"They're such *dear* souls, hearts of pure gold. They exhibit every year at our Festival of Art, as it's such a useful advertisement for their gallery. They met Pamela and took her under their wing. They were warned about the light-fingers problem but took it in their stride. I'm sure Pamela was happy there, but I didn't know about her move to Selsby-on-Thames."

"Neither did Fran or Fliss."

Hannah frowned, looking troubled. "But what made her go there, Glen? And for her to die like that? I hope she found peace."

"She found friendship," I said. "In fact, with several people in Selsby, my sister among them."

"That's something to be thankful for. The poor woman." She glanced at me keenly. "Glen, why are you looking for Marla?"

"I want to make sure all's well with her."

As I spoke, I knew I wouldn't be able to palm her off with that. I felt I had to level with her to an extent. I told her about my involvement with Roland Pettifer, the accident, and his last words: *"Warn – Marla."* I added that I still had no idea what he wanted to warn her about.

Hannah seemed taken aback and looked at me helplessly. "Oh, Glen, I wish I could give you some guidance. But Marla simply went away, and no-one has heard from her since."

"And this was when?"

She thought about it. "Something like four years ago, not long after I first came here."

"Do you think she might have gone back to her old lifestyle?"

"I hope not. I didn't know her previously, but I believe she was – chastened – by Hal's death. She was devastated that she'd been unable to save him. I think she needed to move away from familiar territory and make a fresh start."

I asked Hannah if she felt that Reverend Melford might be able to add anything to what she'd already told me?

"Probably not." She smiled fondly. "He's just a *little* forgetful these days. But you never know. I'll get his phone number for you. He's in a retirement home up in the north-east."

I thanked her for her time. Things were starting to get busy, with people already drifting in. She gave me the old clergyman's phone number and asked me to keep her informed if I found out more about Marla. As I left, she was moving along the queue of incomers, greeting each by name with a smile and kind word.

I got caught in the rush hour fighting my way back to Paddington, so it was early evening when I reached Selsby. Roz was waiting with a glass of wine and a hot meal, both which were most welcome. She was eager to find out what I'd learned from my visits to Jem Stander and St Agnes Church.

Marla had left Stepney in a hurry. We agreed that, still grieving for Hal, a renewal of hostilities with Pamela had probably contributed to her precipitate departure. Roz wondered if she might have returned to Holland and the old ways, but Hannah Ainsley had felt she'd put all that behind her.

So, a new Marla? A change of heart, change of direction? Yet the picture drawn by Venetia Hartman suggested that the daughter who'd not long before come back into her life was similar in outlook to the Marla of sixteen years previously, as recalled by Shirley and Kirstie.

And there was still no clue as to about what or whom Roland had intended to warn Marla…

Or was there?

I thought back to that evening, when I'd crouched over Roland's body, as he'd lain in the road. I wondered if he'd been trying to say something more.

As he'd struggled with fading consciousness, his words had been indistinct. I'd caught 'warn' and 'Marla', but now recalled there'd been a gap between those two words. His lips had been moving feebly, but no sound had come out. Had he been trying to utter some other name? Had he been trying to warn Marla about someone?

Or to warn someone about Marla?

I said as much to Roz, but we agreed that we might speculate all evening and still shoot wide of the mark.

Perhaps the answer lay in Selsby rather than London. Pamela had been plainly advertising Marla's locket and the Hannon necklace, both which had been returned to their respective owners. Had the sight of one of those items seriously rattled someone's cage? Morgan and Lorna Tambling, Barbara and Kirstie Ryde, Shirley Newbury, Roland Pettifer: none of them had seen Marla in the last sixteen years, although perhaps slightly less in Morgan's case. Did one of them hold the key to the mystery of Marla's whereabouts, for despite Venetia's spasmodic contact with her, she was notoriously elusive?

I gave Roz an account of the incident earlier that afternoon at Green Park station, leaving out Kirstie's not unwelcome gratitude. If Rupert Blount had been responsible for that shove in the back, what could his motive be for wanting either Kirstie or me out of the way?

And why was he looking for Marla?

22

The following day saw Roland Pettifer's funeral take place in the little Norman church behind Selsby's main street. A distant relation had been traced, who'd known Roland from before the war, and he and his wife came along, the only representatives of the family. The rest of the congregation was made up from the clientele of the Frobisher Arms, including Roz and myself.

Morgan Tambling read the lesson, and the vicar, whose church, my sister informed me, Roland had studiously avoided for as long as anyone could remember, delivered a warm eulogy on Roland's service as a war correspondent for the *Daily Post,* and how both Selsby and journalism would be the poorer for the passing of this greatly talented man. Would Selsby, the vicar wondered, ever see his like again? I noticed Shirley Newbury, sitting across the aisle from us, looking on with pursed lips and furrowed brow.

After Roland's coffin had been lowered into the grave in the little churchyard, we all repaired to the Frobisher Arms. I walked with Roz, who clung to my arm. She was sniffing back tears she'd never have admitted to, if challenged; but I declined to comment, because I knew she was unable to persuade herself that she hadn't been in some way responsible for Roland's death.

I felt downcast too, sad for a man I'd hardly known, who, for all his bumptiousness and small conceits, had lived a very lonely life, with no loved ones to mourn him at the end.

But I was angry too, for I'd reached the conclusion that someone had deliberately pushed him under the wheels of my sister's car.

Kirstie and her mother had hurried back to the Frobisher ahead of everyone to set out a buffet for the wake, which had been generously supplied by the Tamblings. "Given the amount the poor old boy must have spent in here over the years," Morgan had quipped with a rueful smile, "it seemed the very least we could do."

Once we'd settled into our seats with food and drinks, Kirstie came over to join us, squeezing on to the seat beside me and bringing a knowing little grin to my sister's face. I asked how her audition had gone the previous day.

She wrinkled her nose prettily. "Not great. I think I was spooked by what had happened on the escalator." She peeped round at Roz. "I presume Glen's told you?"

"We have no secrets," Roz replied enigmatically. She was already into her second glass of Chardonnay.

"Glen, do you really think it was him – the guy who called on Morgan?" Kirstic kept her voice low, although there was no-one in our immediate vicinity who'd know what we were discussing.

"Rupert Blount? The description was pretty loose, but the blazer and white hat seem to suggest it." I hesitated, afraid that I might spook her further by what I was about to say. "Kirstie, there's no way he might have been targeting you rather than me?"

"But I don't *know* him," Kirstie replied, placing an anxious hand over mine. "I've never met him and wasn't even in here that day you saw him with Morgan."

I wondered if he'd been after both of us: two for the price of one. But I didn't mention it, as it wouldn't have set her mind at rest.

"Then it must be me," I concluded. "I've been openly inquiring about Marla and," I looked at Roz, "he turned up before us at Venetia's the other day looking for her too."

I made a private resolution there and then to keep alert for any future encounter with Blount.

Beer and wine flowed, as the Tamblings had intended, and the buffet reduced to a few sandwiches which, on this warm day, soon began to curl at the edges. Roz moved off to join Shirley and Lorna at the bar, bestowing me a subtle wink as she left me alone with Kirstie. We spent a happy interlude, discussing more theatres we'd worked in and actors we knew. Finally, as the room began to thin out, Kirstie left to help Barbara clear away.

While we'd had our heads together in close discussion, I'd happened to notice Morgan watching us. He'd been behind the bar, joking away with several locals, as well as playing host to Roland's distant relatives, who'd by now gone on their way. I was sure he'd witnessed the parting kiss Kirstie had planted on my cheek before going off to help her mother and giving him a wide berth. As I approached the bar to collect my sister, he grinned at me pleasantly enough; but I sensed a wariness, bordering on antipathy, about him.

Managing to detach my sister from her wine glass – she and Lorna had been chatting away like old friends, so I'd no idea how much she'd had – we said our goodbyes and headed home. Unsurprisingly, Roz's glum mood had lifted.

"I'm going to put my feet up for a while," she declared. "There's meat pie in the fridge for tea, and I might just crack open another bottle. Your choice: Sauvignon Blanc or Pinot Grigio?" I guessed she'd probably open both.

"I thought you had a deadline to meet?" I replied, recalling her recent meeting with her editor.

"Oh, that can wait," she said dismissively. "In any case, I work better in the mornings."

As we turned down Burnage Lane, a rust-spotted, ageing Vauxhall Viva came bucketing past us. The driver tooted the horn and waved a hand through the open window. We were far enough down the lane to see it swing on to Roz's drive.

We exchanged glances. Mine was puzzled, Roz's incredulous. She groaned. "Oh, no. It *can't* be." Then she hurried on, leaving me trailing in her wake.

On reaching the bungalow, I encountered Roz, hands on hips and amused and exasperated in like measure, confronting the individual who'd just clambered out of his car.

He was smiling, as was usual with him, short and scruffy in stone-washed jeans and an Iron Maiden T-shirt, his slightly greying hair tied back in a ponytail and a scraggy beard round his chin.

Roz cast me a swift glance. "Tell me, Glen, have I been so wicked that I deserve this?"

'This' was Perry Blakeman, my sister's errant husband, who now took a step towards her, arms outstretched.

Roz's answer was to skip back out of his reach, and Perry, unoffended, turned his boyish grin on me. "Glen – how's things?" He thrust out a hand, which I shook firmly.

"Not too bad, Perry." *Listen to the eternal optimist.* "Yourself?"

"Mustn't grumble."

"I must," Roz interrupted. "Perry, what are you *doing* here?"

"Oh, on my way to answer a job ad up near Oxford. As I was passing, I thought I'd call in and see how you were."

"Well, now you have. And I'm a lot worse than I was five minutes ago. What's wrong with London? Too hot to hold you?"

"No – just missed being in this area. London's okay, but I miss the country."

I didn't think it was the country Perry had been missing, so much as Roz, and felt he should be given the opportunity to say so.

"Roz, would it be easier if I -?" I began timidly.

She whirled round on me. "No! Don't even think it! You're staying here." Turning back to Perry, she sighed and added more reasonably, "Now you're here, you'd better come in for a cup of tea."

I'd always liked Perry, a generous guy, probably too easy-going for his own good. I knew for a fact that Roz liked him too, but she was too proud to cave in. Perry was a chef, a good one, and I think his ambition had been, probably still was, to run his own restaurant. London and a lack of funds had obviously thwarted that.

A couple of gossipy neighbours had appeared on next door's drive, talking in low, gleeful whispers. They'd noticed that *he* was back. Roz's basilisk stare left them unmoved, and she impatiently ushered Perry and me inside.

"Just a sec." Perry dived back into the car and emerged with a sad-looking bouquet, which had been languidly wilting in some service station along his route. He proudly presented it to Roz, who took and examined the flowers disparagingly.

"I'll pray for their resurrection. Come on. Inside."

Once indoors, I escaped to the kitchen to make some tea, leaving them to talk. They'd separated a few months previously by mutual consent, and I was certain no third party had been involved. Perry had found a job in London, but the commute had meant long days and late nights. This had coincided with a period of writer's block for Roz, and she'd been hard-pressed to meet her deadlines. Tempers had frayed – well, hers had, which was no surprise – they were both dead on their feet and had made the (to me) rash decision to live apart. Neither of them, however, had closed the door on their relationship.

They were talking in low, earnest voices, although neither would have wished to exclude me. Roz and I had always been close, and I was still a great fan of Perry. As I came through with the tray of tea, making no secret of the fact that I was on my way, Roz had been asking if he was all right for money. I observed in her voice a genuine concern, which didn't surprise me. My sister has a heart of pure gold, only sometimes one has to excavate very deep to unearth it.

"I'm fine, sweetheart. Just scouting around the area for job prospects. Somewhere to stay'd be good?"

"Well, you can't stay here." She seemed flustered, and her reply a little hurried. "Glen's in the spare room."

Perry must have looked his question, while I was occupied with setting down the tray and pouring, for Roz's next utterance was an implacable *"No"*.

"Listen," she went on, after a slight pause. "Why not try the FA? They've been pretty busy of late and might be able to offer some work in the kitchen, provided you don't tread on Barbara's toes."

"I'm not feeling suicidal," Perry replied lightly.

"And keep your hands off the waitress. She's spoken for."

I was in the throes of handing around the tea and sensed an impromptu reddening around the ears.

Perry grinned at me laddishly. "Little Kirstie Ryde? Very nice too."

"And don't let Lorna tempt you down to the cellar. She won't waste an opportunity to beat Morgan at his own game. She's already giving Glen the glad eye."

"Hhmm, Morgan. Yeah, ran into him in some pub down in the smoke just a couple of weeks back. Looks like he's up to his old tricks."

"Same as ever. Some things don't change."

We sat and chatted companionably over our tea, until Perry decided he ought to make tracks. I didn't think he held out much hope for the Oxford job; indeed, he phoned later to say it had already gone, but that Morgan had offered him some temporary bar and kitchen work. Perry looked forward to seeing us in the FA before long.

I shook hands with him, and Roz went outside to see him off, while I remained diplomatically inside. I heard her tell him to take care of himself and suspected there was a parting kiss.

She was looking a bit misty-eyed on her return.

"Pity he's never grown up," she said, trying to sound dismissive.

"He's a decent bloke," was my considered reply.

"And what would you know?"

She changed the subject. But I got the impression that the issue remained open.

*

I telephoned Reverend Melford later that afternoon. He seemed a decent old boy, and whether or not, as Hannah Ainsley had suggested, he was losing his marbles, he remembered Marla.

"Such a pretty child, but, oh, with the cares of the world on her shoulders, having had to nurse that young man of hers for so long."

She'd left Stepney in a hurry, practically overnight. One of the tenants in her block of flats had seen her leaving and thought she'd appeared in some distress. She'd had a visitor the previous day, a woman, and the neighbour had heard raised voices.

Clearly, Marla had felt she had to get away, and Hubert Melford had left it there, feeling it only right to respect her wishes.

All which left us no further forward to knowing where Marla was now.

23

I could tell that Roz had been affected by Perry's visit, particularly over the uncertainty of how things might pan out now that he was, if only for a while, back in the village. However, she typically made light of it, and I didn't allude to it, knowing that she'd confide in me when she felt the time was right.

That time wasn't now, and Roz needed an escape hatch. Marla Hartman was the topic of the moment and, over more tea, we sat down for a serious discussion.

Warn – Marla. Did it mean she was in danger, or someone in danger from her? If someone was out to get her, who might have a motive? Morgan Tambling had gone chasing after her to London and had come back with his tail between his legs. Marla had rejected him. Might she somehow have humiliated him? And seriously enough for him to seek a summary revenge? Or might *she* be out to get *him* for whatever reason?

Lorna had been jealous of her, no love lost between them. Marla could have taken Morgan away from her at any time. Barbara Ryde had lost her son. Sixteen years on, she still blamed the girl for his death.

"We mustn't forget Shirley," I added, wondering how Roz might react to her friend's inclusion on the list of suspects. "Was she more interested in Jamie than she let on? Might she want to get back at Marla, believing her to be responsible, as Barbara does?"

"From what she's said," Roz replied thoughtfully, "she'd given up on Jamie some time before he died. She'd certainly had a crush on him, but she's not vicious like Lorna. I wouldn't put any money on it."

We then moved on to the subject of Pamela Segrave. From what Jem Stander had told me, there was more of a connection between her and Marla than Pamela's possession of the locket. They'd known each other and clashed over Hal Page. Marla had stolen him from Pamela. Might Pamela have harmed her in some way? It was an avenue which needed further exploration.

"Where was everyone on the night Pamela was killed?" I asked, moving to a different tack.

"You've got to look at Ned Braley in the first instance," Roz said. "He didn't leave any fingerprints because he wore gloves. And the murder weapon, the statuette, was in his pocket. The pub closed at ten-thirty, and there weren't many customers that night, so either Morgan, Lorna or both could have got away early. Barbara had already left and gone home. Ned was her cousin. Might there have been collusion between them? And Shirley was visiting her parents at their retirement flat in Didcot, so she's not in the frame."

"Roland?" I suggested.

"Hhmm." Roz frowned. "That's a point. He was at the FA with Pamela and me. Ned came in and left early. Highly likely he was at her bungalow when Pamela arrived home. But why was Roly *passing* at the time? He lived at the other end of the village."

"We wondered earlier about a nocturnal visit to Pamela?"

"I don't buy that, Glen. He liked Pamela without any doubt. It may be that he saw the way Ned was studying her necklace and went along to ensure he wasn't contemplating breaking in and stealing it. In which case, he was way too late. But did he *really* see a shadowy figure bending over Ned's body? Or was he simply hyping it up to make a good story. He didn't do too badly out of it, managed to sell it on to a couple of bigger papers."

"I'm wondering if Pamela helped bring about her own death," I said. "It seems no-one actually thought she *was* Marla, but the way she kept showing off the locket – for someone who, for whatever reason, didn't want the subject of Marla to come up, that might have been a danger sign."

"And don't forget the Hannon necklace," Roz reminded me. "A local theft, fifteen years ago. That might have stirred someone into action. But who?"

"And is Marla involved? Which begs the question: *where's Marla?*"

"Venetia's in touch with her."

"But *only* Venetia. Otherwise, no-one has seen or heard from her for quite some time."

And that, we agreed, was suspicious in itself.

*

Over supper that evening, Roz opened the bottle of wine, which she'd threatened to do earlier, with the result that she slept late the following morning. Awaking early, as I often did, I decided to make the most of the crisp, sunny morning and headed for the woods lining the riverbank, where I'd enjoyed a stroll on a couple of previous mornings.

I'd not been walking long before I realised I wasn't alone. This wasn't unusual, as the woods were a favourite haunt of dog-walkers from the village and around, but my immediate impression was of someone treading stealthily, and for no real reason that put me on my guard.

The crackle of twigs caused me to turn. Through the screen of trees, I made out a parallel track about ten or fifteen yards farther up into the woods. I drew to a halt and, moments later, glimpsed a flash of something white.

I walked on cautiously. The figure was hurrying, trying and failing to make no noise. Whoever it was had passed beyond me by now and, as I came to a bend in the path, he appeared, leaping clumsily out from behind a clump of bushes.

Rupert Blount.

It was the first time I'd encountered him face to face. He was smiling, and I didn't like the smile. I wondered what lay behind it.

"Good morning." His voice was hearty in its greeting, but I distrusted it and him. "No need to be alarmed. The name's Blount, but my friends call me Roop. You're the actor chappie, aren't you?"

Shirley Newbury had described Roop as a big man in his younger days. He was bigger now, fleshy, bordering on overweight. He was smartly enough dressed in blazer and flannels, but the trademark white fedora was looking a little worn, and his face bore the reddening hue of the serial drinker. His eyes were small and restless: they didn't smile.

"I'm Glen Preston, yes," I threw back coolly. "But I rather thought your name was Smythe."

His laugh sounded hollow. "You must forgive my little deception, Glen. I recognised you from Venetia Hartman's place the other day, and I believe I spotted you in Morgan's hostelry very recently."

And I you, as well as at Green Park tube station, I didn't add, although I was saving it for later. "What of it?" I asked stiffly.

The smile stretched wider: the 'we're all mates together' approach, which I always distrusted.

"I believe we have a mutual interest, Glen. Rather a pleasant one, too. A little bird informs me you've been seeking the whereabouts of Marla Hartman."

A little bird? I'd hardly have described Morgan as that; although Lorna seemed the type to capitulate easily under a charm offensive. I shrugged. I'd already decided to give away as little as possible to Roop.

"Well, you know how it is, Glen. You see, Marla and I were once an item. Circumstances forced us apart. I've spent time in Australia making my pile, and now I'm back I simply want to renew acquaintances. I'd very much like to find her, so what say we pool our resources?"

It might have been my imagination, but I sensed an air of desperation about him. I didn't believe him, regarding Australia. Jem Stander had spoken of the 'posh guy' chasing after Marla. He reckoned he'd been dealing and had either OD'd or got arrested. Roop certainly hadn't OD'd, but I suspected Australia might be a more palatable alternative for Wormwood Scrubs.

"I'm afraid I can't help much there," I said. "Venetia was my last hope. She seems to be the only one who has any contact with Marla."

Roop looked thoughtful. "Hhmm. That's what I gathered. Venetia gave me an address, which I followed up, but Marla hasn't lived there in years. The poor woman seems sadly out of touch with everything but the bottle. But, Glen, may I ask about your interest in Marla? Did you know her from way back?"

"I don't know her personally," I replied. "It's all linked to something else."

I was determined to say no more, and he seemed to get the message. "Oh, well." It was his turn to shrug. "I'll go on sniffing around and give you the heads-up if I find anything."

I doubted he'd make good on that promise. "I'm in Selsby for another week or so," I told him, well aware that it could be a month, waiting on Eric Dim. "I'm down at the Frobisher most evenings." I waited until he turned to go. "Oh, er, Roop," I added, my tone dangerously casual. "Didn't we bump into one another in London a couple of days back? At Green Park tube station? I'm sure that was you."

He turned sharply, almost overbalancing with the sudden movement. He looked puzzled. "No, old son. Don't think so. Haven't been near there in yonks."

We wished each other a desultory goodbye, and he returned the way he'd come, crunching heavy-footedly along the rough path. I strolled on, intending to return to Selsby by a different route, distrusting him and his motives.

Although as I walked, I slowly reached the conclusion that when Roop had said he'd not been at Green Park tube station, he hadn't been lying.

24

I walked along the towpath to Selsby bridge. A familiar figure was leaning against the parapet, dragging nonchalantly on a cigarette, his attention drawn to the white-hatted walker a couple of fields distant, who was heading back in the direction of the Frobisher Arms.

Perry Blakeman turned, as he became aware of footsteps behind him. "Hi there, Glen. Out for an early ramble?"

"Clearing away the cobwebs," I replied. "It's a lovely walk through the woods back there, high above the river."

"Doesn't Roz come with you?"

"She hadn't surfaced when I left. Mainly because of last night – something white and chilled in several glasses."

He grinned wryly. "Dare say you can blame me for that. She wasn't too chuffed to see me, was she?"

"It's nothing you did, Perry." I felt sorry for him. He was an honest guy but naïve too, if he expected my sister to welcome him back with open arms. "And I wouldn't say she was altogether displeased."

"Thanks, Glen." He'd guessed I'd be on his side, although I was actually on both their sides. He nodded in the direction Roop had gone. A car started up and, gunned into action, drove away through the village towards the dual carriageway. "That guy, Glen? Did you get a good look at him?"

"It's a long story, Perry, but I just met and had a chat with him in the woods. His name's Rupert Blount."

"Hhmm. I wouldn't know about that. I've just come from the FA. Morgan and Lorna agreed to put me up for a while, in exchange for a few hours' work, covering days off and helping out at weekends. They also want my advice on freshening up the evening menu."

"Barbara Ryde'll love you for that."

"I dare say, but I'll take my chance." Perry paused, jabbing his dwindling cigarette in the direction Roop had gone. "He was there."

"Where? At the FA?"

"Yeah. First thing this morning, I slipped out on to the patio for a drag, and he was sitting in the restaurant with Morgan. Luckily, they didn't see me."

"Wasn't Lorna around?"

"Apparently, some mornings she pops round early to see her mum and dad. Listen, I didn't mean to eavesdrop, but obviously they thought no-one else was about. All seemed a bit suspicious to me, and I don't like the look of that guy."

"You're not alone. Did you hear what they were saying?"

"Well, for a kick-off, Morgan handed over some money and wasn't happy about it. Said something like, "You should be paying me. If you want to know more about -," oh, some woman's name?"

"Marla?"

Perry looked at me keenly. "Hey, that was it. He went on, "Then you'll have to stump up." And this Rupert guy fired back something like even though it was a while ago, if it came out "you've got more to lose than I have.""

"They might have noticed me at any moment, so I slipped quietly away and didn't hear any more. All sounded a bit heavy. Have you any idea what's going on, Glen? And that name they mentioned – Marla? Haven't I heard something about her living here years ago, and that Morgan had the hots for her?"

I had to make a quick decision. I didn't feel as though I could fob Perry off with some superficial explanation or a white lie. After all, he'd just given me a rather interesting titbit: that Tambling and Blount had at one time been involved in something shady. Morgan was, to all intents and purposes, paying him hush money.

I told Perry about my meeting with Roly Pettifer, our journey back on the train, his accidental death under the wheels of my sister's car and his dying words: "Warn – Marla."

Perry wasn't the inquisitive sort. He took it all on board, but his main concern was for Roz. "It's easy to say, but obviously she wasn't to blame. Typical of her, though, that she'd be blaming herself."

"You're right," I replied. "It wasn't her fault. Particularly as I'm of the opinion that Roland might have been pushed."

He let out a long, low whistle and flashed me a sharp glance. "You don't say?"

"But it's a suspicion, nothing more," I insisted.

"And where's Marla? Have you located her?"

"Her mother's the only one to have seen her in some while. Venetia Hartman. Remember her?"

"Before my time here. But I've heard people talk about her. Not the most reliable, eh?"

"You can say that again."

We began strolling back towards the pub. Perry promised to keep eyes and ears open, in the hope of learning more. But he'd helped enormously. From what he'd overheard Morgan saying, I wondered if our affable landlord might not have some idea of Marla's whereabouts.

Perry was looking anxious, as we paused outside the pub. "Y'know, Glen," he said, "I'd really like to get back with Roz. London was a mistake. I mean, nothing happened, there was never anyone else involved. It was just me being impetuous. I should have given it more time. Roz had hit a bad patch, tempers got frayed – you'll know what I mean."

"I'm with you, Perry," I assured him. "You're a darned good chef and you can find work somewhere in this area. But I can't influence Roz and, with all respect to you, I'm not going to try. As you know so well, she's her own woman." He nodded, accepting that. I promised to look in at the FA later, and we shook hands and went our separate ways.

I returned to the bungalow to find that Roz had finally surfaced, with a large mug of black coffee for company. However, she perked up on hearing of my unexpected meeting with Rupert Blount and Perry's account of the conversation between Roop and Morgan Tambling.

"I'm off with Shirley this morning to visit her parents in Didcot," she announced. "They were really good to me when I first came to Selsby, and I haven't been to see them in a while. Shirl and I will probably stop off for a spot of lunch on our way back, so I'll find out what I can about your friend Roop." She hesitated before adding with obvious reluctance: "I suppose I might be able to get a bit of background from Desmond Burge…"

"Oh, he'll be only too pleased to help you out, *my dear.*"

Roz pulled a face. "S'pose I'll have to take it on the chin. After all, Roop's involved in this somewhere, isn't he, Glen?"

"He and Morgan both, for my money. I'll pop down to the pub for a lunchtime sandwich."

"Hhmm, you might get something from Lorna."

"That's what worries me."

"And I'm sure Kirstie'll do *everything* she can to help you. I do believe you've made an impression there. Honestly, these handsome, virile actors…"

"I'll be on my guard – don't want one of them muscling in. But, yes, I like Kirstie. Feel sorry for her too: Barbara's a right grouch."

"Always has been, so I've heard. Kirstie would love to be able to get away, settle in London."

Shirley called for Roz a little later, and soon after midday I strolled round to the Frobisher Arms. The first person I met was Perry Blakeman, in chef's regalia, enjoying a coffee on a bench outside the front door.

"Barbara's day off," he beamed. "Which gives me the run of the kitchen. He cast a glance through the side window into the almost empty pub. "All I need now are some customers."

"You can rustle me up a ham and cheese baguette," I grinned back. "Although that'll hardly test your culinary skills."

In the next instant, our amusement evaporated as we heard a scream. Perry leapt to his feet. "The kitchen," he exclaimed.

We dashed inside. Lorna stood behind the bar, where she'd been conversing with a customer. Her face was like thunder. "If that's what I think it is -!" she snarled.

Perry was ahead of me, as we hurtled into the kitchen. Kirstie stood before us, looking frazzled. Morgan, beside her, looked the picture of bumbling guilt.

We stared our question, guessing the answer. Kirstie's eyes, holding an appeal, fixed on me. As she struggled for words, Morgan cut in.

"Pure accident, I swear," he gasped. "I came up from the cellar and stumbled on the top step as Kirstie came past."

"A likely story." Lorna's voice boomed from the doorway. "And as feeble an excuse as any I've heard." She glared at the girl with contempt. "You can get on home, Kirstie. We shan't need you today."

"Lorna, honestly, it *was* an accident -," Kirstie began.

"Oh, I'm *sure,*" Lorna sneered. "Along with all the other *accidents.* Not as if you haven't been leading him on. Go on, get along home." She turned angrily on her husband. "As for you, we shall be having words, once there's no-one else around to hear them."

"Lorna, I can explain all this." Morgan had edged away from Kirstie to stand red-faced before his wife, hands dangling helplessly at his sides.

"Oh, you will," she promised dangerously. "Later." She turned on her heel and went back to the bar.

Morgan looked round at the three of us, not quite able to meet our eyes. "All a mistake," he whined. "I'm sorry." He slunk miserably away, leaving the three of us together.

Kirstie looked distressed. "It really *did* happen the way he said," she exclaimed. "Not that she'll listen. I think she's just given me the bullet..."

"I don't think she has," I replied. "Let me speak to her when she's calmed down."

"Perhaps it's best if I do," Perry piped up. I read his meaningful glance correctly: he was impartial, and Lorna might listen to him. She knew that I was friendly with Kirstie and might react negatively to any appeal coming from me.

"Might be an idea," I concurred. "Come on, Kirstie. Let me walk you back. Morgan's his own worst enemy, and Lorna jumped to the obvious conclusion. Perry'll talk her round."

Kirstie collected her handbag, we both thanked Perry and left through the main door, avoiding the bar. I'd thought Kirstie might reject the offer of my company, but she wanted to talk and was glad of a shoulder to lean on.

"I actually feel sorry for Morgan," she confided, as we crossed the road and turned down Selsby's main street. "He's tried it on a few times – just one of those men who can't keep his hands to himself. This time, though, it really wasn't his fault."

"Sadly, his reputation goes before him," I replied. "But I'm confident Lorna will listen to Perry."

"Oh, you bet she will," Kirstie hit back spiritedly. "She's more than happy to have another man about the place." She smiled up at me, slipped a hand into mine. "In any case, it's not going to matter in the long term. Unbelievably, that audition worked out better than I'd hoped."

"You got the part?"

"Two, actually, and both small. But there's understudying as well. Oh, no great shakes, but at least I'll be back in London and treading the boards."

"But that's great news, Kirstie," I enthused, wondering if I should be giving Eric Dim another wake-up call. "I'm really pleased for you. I'll be sure to come and see you once the play's up and running."

"That'd be nice. Thanks, Glen."

We'd turned off the main street and reached her house by then, pausing awkwardly outside the front door. Going by previous experience, I doubted if she'd want to invite me in and, impulsively, I took her in my arms. We kissed lingeringly, reminiscent of the Green Park experience but minus the bruises.

"Would you like to come in for a coffee?" she asked, and I didn't mistake the invitation sparkling in her eyes. She must have sensed my slight hesitation. "Mum's out for the day," she reassured me. "Shopping in Reading." She unlocked the door and took me by the hand into a room which, despite the obvious longevity of sofa, armchairs and Welsh dresser, was airy and spotlessly clean.

"A palace compared to my flat," I commented, as we sat over coffee and a sandwich in the kitchen.

"You're very kind," Kirstie said.

But it was no idle compliment. The house was well upkept. In fact, I was so impressed, I stayed there a while.

*

Roz arrived back late afternoon in high spirits. She'd had a long chat with Shirley, and together they'd called in on Desmond Burge. It turned out that Rupert Blount's parents had been good friends with the Hannons, and Roop had been a guest at the Hall on several occasions. Shirley had dug out from the *Bugle's* archive a photograph of him with his parents at a Hannon Hall garden party in May 1971, a month before the burglary there.

Burge had done some checking for them, confirming that Roop had been imprisoned for drug trafficking and dealing for six years between 1973 and 1979. He'd made himself scarce since then, forming various companies, none of which had lasted long. The Metropolitan Police had kept a weather eye on him since his release from prison and, while some of his dealings had appeared decidedly dodgy, he'd committed no punishable offence.

Roz hadn't shared her opinion with Shirley, but it was her guess that Blount and Morgan Tambling had had something to do with the Hannon Hall burglary. Between them, they'd have had a good idea of the layout. Also, on the weekend in question, the Hannons had been at Glyndebourne with Roop's parents.

It was speculation, although it offered an explanation for Rupert Blount's hold over Morgan. What we couldn't answer was why Blount was so keen to find Marla. We didn't believe his excuse that he merely wanted to renew old acquaintances.

And from what Perry had overheard, did Morgan know where Marla could be found?

A little later, as I cooked supper in the kitchen, the phone rang in the hall. I heard Roz answer it, heard the note of astonishment in her voice and was intrigued.

I wasn't on tenterhooks for long. Soon, she burst into the kitchen, clutching a shortly-to-be-opened bottle of wine.

"This is a cause for celebration, darling brother," she enthused. "Guess who phoned just now?"

"Er, Eric Dim?" I suggested, without hope.

"Even better. It was Venetia, inviting us to Knightsbridge tomorrow evening. We're going to meet Marla."

25

Roz went on to explain that Venetia had decided to host a get-together for two of her neighbours, who'd just returned from a month-long cruise. They'd only met Marla briefly on a previous occasion and, as Marla had only that morning telephoned Venetia to say she was calling round, her mother had put the idea to her and wondered if she might also invite a handsome famous actor, who was simply dying to meet her. Marla had professed to be delighted at her mother's initiative, and Venetia had phoned Roz to invite us both along.

My sister's mood was buoyant: Marla had resurfaced, and we might finally discover an answer to Roland Pettifer's dying words. But why had she been so elusive? Was she already living in fear of someone? Here was an opportunity to meet her face to face and ask some direct questions.

I couldn't define what it was, but something was holding me back. Roz and I had been trying to track down Marla with limited success. And yet, suddenly, here she was, and we were on the cusp of making her acquaintance. It seemed too good to be true, almost as if the situation had been engineered to culminate in this meeting. Perhaps that was simply my suspicious mind at work: time would tell.

Our invitation was for early evening, and we had the day before us. So, we took Roz's car and drove to Oxford, had a wander around a couple of colleges and the botanical gardens, and a picnic lunch on the banks of the Cherwell. It was a welcome break from our investigations, but part of me would have settled for popping down to the Frobisher to make sure all was well as far as Kirstie was concerned. However, because Perry was there, Roz wasn't so keen, and I bowed to her wishes, hoping that time might heal things between them.

We arrived in Cavanaugh Close a little after the stated time, gave our names to the concierge, were told we were expected and fired up in the lift to the third floor. The first ring of the bell brought Venetia to the door with a squeal of delight, as she shepherded us into the hallway. Her greeting was too effusive for my liking, although in my profession I was well used to the inhalation of concentrated alcohol fumes.

Venetia, glass welded to hand, was, as before, the epitome of gush and swirl. Dolled up to the nines with crimson lipstick, electric blue eye shadow and a ton of blusher, she twizzled around in a brilliant white sari with a few thousand pounds worth of diamonds nuzzling her throat.

"Come in, *do* come in," she pleaded, leading me by the hand, with my smirking sister behind me. "I simply *must* introduce you to my lovely neighbours."

They turned out to be Bernie and Belinda Ballenheim, he a retired financier, she a retired financier's moll. They'd been in conversation with a third person, whose torso I'd glimpsed as the Ballenheims rumbled forward to greet us.

I say 'glimpsed', because they were large enough to obscure my view. Bernie was bald, seventyish, triple-chinned and affable in a tuxedo with a maroon cummerbund; Belinda twenty years younger and not much slimmer, very blonde and made-up, swathed in a furlong of silky, rose-patterned material and wobbling on amazingly high heels. She was drinking Chardonnay, as the three-quarters empty bottle on an adjacent sideboard testified.

The Ballenheims were over the moon at meeting their ditzy neighbour's 'very own' famous actor and novelist siblings, although I felt sure they'd never heard of either of us. Venetia twittered around between gulps of gin and then conjured out from behind the screen of Ballenheims the other, hitherto virtually unseen guest.

Morgan Tambling.

Venetia diverted Bernie and Belinda to more drinks and a lavish buffet, the latter undoubtedly supplied by caterers, as I was hard-pressed to dredge up an image of Venetia, with her long fingernails, slaving away in a kitchen; particularly as one hand would be already occupied.

Meanwhile, Morgan greeted Roz with a hug and me with a firm handshake, before drawing us over to the bottle-laden sideboard and providing us with drinks.

Roz had recovered her wits quicker than I. "Lorna not with you tonight, Morgan?"

"Venetia invited her," he sighed. "But she and Marla were at daggers drawn. I thought I ought to put in an appearance for old times' sake."

Roz's expression told me that she thought that was another likely story.

Morgan turned to me, looking rather serious. "Glen, my apologies about what happened yesterday. Or rather, what didn't happen. Once Lorna had calmed down, she let me explain. I tripped on the top step, as I came up from the cellar, and alarmed Kirstie, who happened to be passing at that moment. By the way,

Lorna phoned Kirstie this morning to apologise for jumping to conclusions, and all's well again."

"Thanks, Morgan," I said. "I'm glad to hear it." I shouldn't think Kirstie had let on that she'd shortly be going back to London again; nor that she'd be hoping the new play would enjoy a very long run.

"Let's get some food," Morgan resumed heartily. "Typical that Marla's late. Some things never change. But she'll make the grand entrance, like she always used to."

We followed him to the table where the Ballenheims were busy loading their plates and Venetia was nibbling at a vol-au-vent. Roz threw me a puzzled look, which I returned with a shrug. I was content for the evening's events to take their course. Things *were* puzzling; but interesting, nonetheless.

Everyone stood around for a while, munching and drinking, Bernie and Belinda big on conversation, as well as everything else; Venetia simpering and mainly drinking, and Morgan skulking on the group's perimeter, wearing a sly smile and looking pleased with himself.

And then the doorbell rang.

Venetia beamed at us regally, as she wheeled round and swept out into the hallway. We heard the door open, her words blasting out in a delighted whoop. "Marla – *dah-ling. Do* come in. Oh, they'll all be so *thrilled* to meet you."

She returned to the lounge, pulling her daughter by the hand. Roz and I had never met Marla, but the woman before us tallied with the descriptions supplied by Shirley and Kirstie, making allowances for the years which had passed since they'd last seen her.

Her blonde hair tumbled over her shoulders, and blue eyes appraised us cautiously. Her red mouth had frozen in a wide, somehow superior smile. She'd gone big on make-up, although falling short of her mother's excess, and I supposed the years of high living and drugs had eroded her youthful beauty. However, she was still an extremely attractive woman. She wore a blue velvet dress with a heart-shaped neckline, which showed off the gold locket I'd never seen but had heard so much about. She slipped off the mink stole from around her shoulders and draped it carelessly over a chair.

Venetia introduced the slavering Ballenheims. "Oh, how lovely to meet you," Belinda oozed. "I can see where you get your looks from," Bernie gushed, earning an excited little giggle from our hostess.

Morgan had deftly woven his way between Roz and I to stand before Marla, who, having finished being adored by the neighbours, turned, saw him and gasped. "Morgan! It's you! Oh, what a lovely surprise!"

"Marla! Great to see you again. It's been far too long. But, my goodness, you're more beautiful than I remember, and that's saying something."

"And you're still devastatingly handsome…"

They embraced like long-lost lovers (perhaps they were?), while I marvelled at Morgan's performance. Suavity and easy charm bubbled from every pore. He was a ladies' man to make the flesh crawl, and I found myself feeling sorry for Lorna. I busied myself making mental notes for some future supporting role, in the hope of improving on a previous one. *('Preston's cameo as a lounge lizard was eminently forgettable. It was a relief when he departed to creep back under his stone.')*

"Allow me to introduce my friends." Morgan steered Marla in our direction, as Venetia and the Ballenheims gazed on us benevolently.

"We find ourselves in distinguished company, Marla," Morgan went on. I suspected he was having a laugh and could cheerfully have punched him on the nose. I could tell Roz felt the same, for she was trying to transform her murderous expression into something resembling a gracious smile. "This lady's Roz Blakeman, known to the world as Rosa Peyton, the romantic novelist."

Venetia had materialised at Marla's side. "Yes, darling. You'll remember I mentioned her books to you when you phoned the other week?"

"Delighted to meet you," Marla declared, offering a hand. "Yes, Mummy, of course I remember. I'm sure I've read some."

Roz's grin was not unlike a crocodile's. "And I'm pleased to meet you, Marla," she replied. "I've heard so much about you. You must come back to Selsby one day. Lorna, Shirley and Kirstie would love to have a chat."

"Oh, dear little Kirstie. She was an adorable child. Mummy tells me she's making a name for herself as an actress."

"And this wonderful man is none other than Glen Pressman," Venetia went on. "He's appeared in *oodles* of films."

"Preston, actually," I corrected with a patient smile, noting Marla's amusement. "Not sure about the oodles."

"Oh, but I've seen you on television," Marla enthused back. She named a couple of shows in which I'd had a small role.

I was pleasantly surprised. "You must have a good memory," I complimented her.

"Well, you've got a familiar-looking face."

"People often say 'what have I seen him in?' Roz cut in.

"And it's never anything memorable," I added, making everyone laugh. I felt Marla's amusement was genuine, with a hint of relief, possibly because we'd broken the ice; while Morgan's was forced and sycophantic, and Venetia's gin-laden. The Ballenheims were momentarily absent, replenishing plates and glasses.

"Marla, darling, your nasty old Mummy's forgetting her manners," Venetia declared. "Let me get you a drink. G & T?"

"Oh no, Mummy. Just a small white wine spritzer. I've brought the car, as I'm going on somewhere shortly."

"Allow me to get it," Morgan offered gallantly.

"Morgan, dear, you're so kind," Venetia replied. "And then perhaps you young people would like to go outside for a chat. Bernie and Belinda will want to tell me all about their Caribbean cruise."

She blundered away, while Roz and I followed Marla out on to the balcony, where we sat round a small, glass-topped table. It was a balmy evening, the sun beginning to go down, and the lights and sounds of the vast city twinkling and reverberating below and beyond us.

Morgan brought along Marla's drink and a fresh one for himself. He was going into overdrive to ingratiate himself, harking back to the time she'd spent in Selsby.

"Oh, but Morgan, those discos were completely awful – so very amateurish."

"You've got to admit that the one I gave at the pub was pretty cool – you seemed to be having a good time."

"Oh, sweetie, what planet were you on? I was being polite. Remember when you came down to London? Now, *that's* what partying was all about."

"Yes, and as you well know, I didn't stay in London long enough to savour it."

Marla gave him a mock-pitying look. "You could have stayed."

"Not after you rejected me." He glanced appealingly at Roz and me. "Utterly heartless, this girl. Had eyes for one person alone."

"Darling Hal." Marla was fingering the locket, a faraway expression on her face. She quickly snapped out of it. "Morgan, we're boring these good people out of their minds. Go and get them more drinks, and you can fetch me a small plate of something, unless the boozy Ballenheims have demolished the lot."

"Fair maiden, your wish is my command." Morgan got up and performed a deep bow. In my opinion, he was overdoing it, and then some.

Marla waved him away. "You always were a charmer. Some things never change. Get on with you." She turned to me with an appealing smile. "Let's talk about some of your roles, Glen. You've probably been on TV an awful lot?"

Roz gave me a brief nod, a prearranged signal, and rose from the table. "Why don't I lend Morgan a hand?" she suggested. "I believe there was something you wanted to ask Marla anyway, wasn't there, Glen?"

"Oh?" Marla looked intrigued.

Morgan had already moved away, and Roz took off after him. "Yes, there is," I said. "Marla, do you remember Roland Pettifer?"

"Roly? Wasn't he the journalist guy? I remember him from way back. Always found him a bit creepy. I know that he and Mummy stayed in touch." She stifled a giggle. "I think he fancied her."

I gave her brief details of Roland's accident, recounted his dying words. I asked if she knew of anyone who might want to harm her?

She looked stunned. "Well – no. I've a large circle of friends, but no-one I've *quarrelled* with. Are you sure that's what he said?"

"Pretty sure. No-one from way back? From the time you lived in Selsby, for instance?"

Marla laughed incredulously. "How ridiculous! Glen, that was *sixteen* years ago."

"Even so?"

She frowned, took an anxious pull at her drink, then a quick look over her shoulder to make sure Morgan was still occupied. He would be: it was part of Roz's brief. She leaned towards me confidentially.

"There was Lorna, of course. To be frank, she hated my guts, thought I was hell-bent on stealing Morgan away from her. Between you and I, Morgan was never part of my plans. Then there was that sour-faced Ryde woman. The way she blamed me for poor Jamie's death, even threatening to kill me. Glen, honestly, that was just a tragic accident."

"No-one else?"

"That friend of Lorna's – plain-looking cow. What was her name?"

"Shirley Newbury."

"She didn't like me. Not sure if she really fitted in with any of us. But I don't think she *hated* me. No, it's too absurd."

Marla dismissed the idea with an expressive sweep of her hand, succeeding in knocking over her empty glass. As it toppled, I snatched at it but only managed to help it on its way over the balcony rail. With a gasp, I watched it plummet and smash on the dark pavement below.

Marla claimed my attention, patting my hand. "Don't worry," she drawled. "It's only a glass."

There was something in her veiled expression which I couldn't define. Something akin to anxiety. Her gaze raked my face, as if looking for a clue to what I was thinking.

But I couldn't tell what I was thinking either. The dying fall of the glass, its expiring tinkle on the pavement: something there had alarmed me, breeding a suspicion of what might be to come. But what? Certainly nothing good.

And Marla had seen and recognised it.

26

Looking back into the lounge, I saw that Roz and Morgan were finally making their way back towards us. She'd done a good job in stalling him, but I wasn't quite through with my interrogation. I asked Marla if she'd run into Rupert Blount.

She looked distracted. "Sorry – who?"

"You might have known him as Roop."

"Oh – *Roop.* No, not for years. We – um, lost touch. I've no idea where he might be."

"Well, he's turned up in Selsby, looking for you."

Roz and Morgan had reached us, setting drinks and plates on the table, but I'd already witnessed the flash of alarm in Marla's eyes. The mention of Roop had sparked it. Did she for some reason *fear* him? She glanced up at Morgan. "You took your time." The note of accusation was plain.

"Just being sociable." He looked amused. "Bernie and Belinda are well on the way."

"I should imagine they're as bad as Mummy. Ah, food. I'm starving." She picked up a sandwich and bit into it energetically, appearing relieved at the change of subject.

Roz switched me a sly glance. "That's a gorgeous locket, Marla," she remarked. "It must be the one that -?"

It was a deliberately unfair observation as, at that precise moment, Marla was trying to cope with a large mouthful of salmon-and-cress sandwich. Morgan, however, rode gallantly to the rescue.

"Spot on, Roz. The one poor Pamela had somehow -er, acquired."

"I didn't miss it for yonks," Marla declared, once restored to parity. "It must have been taken soon after I lost Hal. I left it in a drawer, and when, finally, I came to look for it, it had gone. But that poor woman… I mean, we weren't exactly friends, but I was absolutely floored when Mummy told me what had happened. Did you know her well, Roz?"

"She was difficult to get to know," my sister replied. "But I hope that, along with Shirley, I helped make those last months in Selsby at least bearable for her."

Venetia had swayed across to join us. "Darlings, Bernie and Belinda are about to leave. They're going on to dinner. Perhaps you'd all come over and say goodbye."

We dutifully trooped back into the lounge, where the beaming Ballenheims awaited us. The contents of the buffet had been decimated. We four hadn't exactly gorged ourselves, and I suspected Venetia's diet was at least ninety per cent liquid. Bernie's face was a deeper shade of red than earlier, and Belinda looked replete. *And now dinner?*

They were full of compliments for Marla. "So *wonderful* to properly meet your bea-ootiful daughter," Bernie rumbled. "And to be in the same room as a top novelist and a film star – well, it's simply blown us away."

I felt it would take a hurricane to do that, but we chatted away, smiled chummily and made the right noises, until the Ballenheims had been despatched back down to their floor in the long-suffering lift.

I took the opportunity to draw Roz aside. "Go back on the train with Morgan and don't leave just yet," I murmured. "There's something I have to do. I'll catch a later one."

Avoiding her questioning stare, I moved across to join Venetia and Marla, just as Marla declared that she really ought to dash, as she was meeting someone.

"He's a lucky man," Morgan drooled.

"Oh, but darling, when shall I see you again?" Venetia whined. "You forgot all about my birthday, you wicked girl. I'd so have loved to have gone to Radolfini's for a meal."

"Then I'll take you next week," Marla promised. "Why don't we say Tuesday?"

"Oh, sweetie, that would be *marvellous*," Venetia gushed. "I'll *so* look forward to it. And now you must go. Mustn't keep your admirer waiting."

"I'd better be running along too," I apologised. "I'm meeting up with a friend from way back. You may have heard of Jem Stander? I believe he may have a role for me."

Marla smiled engagingly. "I'll wish you the best of luck, then."

"And it's been great meeting you," I enthused. "Venetia's told us so much about you. We're so grateful for the invitation."

"An absolute pleasure, Graham," Venetia cooed. "You really must come again."

I edged towards the door. Marla seemed to be heading that way but suddenly had second thoughts.

"Oh, Mummy, I've just remembered. That bracelet we spoke about last time. The one that was Grandma Hartman's?"

"Of course, darling. It's in the bedroom wall safe. Let me get it for you."

"I'll come with you." Marla turned to me. "Glen, it's been super meeting you. I do hope your friend gives you that role. I'm sure you'll be utterly magnificent."

I was being dismissed. Marla was full of charm, but for some reason she wanted to avoid accompanying me down in the lift. It didn't surprise me. I cheerfully wished everyone a good evening and saw myself out.

Marla had said she'd driven there, and I was sure she'd have parked in the basement garage. I believed she intended making a quick getaway, and my aim was to follow her. There was a convenient taxi rank just across the road.

I wished the concierge a good evening, went outside and scuttled down the ramp to conceal myself behind a pillar. The garage was dimly lit, with a sprinkling of cars. I didn't envisage Marla driving a Bentley or Daimler, so reasoned that she'd parked at the far end of the garage.

After about five minutes, I heard the *whoosh* of the lift descending, the clatter of heels and the sound of a car door closing.

A car started up, moved off. As it swept up the ramp, I registered that it was light blue, possibly a Renault or Fiat, and clocked part of the number plate, as it turned into the street: A453. The colour made it easy enough to follow: I was in business.

I hared up the ramp, intent on gaining the taxi rank, when a shape lurched out from behind the next pillar. It was a large shape and, as it collided violently with my shoulder, solid enough to deposit me in a welter of arms and legs on the concrete floor of the ramp. I had enough presence of mind to glimpse a dark figure loping away across the street and signalling frantically for a taxi. The white fedora betrayed the identity of my assailant.

Painfully hauling myself to my feet, I watched a taxi speed away. Both Marla and the fedora were long gone. I dusted myself down, hobbled to the nearest tube station and returned to Paddington.

I was sure Morgan and Roz would have taken a taxi and were, in all likelihood, on the Reading-bound train pulling out of the station as I arrived. That suited me. I was sore and crotchety after my recent adventure, and my mood was only slightly improved by the swift despatch of a large brandy in the station bar.

Roz was awaiting me at the bungalow and realised plans had gone awry the moment I trailed in. She sat me down, bathed and dressed a nasty graze on my elbow and fed me more brandy. She'd journeyed home with Morgan, and both had kept the conversation on a superficial level. Like us, he'd been surprised to receive Venetia's invitation to meet up again with Marla. He'd not set eyes on her since that time in London more than fifteen years previously. He reckoned she was more beautiful than he remembered. That was typically Morgan, but Roz felt inclined to give him the benefit of the doubt.

For my part, I wasn't so sure; and neither was she, when I told her my assailant had been Rupert Blount.

"But how could he have known -?" she began.

"Precisely," I cut in. "It has to be through Morgan."

"So, Blount's on Marla's trail."

"Hhmm." I threw her one of my superior smiles: I don't get to practise them very often. "I wish him luck with that."

Roz frowned, puzzled. "Glen – what on earth do you mean?"

"Because, dear sister," I went on, "despite the fact that the woman we met this evening dazzled us with a first-class performance, in my humble opinion *she's not Marla.*"

27

Roz's answer was to pour herself a stiff drink and plump down opposite me, looking severe. "Glen, when you collided with Blount this evening, are you sure you didn't suffer a nasty bang on the head?"

"Quite sure."

"Because Marla seemed pretty genuine to me. Just the way she's been described to us."

"Oh, she undoubtedly made a good job of it." I leaned back in the chair and savoured my brandy. Two in one night, and both large ones: I expected to be reminded of them when I awoke the next morning. "But didn't you notice the glaring omissions?"

She shook her head, frowning. "No?"

"For instance, when I mentioned that I was about to visit Jem Stander?"

"So?"

"Roz, *she didn't know him.* Her expression was blank. Yet he played guitar and shared vocals in their pop group, *Daze of Sorrow.* They cut several singles and an LP, so must have been together a while. Also, Jem's a good-looking guy – most women wouldn't have a problem remembering him. On top of that, she didn't recognise Rupert Blount's name right away, and going back to the conversation I had with him, they were once an item. At least that's the way he tells it, but the bottom line is that she *knew* him. And then, of course, she'd forgotten her mother's birthday."

Roz nodded as she took this all in. "So, if you're right, how come Morgan was convinced?"

"Because Morgan's in this up to his neck. Listen, Roz, we need to locate Marla and discover where Blount fits in. As for Morgan, we play along and don't let on that we're suspicious."

"And how exactly do you intend to track down Marla, having let her slip through your fingers last night?"

My sister's tone can be cutting, but I shrugged it away. "Apart from scouring London, there's not a lot we can do. If there's some link over this between Morgan and Blount, it's not going to be long before Blount turns up in

Selsby again, or Morgan returns to London. We stay on the alert, and maybe pull Shirley, Kirstie and Perry into this. If Morgan hops on a train, I intend to be right behind him."

The brandies I'd consumed contributed to a good night's sleep. Roz and I went for a brisk country walk in the morning and stopped off at the Frobisher Arms for a light lunch.

Morgan greeted us like old friends: to me, that was guilt talking. However, Lorna was out to lunch with the landlady of a pub in a neighbouring village, and her absence no doubt contributed to his light-hearted mood.

"Hi, Roz, Glen," he enthused. "Enjoy last night's get-together? Good, wasn't it? Dare say you'll agree Marla's quite a dish, eh, Glen? Hasn't lost any of it, in my opinion. And how about your meeting with your showbiz pal? Did that work out okay?"

"Oh, Jem's come up trumps for me," I lied cheerfully. "Only a small part, but no matter. I'm quite used to that. It means," I added, leaning forward confidentially, "that I'll be on my way back to London before long."

"Well, congratulations! Really glad to hear it. Now, what can I get you both?"

I had the feeling that what Morgan was glad about was the news of my impending departure. However, I placed an order for our drinks, just as, having heard our voices, Perry came bouncing out of the kitchen with the exuberance of a two-year-old. He had the kitchen to himself again, as Barbara Ryde had gone to London to meet her sister, who was up from Cornwall for a few days. He took the order for our baguettes and disappeared back to the kitchen, while the genial Morgan served our drinks.

I could tell Roz was still a mite uncomfortable with Perry around and bore her drink over to where Shirley Newbury was sitting with her colleagues, Deirdre and Penny.

Kirstie was on duty in the restaurant. I happened to catch her eye, and she beckoned me over, out of Morgan's line of vision. She was looking glum.

"You okay?" I asked, although I could tell right away that she wasn't.

"Could be better," she replied, without much enthusiasm. "Be off duty in a couple of hours. Did I overhear you saying just now that you've landed a part?"

"Jem Stander's got something lined up for me." I hated lying to Kirstie, but it was necessary to maintain the fiction. Walls might not actually have ears, but pubs certainly did.

She smiled back wanly. "Well done, you. So, before long, we'll both be back in the big city. In fact, I'm on my way early next week." She flicked a quick glance at the figure behind the bar. "Can't wait."

"Listen, has he been making a nuisance of himself again?"

Kirstie raised her eyebrows. "When hasn't he?" Sensing my anger, she stalled me, a hand on my arm. "Just forget it, Glen. I'll soon be out of here and away from him."

I felt like punching him on the nose for more reasons than one but gave in to her wishes. "Hopefully see you before you zip off to London?" I asked.

"You will." She was smiling brightly again, and we parted with a quick kiss. I took my drink into the lounge and sat with Roz, Shirley and co. Kirstie served our baguettes and, before long, lunch was over, trade in the pub was winding down and we were walking back to Roz's bungalow.

The moment we let ourselves in, the phone in the hallway started ringing. I was ahead of Roz and picked up the receiver.

"Hello?"

"Hello? Glen?" It was Shirley, sounding very agitated. "Can you and Roz get back down to the FA right away? I can't explain now. All hell's broken loose."

I told her we were on our way and put the receiver down. I felt my anger returning, certain that Morgan was up to his old tricks again. This time I was determined to sort him out. Roz looked at me questioningly. "Back to the FA," I said. "And quick. Sounds like trouble."

We hurried back the way we'd come. A Panda car had drawn up in the car park, and a siren wailed in the distance. As we approached the entrance, an ambulance hurtled round the bend in the road and lurched to a halt beside the police car.

Desmond Burge appeared in the pub doorway, hustling a forlorn figure along in front of him, as two paramedics spilled out of the ambulance and dashed past them. Roz gasped as she caught sight of the first figure. "Perry! What*ever's* going on?"

A small crowd had gathered on the perimeter of the car park, but Roz was oblivious to them. She rushed forward and latched on to Perry's arm. "*Please!* Will someone tell me what's happening?"

I'd followed her over, and Perry, his chef's tunic smeared with traces of culinary exploits, as well as an ominous slash of glistening red, turned a face of anguish towards us. "Roz – Glen – I *swear* I didn't do it!"

My sister's face was suffused with fury, which she directed at Desmond Burge. "Sergeant Burge – I demand to know what this is about. Why have you arrested my husband?"

Burge assumed his best constipated expression. "I'm sorry, Rosalind. I'm not at liberty to say. Mr Blakeman is helping with inquiries. Into the car, if you please, sir."

Perry stumbled helplessly towards it, Burge reaching across to tug open the rear door and bundle him inside. Closing the door he stood on guard beside it, unimpeachable, awaiting a CID presence from Reading.

Roz didn't seem prepared to let the matter rest there, however, so I wrestled her away, noticing out of the corner of my eye that Shirley was waving at us from the pub's patio door. I steered my sister over there, and Shirley pulled us inside. The lounge's only other occupant was Kirstie, sitting tearfully at one of the tables.

Through in the restaurant area, I saw the paramedics carefully loading someone on to a stretcher, with Burge's constable in attendance.

"It's Morgan," Shirley informed us in a low, tense whisper. "He's been stabbed."

"Oh, dear God!" Roz exclaimed. "What – do you mean he – he's *dead?*"

"We don't know. They're taking him to the Royal Berks at Reading. I've phoned Lorna, and she's heading straight there."

"But what *happened?*" I asked. "And surely you're not going to tell me it was Perry who -?"

Kirstie looked up, tears streaming down her cheeks. "Has – has Burge arrested him?"

"It looks like it," Shirley replied.

"But Perry *wouldn't!*" Roz protested. "Simply wouldn't! He's one of the gentlest men…"

"It wasn't him," Kirstie sobbed. "It *wasn't*. I *know*. I was there."

"Then who was it?" I asked gently, seating myself beside her and laying a hand over one of hers.

Shirley had fetched a glass of brandy from behind the unpopulated bar and encouraged Kirstie to take a sip or two. Once she had, she seemed to collect herself.

"We were about to close," she said. "The last customers had left the restaurant, and I was clearing away."

"There was no-one in the lounge bar either," Shirley confirmed. "I was last to leave – was actually just outside the front door when it happened."

Roz threw Kirstie an exasperated glance. "Morgan?"

She nodded glumly. "You've guessed it. With Lorna out, he'd been making flirtatious remarks all morning. Once the customers had left, he grabbed me from behind and swung me round to face him. I ought to have screamed but could only gasp, because he'd taken me by surprise. Perry saw us as he came out of the kitchen. Then this guy seemed to appear from nowhere – he was there and gone in an instant. He must have stabbed Morgan in the back, because Morgan groaned and let go of me. Perry rushed forward and caught him before he fell."

"That explains the blood on his tunic," I said.

"I was out in the car park, when I saw someone run out of the patio doors and away through the side entrance," Shirley said.

"Did either of you see who it was?" Roz asked.

Both shook their heads. "He was there and gone so quickly," Kirstie mumbled dejectedly.

"All I noticed was that he wore a white hat," Shirley answered, prompting Roz and I to exchange a swift glance.

Rupert Blount.

Police reinforcements had arrived, and Perry had been taken away. Burge blundered in, notebook in hand, shaking his head sorrowfully.

"Dear me," he groaned. "This is a bad, bad business."

"Is there any news on Morgan?" Shirley asked.

"Well, he's alive, at least," the sergeant answered. "But they won't be able to tell how serious it is before they get him to hospital. And you can take my word for it, it looked pretty darned serious. Now, Miss Ryde, if you're feeling up to it, I shall need a statement from you. You too, Miss Newbury."

Kirstie looked up defiantly. "Now's a good a time as any, Sergeant Burge. Because one thing's for certain. I saw everything that happened, and I can tell you you've arrested the wrong man. Perry Blakeman didn't do it."

Roz's expression was one of relief, and she clung to me for support. As we were surplus to requirements, I told Burge I was taking my sister home. We'd arrived too late to witness anything, but he knew where to find us if we were needed.

We said our goodbyes and walked back, with plenty to think about.

28

Things settled down over the next twenty-four hours. Morgan Tambling had been critically wounded, but his condition had stabilised, and the doctor was hopeful that he'd pull through. He was, however, some way off being able to receive visitors, which included the police. Lorna was extremely relieved and called in on all her friends and neighbours to thank them for their support and good wishes.

Thanks to the witness statements of Kirstie and Shirley, Perry Blakeman was released from police custody later in the day the attack happened. As the Frobisher Arms was a crime scene, it had to remain closed, which was likely to be the case for a while. It left me in a dilemma, as Perry had nowhere to go. I offered to vacate the spare room, but Roz was having none of it. In the end, Shirley kindly offered to put him up for a while, for which we were all grateful.

However, it wasn't as if Roz didn't want anything to do with Perry. On the contrary, she fussed over him like a mother hen. I'd seen signs previously that her attitude towards him was beginning to soften, and Shirley and I agreed that we'd like to see them back together again.

The description of the fugitive, which Shirley and Kirstie had given the police, was rather sketchy, but Lorna was adamant that it must be the same man who'd visited Morgan at the pub days earlier. Sergeant Burge informed us that the case had been turned over to the Met, who were now actively seeking Rupert Blount.

I went round to see Kirstie. Barbara was at home when I called, and in a surprisingly pliant mood; and the three of us sat together over tea and cake. The attack on Morgan had upset Kirstie, and she'd made the decision not to return to the Frobisher Arms or Selsby. Her rehearsals were starting in London that week, and she'd stay at a girlfriend's flat until she could find one for herself and sort out a temporary job for when she wasn't acting.

As for Barbara, she'd met up with her widowed sister at the weekend and had finally been persuaded to go and live with her in Cornwall. With Kirstie leaving, the time had come for Barbara to move on.

I wished them both the very best, and Kirstie saw me to the door, where we lingered over our goodbyes. I hoped it might be *au revoir,* as I passed her my business card with my London address and telephone number, and she promised to keep in touch.

That evening, with Perry exonerated, we celebrated with a meal at the bungalow, which he insisted on providing. We invited Shirley to join us, and she and I sat smiling and nodding sagely over our drinks, as Roz helped her husband in the kitchen, with accompanying laughter and merry banter. I was beginning to feel *de trop,* and it was my intention not to put upon my sister for much longer. In any case, Eric Di Mario had been far too quiet of late, and I wanted to interrogate him face to face over the 'wonderful' role he'd practically promised me.

But there was still the matter of Marla. Might it be that Blount had caught up with her, before coming to Selsby to make his attack on Morgan? Had they all been involved in something together, and Marla and Blount had agreed to dispense with Morgan's services? I'd wondered the previous night about laying the whole matter before Sergeant Burge. Roz had only just left off laughing at that suggestion. But we'd about reached the end of the line, and I still felt that we should at least inform the police of our suspicions.

Until a chance conversation among the four of us, as we sat over our meal that evening…

It began with Shirley. We'd just finished our main course, steak *au poivre,* cooked to mouth-watering perfection, when she brought up the subject of Morgan.

"It looks as though his sins have finally found him out. Lorna's so relieved that he's likely to make a full recovery, but she was telling me she'll be keeping him on a short leash from now on. I doubt if he'll be gallivanting off to London quite as much. I never mentioned it to Lorna, but I ran into him a few weeks back in a pub in Shoreditch. I was down there interviewing a student from Selsby, who'd just won a top award from her college. Morgan pretended he hadn't seen me, because he was ensconced at a corner of the bar with some woman, who I'm sure must have been the landlady. They certainly seemed rather friendly…"

Perry looked up sharply. "Did you say Shoreditch, Shirl? Wasn't by any chance the Parrot & Cage?"

Shirley stared at him in surprise. "That's right, it was. Do you know it, then?"

"I went there back in June in response to a job ad, but the position had already been filled. Story of my life, I suppose. It was the landlady I saw – Thelma something; and Morgan was with her. I put it down as some sort of business meeting. He couldn't pretend he didn't know me, of course, and he came across as his usual amiable self. But I wondered at the time, knowing Morgan, if there wasn't some ulterior motive. She was an attractive woman."

"Yes, our Morgan certainly got around," Roz remarked, as she passed a second bottle of wine round the table. "Let's wish him a speedy recovery, although I guess he'll find life a bit more regimented, once he comes out of hospital."

The rest of the meal passed off very pleasantly, with Shirley and I maintaining a respectful distance, as Roz and Perry said their goodnights. As we waved him and Shirley on their way, my sister turned to me with a triumphant grin.

"London?" she suggested.

"My thoughts exactly," I replied.

The next day, I caught a mid-morning train alone. Roz had a deadline to meet and, after the excitement of the last few days, was having to play catch-up. "Besides," she teased me, "from the sound of her, Thelma would probably be more responsive to being questioned by a man. And you're not exactly repulsive."

I thanked her for that and set off.

*

The Parrot & Cage was a large Victorian pub in a street off Kingsland Road. The bright hanging baskets and green-tiled walls outside, the high, crafted ceiling, parquet floor and majestic sweep of its polished mahogany bar inside, all lent it atmosphere. As I arrived, the lunchtime trade was just kicking in, but the landlady was happy to spare me a few minutes and came to sit with me at a corner table, as I lunched on pasty and chips and a pint of shandy.

Thelma Woodfull was certainly glamorous: tall, bottle blonde and busty, in a blouse not quite opaque, a tight grey skirt and killer heels. The view from a distance suggested she was in her mid-thirties, but at close quarters and despite skilfully applied make-up, she looked ten years older. I could see the attraction for Morgan.

"Yes, lovey, how can I help? What did you say your name was?" The gleaming smile and coquettish flutter of eyelashes sought to bring me under her spell. I saw how it might work for Morgan, but Calista was too fresh in the memory for me to be swayed.

"My name's Glen Preston," I said, "and I'm trying to track down an old acquaintance. A friend of mine told me he'd bumped into him in here not long ago and thought you might have had dealings with him? His name's Morgan..."

I'd uttered a very bad word. Thelma's bright smile somersaulted into a scowl. "Say no more. Morgan Thompson. 'Fraid you'll have to go on looking. I don't know or care where he is, and I don't want to see him ever again."

"Oh?" I pretended to be surprised. "Morgan *Thompson?* I'm not sure we're talking about the same person here." Although I was – *very* sure. "The chap I'm looking for is called Morgan Tambling."

Thelma blew out an exasperated sigh. "I might have known it."

"I'm really sorry." My sympathy was genuine. I'd been betrayed and two-timed on several occasions and knew how she felt.

She worked on a smile. "You know, lovey, there are no flies on me." *I could well believe that.* "I met him at some brewery do, three or four months back. He was single – he said – good-looking, charming and scouting around for a business opportunity in London. Well, I've been around these parts all my life and offered to help him. One thing led to another, and, well -," another flutter, "you're old enough to know the form."

"So where did it all go wrong?"

The smile yielded to her 'hell hath no fury' expression. "The last time he came here – and it was the last, as I told him afterwards in no uncertain terms – we were sitting at this very table. It was getting to the end of the lunch period with business tailing off, when this woman walked in and went up to the bar. She was dressed to kill and seemed to delight in the attention she was getting. Hell's bells, the moment he clocked her, he couldn't take his eyes off her! It was obscene. He got up like someone in a daze and trailed out after her – though not before I'd tweaked his earhole good and proper!"

"Can you describe this woman?" I asked tensely.

Thelma eyed me cagily. "Yeah, I s'pose I can. Here, are you some sort of private detective?"

"I'm actually an actor," I replied. "Glen Preston."

Not a glimmer. But I wasn't there to be recognised and cooed over. "All I'm trying to do is track Morgan down," I lied, knowing full well that he was currently immobile in the Royal Berks hospital. "His wife's concerned about him…"

"His *wife?*" Thelma screeched. "Oh, the bastard! And to think that I -?" She shook her head, her stern features giving way to a rueful smile. "Listen to me banging on. Dare say you've been there too, haven't you, lovey?" I nodded my agreement.

"Well," Thelma swept on. "For what it's worth, in my opinion dear Morgan Tambling-Thompson's probably shacked up with the floosie he went panting after two or three weeks ago. I've never seen her since, but here goes."

She launched into a description of the woman Morgan had followed out of the Parrot & Cage. There was very little detail, but I had no problem working out who the woman was.

Thelma was describing Marla.

29

"You look as if you know her." There was a hint of accusation in Thelma's tone.

"I think I may have met her," I replied evenly. "Although I'm not sure of her name. Did she have a car outside? Hailed a taxi, perhaps?"

"Oh, I don't reckon she lived far away. She turned right down Kingsland Road, though I couldn't tell you where she went after that. She'd bought a baguette at the bar, so I guess she'd have been off home for lunch, or back to the office. I watched him go after her. I mean, I was absolutely flabbergasted at the way he'd just walked out on me."

"Did Morgan catch up with her outside?"

Thelma shook her head. "Not him. He kept a few yards back, almost as if he was stalking her, the creep."

I thanked her for the information: she had no way of knowing what a tremendous help she'd been.

"Any time, lovey." The smile was back, and dangerously welcoming. "You're an actor, you say? Glen -?"

"Preston."

I could tell she was racking her brains to put the name and face to some TV series or other. *Best of luck with that.*

"Not on TV so much," I said. "Only bit parts. Most of the time I'm on stage."

"Hhmm. Have to say I like a good play. You must call and let me know when you're next on in London – Glen. I'll take the night off and pop along to see you."

"Er, yes, of course. That'd be nice." I made a mental note to avoid Shoreditch as a priority.

Her smile broadened, bordering on feline. "Oh, and if you happen to report back to that creep's wife, you might suggest she should..."

An ambulance careered past at that moment, the blare of its siren drowning out her words. But I got the gist. It brought tears to *my* eyes, let alone what it might have done to Morgan Tambling-Thompson, if Lorna ever took up Thelma's suggestion. Hell hath no fury, indeed.

I made my way on to Kingsland Road and walked down it without a clue as to where they might have gone from there. I wandered aimlessly for a few minutes, before it struck me that some of the street signs and shop fronts were familiar. I'd been along here before; and recently.

I struck off the main thoroughfare into a maze of side streets, not quite sure what I was looking for, but hopefully something which might point me in Marla's direction. From what Thelma had told me, she could well live or work in this area.

As I walked, part of my mind was busy pondering the deviousness of Morgan Tambling. And that started another train of thought: Shirley's account of what had happened in Selsby sixteen years previously.

Jamie Ryde's death had been an accident. *Or had it?*

I'd told Roz I was confident that the woman at Venetia Hartman's soirée, whom Venetia believed to be her daughter, wasn't Marla.

I wondered if my judgement had been premature. All right, so Marla hadn't reacted when I'd mentioned Jem Stander's name; and she'd forgotten her mother's birthday. It proved nothing. She hadn't seen Venetia in years, and she'd lived in a drug-fuelled haze for some time after she'd played with Jem in *Daze of Sorrow*.

Another theory had come to the fore, and it involved Morgan, whose name was becoming synonymous with 'shady'. Morgan had seen Jamie Ryde as an obstacle in his path to Marla. What if he'd removed that obstacle, diving into the river ostensibly to rescue the unconscious Jamie, and then *holding him down so that he drowned?* Marla had seen what happened, and because of it rejected Morgan's advances when he'd chased after her to London. And Rupert Blount? He'd known Marla too. What if she'd told Blount about what had happened, and he'd come to Selsby to blackmail Morgan, stabbing him when he wouldn't pay up?

And then I shelved that startling hypothesis in the dusty archives at the back of my mind. Because, as I chanced to glance down a narrow side street, I happened upon Marla's car.

It was a light blue Fiat Punto, not an uncommon make or colour. But I'd succeeded in getting a partial number plate reading the other night, and it tallied with what stood before me now. Also, somewhere in the foggy reaches of my brain, a bell was ringing. I sought out a telephone kiosk and called my sister.

I gave her a brief account of my meeting with Thelma Woodfull at the Parrot & Cage. Morgan had followed Marla, and it had been Thelma's opinion that she lived or worked locally. My discovery of the car confirmed it.

"Something's nagging at me," I said. "Has anyone over the last ten days mentioned a light blue car? This one's a Fiat Punto, registration number A453 GNO?"

Roz was silent for so long, that I thought she'd either given up on me or nodded off. It transpired she'd been deep in thought.

"Glen!"

I leapt several inches and nearly dropped the receiver.

"Of course!" she swept on. *"That's* why it's ringing a bell. Can you remember? When we were talking to Dismal Desmond? He mentioned a light blue Fiat - *the car which ran over Ned Braley back in May.* But is it likely it's the same one?"

"Get on to him now, Roz," I urged her. "He must have a note of the registration number." I repeated it for her to write down. "He'll have the driver's address as well," I went on, "and I bet it tallies with the part of London I'm standing in right now. What was her name? The girl who was driving the Fiat?"

"He mentioned a surname. A Miss – Bentley? Benedict? No, I've got it. *Blenkinsop!"*

"Okay, Roz. Get those details and call me back." I gave her the kiosk number. "Say twenty minutes?"

"Should be plenty of time, even for Desmond."

We rang off, and I spent the time pacing up and down in front of the kiosk. Roz rang back within fifteen minutes: Burge had been eager to please. The girl's name was Kate Blenkinsop, a freelance journalist, and her address was in Longdale Square, Shoreditch. *Not far away.*

That set off another bell, and not a distant one. "Roz," I said sternly, "there's something very sinister going on. Longdale Mews is where Pamela

Segrave's cousin, Georgia Derry, lives. So, there's a connection between Marla, Georgia and Kate Blenkinsop."

"Then what's happening, Glen?"

"I believe Venetia Hartman's life is in danger."

"Oh, come *on*," Roz cackled. "How did you arrive there? Did you have several large scotches at lunchtime or get starry-eyed over Thelma What-not?"

I calmly recounted the incident at Venetia's flat the other evening, when I'd been left alone with Marla on the balcony, and she'd accidentally knocked a glass over the rail, sending it plummeting down to shatter in the street. I recalled how I'd felt Marla had recognised something – some hint of foreboding? – in my startled expression, which had seemed to put her on her guard.

It could only be a suspicion. But what if that glass had been a person? Someone swaying drunkenly, someone tripping, given a helping hand, falling…? It was a long way down.

Roz was serious again. "So, what do you suggest?" she asked.

"Can you get down to London – like now? Just get Venetia out of that flat and stay with her."

"Hang on. Didn't Marla promise the other day to take her mother out for a meal to celebrate her birthday. Didn't she say Tuesday? That's tonight?"

"You're right. Then it's even more important to get Venetia away from there. Say I need to see her urgently, that Marla knows all about it and will call later. Take her to my flat. Mrs Hawkins on the ground floor has a spare key and knows who you are. I'll phone you there this evening."

"Okay, got that. What are you going to do?"

"I'm going to find Kate Blenkinsop. I have a feeling she and Rupert Blount may be in this together."

"Then be careful. Speak later."

We hung up, and I checked my watch. It was after four o'clock, which meant that Roz wouldn't reach Knightsbridge before six or six-thirty. It would be useful if I could head off Kate/Marla, as of now. With the evidence of the car, I felt they had to be one and the same person.

There followed the question: where did Georgia Derry fit in?

Longdale Mews was in a quiet square, not far from where I'd located the Fiat. It looked as if each terraced house had been converted into two flats. On Georgia's door was a buzzer for 'Derry', and another with no name against it. I pressed 'Derry', and Georgia's voice sounded nervously over the intercom. "Yes? Who is it?"

"Glen Preston. I called on you last week."

"Just a moment."

She admitted me and was waiting at the open door of her flat, dressed in baggy T-shirt and jeans similar to the other day. She looked pale, and her eyes appraised me anxiously.

"What do you want, Mr Preston? If it's about Pamela, I'm not sure if there's any more I can -?"

"It's not," I cut in rudely. "It's about Kate Blenkinsop."

Georgia was on edge. She stood in the doorway with a hand on each doorpost, as if in need of support. "Kate? What about her?"

"She lives here, doesn't she?"

"In the flat above. Why are you looking for her?"

"It's a personal matter. Do you mind if I go up?"

"Well, she's not in." She forced a laugh. "In fact, she hardly ever is. Kate's a freelance journalist, you see. Often away on an assignment."

"Yes, I wondered if she might be. Georgia, would you mind awfully if I had a look in her flat?"

I'd put my request casually. It had an astounding effect on Georgia. Her eyes widened, full of fear. Her grip tightened on the doorposts.

"But – but you can't do that! It's private property! You – you've no right whatsoever…"

"But I'm going to anyway. Unless you feel you ought to call the police?"

She shrank back from me. "Wh-what you're doing is illegal -," she began.

"In that case, perhaps I'll call them, and they can get a warrant," I threatened suavely. There are times when I can be really intimidating. *('Preston's portrayal of a murderous villain pulsated with all the latent menace of a vicarage tea party').*

Georgia gave in, her anxious eyes hating me. "I – I'll let you in. I keep a spare key for her." She turned back into the room and fished around in a drawer of the sideboard. Brandishing a key, she pushed past me and headed up the stairs. "Kate's going to learn of this," she added with asperity. "I shall recommend she makes a formal complaint…"

She unlocked the door on the landing. "There. You can see she's not in."

"Thank you." I carefully insinuated my way past her and into the flat. A strange smell assaulted my nostrils, as I entered a sparsely furnished room. I took a few paces forward, and it became unbearable. I glanced back questioningly at Georgia, who was watching me sullenly.

The smell seemed to emanate from behind a door in front of me. I turned the handle, and the door flew open. Something pitched out into my reluctant arms, making me stagger back under its weight, so that I was hard pressed to keep my balance.

But then, inert bodies tend to be heavy, particularly when they're dead, with cruel-looking kitchen knives buried in their backs.

Too late, I heard a soft footfall behind me and, before I could turn, something hard crashed against the base of my skull. I waltzed into a dizzying darkness, still maintaining a firm hold on my new, dead friend.

30

It must have been the smell that woke me: the nauseating stench of rotting flesh. My head throbbed madly, as if what counted for my brain was ricocheting across every part of my skull.

But that deadly aroma proved the incentive to stir myself to action. Given the absence of Rupert Blount's body, I probably could have lain there and slept for the rest of the day or night, or whatever it was.

I rolled him off me. He ended up on his side, fixing me with an accusing stare, his flesh beginning to turn green. I had no experience in such matters but guessed he'd been dead since before the weekend; maybe that Friday night in Cavanaugh Close, when he'd hared off in pursuit of Marla. Blount's trademark fedora must have fallen out of the cupboard with him. It now rested fittingly at his elbow.

The thumping headache was the least of my worries. My hands were tied behind my back and a strip of duct tape placed across my mouth. Insurance, no doubt, against my crying out for help, if I'd happened to regain consciousness quickly, and I hadn't done that. A downward glance at my watch informed me that it was after seven p.m.

A bed stood against the window. I stumbled across and pitched down on it, working at my bonds. I was sure they'd been tied in a hurry and that I could loosen them.

Several minutes and much wriggling later, my hands were free. I ripped the tape from my mouth, yelping in agony as it came away. But my problems weren't over. A visit to the door informed me that it was locked. I cast about the room for something heavy to wield at it. A wardrobe stood at the end of the bed, one door hanging open. I went across to see what might be in there.

And made another discovery.

The wardrobe contained a quantity of dresses, slacks, blouses and shoes, belonging, I presumed, to Kate Blenkinsop. But on the top shelf sat a white fedora, twin to the one currently lying at Roop's elbow. And among Kate's clothes hung a blazer the same colour as the one he was wearing.

Then had my assailant on the Green Park escalator been, not as I'd suspected, Rupert Blount, but Kate Blenkinsop?

It put a whole new spin on her involvement in Ned Braley's death and the reason for her being in Selsby on that fateful evening. But trying to figure that out would have to wait. Other, more important things   were on my mind, the first of which was getting out of the room.

On the floor at Roop's feet lay a heavy-looking brass candlestick. The back of my skull felt as if it was that which had laid me out, but it fitted my current purpose. I picked it up and used it in a savage assault on the door.

Whether or not a sense of urgency had lent me a surfeit of strength, the door wilted. More than likely, it wasn't a particularly strong door, but a dozen whacks with the candlestick splintered the panels sufficiently for me to climb through and blunder out on to the landing.

I hurried downstairs and hammered on Georgia Derry's door. There was no response, so I put my shoulder to it. At the third time of asking, the door flew open, and I fell into the room, shoulder starting to throb painfully. Georgia wasn't at home, although I hadn't expected her to be.

By now, it was after eight o'clock, and evening was drawing in. I picked up her phone and rang my flat. There was no reply. Next, I rang Mrs Hawkins in the flat below mine. When she answered, I asked if my sister had arrived. I'd arranged to meet her there but had been delayed. Mrs Hawkins knew Roz from previous visits but hadn't seen her at all that day. I believed her: Mrs Hawkins sees everything.

Alarm bells were ringing loud and clear. *What had happened to Roz?* I rang her bungalow in Selsby but got no reply. The only answer was to head for Venetia's flat in Knightsbridge.

That meant a dash across London by tube. Thankfully, at that time of the evening, it didn't take long. Ironically, the nearest station was Liverpool Street, where all this had begun little more than two weeks ago, with Roly Pettifer's near-accident, which, I was now convinced, had been no accident at all.

As I hurtled down Cavanaugh Close and pulled open the door to reception, who should I almost collide with on her way out, but Kirstie Ryde. She looked as anxious as I felt.

"Kirstie – but what are *you* doing here?" I gabbled.

"Glen! I travelled down on the train with your sister. She seemed rather agitated – something about you asking her to do a mercy dash to rescue Venetia Hartman? I just dropped off my suitcase at my girlfriend's flat and came round to see if Roz needed help. But that man," she nodded towards the stone-faced concierge wedged behind the reception desk, "said that Mrs Hartman was out, and he couldn't let me go up there."

I strode over to confront him, with Kirstie trailing in my wake. I explained about my sister calling on Mrs Hartman. Had they left together, and how long had they been gone?

"A short, blonde lady, is she, your sister?" he asked. "Fairly aggressive?"

"Very," I said.

"Mrs Hartman invited her up. She had her daughter with her…"

Her daughter…

"So, they all left together?" I interrupted.

"I assume so, sir. I knew Mrs Hartman was about to go out but as I've not been at the desk the whole time, I didn't see them leave."

He was about to say more, but I cut in again. "I need to get into the apartment. I believe my sister may be there."

He was already shaking his head stubbornly. "I'm afraid I'm not authorised to let you do that, sir."

I was beginning to feel desperate. I didn't think my shoulder would stand another assault on a door. I strongly suspected Roz hadn't left with Venetia and Marla. She was in that apartment, and I had to get in there. I played my last card.

"Are Mr and Mrs Ballenheim in?" I asked.

The concierge offered to inquire, and, at the mention of my name, Bernie came down to reception. He trundled out of the lift, and approached, hand outstretched.

"Mr Preston – Glen. To what do I owe this pleasure?"

I introduced Kirstie and explained that we were concerned about my sister, whom I was unable to trace. She'd come to call on Venetia, who was out, and I believed Roz was still in the flat. I felt very concerned for her.

Bernie was an absolute brick, taking charge right away. He'd clocked my distress but didn't bother to ask questions. He took in everything with a triple-chinned nod and rumbled over to the reception desk, where the concierge looked up respectfully.

"Hemmings, Mr Preston here is a well-known actor and personal friend. Naturally, he's most concerned about his sister. I'll take full responsibility, but I think we should check Mrs Hartman's flat."

"Very good, Mr Ballenheim." He looked across at Kirstie and me. "If you'd follow me, sir, miss?" He grabbed a bunch of keys from beneath the desk and led the way to the lift.

We heard the noise on approaching Venetia's door: a dull pounding, coming from within the apartment. The moment Hemmings had unlocked the door, I rushed past him and a bemused Bernie, with Kirstie at my heels.

The noise was coming from a floor-to-ceiling cupboard in the hallway. Someone was thumping vigorously on the door and yelling obscenities. I shot back the bolt, yanked open the door and a rumpled, fiery bundle of extreme bad language tumbled out into my arms, pummelling me with manic fists.

"Roz!"

She looked up. Her face was red and blotchy, stained with weeping; but they would have been tears of frustration.

"Glen! Thank goodness! Oh, I've been such a fool."

I guided her through to the lounge and sat her down. Bernie emerged from his stupor, went to the drinks cabinet and fetched her a generous slug of brandy.

"Drink this, my dear. You'll soon feel better."

Roz smiled back gratefully and took a pull at the glass.

Bernie turned to Hemmings. "You can leave the key with me," he said. "I'll return it as soon as these good people are through."

"Very good, Mr Ballenheim."

While Bernie had gone to the door with Hemmings, Kirstie, keeping her voice low, asked, "Roz, what happened?"

Roz obviously didn't want to say too much in front of Bernie, who'd just begun to rumble back along the hallway.

"Venetia let me in," she whispered, "and I said my piece. She went off to the bedroom to fetch her stole, I wandered into the hallway and got clobbered from behind. It had to be Marla: there was a waft of perfume and a flash of blue dress. Next thing I knew, I was in that blasted cupboard."

Bernie was close enough to hear the last few words. "Marla came here earlier," he said. "She's taking Venetia out for a meal. Venetia's been on and on about it all day to Belinda and me."

"Bernie, do you know where they were going?" I asked. "When we were here the other night, Venetia mentioned a restaurant she liked. Something which sounded like – Randolph's?"

"Ah, yes – Radolfini's," Bernie replied. "It's a little way along Shaftesbury Avenue. I've been there a few times. It really is very good."

From the size of him, I imagined he'd been in every restaurant in London, but I expressed my gratitude for all his help. If not for him, Roz might have still been in that cupboard.

"We've got to dash," I told the girls.

"Goodness!" Bernie exclaimed. "Sounds like a matter of life and death?"

"Bernie," I replied solemnly, "you've been tremendous, and I can't say any more now. But you're right. That's exactly what it is."

31

Once again, the tube was our best option. By the time we'd reached Piccadilly Circus, pubs and restaurants were starting to empty, as well as theatres and cinemas, which meant a lot of people.

We made our way along Shaftesbury Avenue, looking for Radolfini's, in the hope that Marla and Venetia might still be inside. Kirstie and I took one side of the pavement, while Roz took the other, just in case they'd already come out. It was imperative not to miss them. I reasoned that they'd have come by taxi or tube, as parking was at a premium.

It was now close on eleven p.m., and only a handful of customers remained in Radolfini's. A waiter intercepted us at the door and told me they were on the point of closing. I replied that we were looking for Mrs Venetia Hartman and gave a brief description.

He grinned indulgently. "Ah, the Mrs Hartman. I know her well. She left a few minutes ago, with a lady who I think is her daughter."

I thanked him and, dragging Kirstie by the hand, wheeled round to catch sight of Roz, almost opposite and gesticulating frantically down the street beyond us. We shouldered our way through the crowd in the direction she was pointing.

I soon caught sight of Marla's blonde mane and, beneath it, the blue velvet dress she'd worn the other evening. As we drew nearer, she seemed to be supporting Venetia, flamboyant in silver evening dress and fur stole. They were waiting to cross the road at a pelican crossing. The pedestrian lights had just changed to red, and traffic had started to thunder past in both directions.

I was struck by the premonition of danger, recalling Marla accidentally sending the glass over the balcony of the Knightsbridge flat.

I dashed forward, leaving Kirstie behind, ploughed through the clutch of pedestrians at the crossing and latched on to Venetia's free arm. Marla gasped as she caught sight of me. "Not this time," I growled.

Venetia beamed up at me blearily. I could tell she was very drunk, more so than on the two previous occasions we'd met. "Oh, Marla, darling. It's that nice Graham Pressman…" Her voice was slurred, and I doubted that she could have stood unsupported.

Marla didn't think I was nice. Her eyes blazed at me, although behind the anger, I thought I detected a glint of fear. Kirstie had caught up with us, looked apprehensively at one then the other. She was wondering what the hell was going on.

"What do you mean, 'not this time'?" Marla asked snappishly. "What right do you have -?"

"Every right," I gave back tersely. The crossing signal bleeped, and the people around us swept past. Roz joined us from the other side of the street. "Come on," I said, "let's get back on the pavement." I steered Venetia round, and Marla had no alternative but to accompany us. Roz and a much-confused Kirstie followed.

"You haven't answered my question," Marla blustered. "This is an outrage! I *demand* an explanation." I was struck by the sound of her voice, was sure I'd heard it very recently.

"Then I'll do so now." I placed a wobbly Venetia in Roz and Kirstie's care and drew Marla aside. "I've every right to save a life," I added.

"And I haven't the faintest idea what you're talking about."

"Oh, I'm sure you have," I countered smoothly. "Callous of me, I know, but I'm thinking along the lines of poor, drunken Venetia lurching under the wheels of a car. The traffic's heavy, and a little push is all it'd take. It's happened before." *Ned Braley. Roland Pettifer.* "All in all, an efficient method of dispatch. Even if it is getting a bit samey."

Marla stared at me as if she expected men in white coats to materialise and bear me away at any moment. She shook her head despairingly. "I really don't know what this is about," she said.

"Might you if I addressed you as Kate?"

My words were softly spoken, for her ears only, but they hit the spot. The shock on her face gave her away. I wondered if she might try to bolt, but in those heels that probably wasn't a great idea. However, at that moment, she seemed incapable of movement.

I beckoned Roz forward. "Take Venetia back to her flat and phone the police," I said. "Send them to 25 Longdale Mews. I'll be there with – with her." I glanced at the former Marla: I guessed she was still reeling at having been unmasked, maybe trying to figure a way out.

I turned to Kirstie. "You'd better come with me in case Kate tries to do a runner. We'll grab a taxi. You too," I added to Roz. "Can't see you getting Venetia back any other way. From the state of her, you'll have your hands full anyway."

"Okay," Roz replied. "You sure you'll be all right?" She nodded towards Kate/Marla, who appeared absorbed in a study of her feet.

"Two of us, one of her," I proclaimed confidently. I was feeling justified, in control and, okay, just a little bit macho. An unusual feeling, that last. Dangerous, too. You know where they say pride always goes.

Kirstie had been watching me, puzzled. *"Kate?"* she asked.

"It's a long story," I said. "Let's get her back to her flat."

We said goodbye to Roz and Venetia, who set off up the street at a snail's pace in search of a taxi. Venetia went uncomplainingly, totally out of it and not even bothering to bid her darling 'daughter' goodnight.

I met no resistance from Kate, taking her arm in a firm grip. With Kirstie bringing up the rear, we crossed the road at the next opportunity and were lucky enough to hail a taxi straight away.

Did I say 'lucky'?"

I was distrustful of Kate, apprehensive that she might make a move at any time, so I needed to stay alert. She was cornered and had everything to lose. It would, therefore, have best suited my purpose for our taxi driver to have been the dour, silent type, who only communicated in grunts.

But we got Merv, bald, garrulous, deplorably cheerful, his vast stomach wedged irretrievably beneath the steering wheel. I gave him our destination.

"Off home after a night on the town, then, cock? Two gorgeous gals you got there. Luckiest bloke in London, I'd say. I'm off shift at midnight, you need any help. Name's Merv, by the way. Here's my card. Any time of the day or night."

I reached forward, took and pocketed it. Kate/Marla was sandwiched between Kirstie and me. As Merv wove deftly through the traffic at a decent pace, I doubted she was capable of going anywhere, other than where we were taking her.

"Boot'ful day today," Merv rattled on. "Marv'llous flippin' sunshine." He stole a crafty glance over his shoulder. "Dare say you girls were taking in the sun, eh? Stretched out in your bikinis in Hyde Park, eh? Cor, a sight for sore eyes, I should wager. Blimey, cock, they don't say much, do they?"

"They don't speak English," I countered blandly, drawing a quirky smile from Kirstie, while Kate/Marla stared sullenly ahead.

That set Merv off again. "Cor! Reckon you're in for a night of it, then! Hey, that blonde's a reg'lar ice maiden. Wouldn't mind the chance of thawing her out."

He chuckled lasciviously. *If only he knew. I doubted the experience would have been good for his health.*

Fortunately, the traffic required Merv's attention. I leaned back in the seat, catching Kirstie's anxious glance. She was confused, which was unsurprising, but I couldn't explain anything yet. I tried to relax her with a reassuring grin.

Kate/Marla continued to stare ahead, unyielding. I studied her face, wondered what she might be thinking. *The ice maiden,* Merv had called her. Yes, I could see that: single-minded, cruel, as cold as ice. And as I watched her, took in her uncompromising features, I saw another face behind the bubbly, ditzy Marla façade.

The face of Kate Blenkinsop.

Then there'd been that voice I'd recognised. And beyond that: *a face I knew.*

Merv dropped us off with another salvo of badinage. I over-tipped him, simply because I didn't want to hang around for change. He thanked me cordially, had probably expected a decent tip anyway. Because, after all, it was my lucky night.

All the while, however, I'd retained a firm grip on Kate's arm, and, with Merv driving back into the depths of the London night, I turned her inarguably in the direction of her front door. She clattered along disconsolately with head bowed. Kirstie walked doggedly in our wake, patient and unable to understand.

Kate made to open her handbag, but I prised it gently from her, searched inside, found the key and opened the door.

"We won't go upstairs," I decided, as we shuffled into the hallway. "It won't smell too sweet." Kirstie stared at me aghast, and I felt I had to at least qualify that statement. "There's a dead body in it," I added, as mildly as I could.

Kirstie's hand flew to her mouth. "Oh, dear God, Glen – *whose?*"

"Rupert Blount's." I turned to Kate. "We'd better use the downstairs flat. But you'll feel at home there, won't you, Georgia?"

Another gasp from Kirstie. "But Glen, how – how can you know?"

The face in the taxi. What a job she'd made of it. But then, Georgia was a skilled make-up artist. Quite an actress, too. And even if I hadn't recognised her in that long, concentrated study of her face, there'd been my experiences in the upstairs flat late that afternoon; the blow on the head, administered by the only other living person in the building…

I opened the door, and she led us into the downstairs flat, seeming not to register the damaged door, hanging half-open. She slumped down in a chair and hauled off the blonde wig to reveal Georgia Derry's short, dark hair.

She stared up at me, defeated, as I steered Kirstie to the sofa opposite and sat down beside her. Kirstie seemed in awe of me, clinging to my hand. *The great detective.* I'd never played such a part before, although I'd once been cast as Hercule Poirot's sidekick, Captain Hastings. *('Hastings is never the brightest star in the galaxy, but Preston's comical portrayal endows him with all the perspicacity of an amnesia victim').*

"It's over, isn't it?" Georgia mumbled, her limp gaze on my face.

"I'm afraid it is," I replied.

She shrugged. "Story of my life, I suppose." She turned to Kirstie. "Any chance of a coffee?" she asked with a half-smile. "I need one after those ruddy cocktails with Venetia." She nodded towards the little kitchen at the back of the room. "Everything's in that cupboard next to the sink. Lots of sugar, please. Need something in it."

Kirstie detached her hand from mine and got up. "Might as well make us all one," she said. "Glen?"

"Please. Better make it black. Two sugars." I was going to need to stay awake for a few hours yet. "Right, Georgia," I resumed briskly. "Over to you."

She sighed. "As you know, Pamela Segrave was my cousin. She'd stolen that locket from Marla Hartman. That's what gave us the idea for the whole thing."

Us? This was becoming interesting. "How did you get to know about Marla?" I asked, conscious that Kirstie stood in the archway to the kitchen, watching us with a frown, as the kettle wheezed into life.

Georgia looked pained, the regrets kicking in. "I met Morgan Tambling, oh, a while back now. He knew Pamela, of course, knew all about Marla too, because he'd spent time in London, chasing after her years ago. He was pretty sure she was dead. She and her boyfriend, Hal, had got into crack and heroin big-time. Morgan had learned I was a make-up artist who'd done a bit of acting, and reckoned I had the right height and figure to pass off as Marla.

"His motive was Venetia Hartman's money. His business was struggling, and he wanted to pay his debts, take off with me and get away from his cow of a wife.

"Our first problem was Pamela. She'd known Marla a lot more recently than Morgan had, and we couldn't let her spoil our plans. There was a possibility Marla might still be alive, and that Pamela might know where she was. So, we had to remove Pamela."

Kirstie joined us with the coffee and set it down on the table between us. Georgia smiled her thanks, and Kirstie re-installed herself next to me. Her hand found mine, as I reached for my mug and took a leisurely sip.

"And you used Ned Braley for that?" I prompted.

Georgia hung her head. "Morgan knew him well, and that he needed money. He – he hit Pamela too hard. I – oh, God…" She shook her head, her face a mask of misery. "I was such a fool to be carried along, but he could be so – controlling. You see, it all went wrong then. Braley must have panicked, just as I arrived to pick him up. I was on the bend, and he stumbled and fell under my wheels. I went right over him…

"Of course, no-one in the village, except Morgan, knew me. Somehow, I managed to keep my head and run to the phone box to call the police. I'd come in the guise of Kate Blenkinsop, so that my link with Pamela couldn't be traced back."

"And with Pamela out of the way, you became Marla again, but only in Venetia's company. Venetia was under the influence most of the time and only too thrilled to have her darling daughter back after so long. I dare say she'd made you her sole legatee once she'd sadly – and I don't doubt suddenly – had departed this life."

Georgia lifted her head and held my gaze. She seemed to have come back to life. "My, you've really got it all worked out, haven't you?" I was alert to the sneer in her voice. "Not only a *famous actor,* but quite the detective as well."

The Great Detective frowned. Georgia's explanation had been quite full, yet, as she'd been speaking, a few seeds of doubt had begun to germinate in my brilliant mind.

Full – but not quite full enough. From what Desmond Burge and other Selsby locals had said, Ned Braley had been a crook, but he'd been no killer. Why should he have broken the habit of a lifetime with Pamela Segrave, who surely would have offered little resistance?

And what about the second white fedora in the upstairs flat? Who'd stabbed Morgan? Not Rupert Blount, because he was already dead. It had to have been Georgia. Because, as she was already ensconced in Venetia's good books as her long-lost Marla, Morgan was surplus to requirements.

But it *still* didn't make sense. Somewhere, I'd taken a wrong turning, been over-confident…

In fact, it was fast dawning upon me that nothing made sense. I couldn't think straight; my brain was turning to sludge. I'd enjoyed my coffee, even though it had been a bit strong, but as I placed the mug back on the table, I began to feel rather odd.

Across from me, Georgia sat back in her chair, arms folded, waiting. She was smiling. I didn't think it could be a pleasant smile, but her features were suddenly so hazy, that I couldn't tell.

I found myself slipping helplessly down in my seat. I mouthed words to warn Kirstie, but they were just a meaningless babble. I tried to take her hand in a firmer grip, but it wriggled out of mine; and then she was standing over me, her face blurring. I felt her gentle kiss on my forehead, heard her whisper, "I'm sorry, Glen." Was there genuine regret in her words? I couldn't tell. By then, I didn't care.

So much for the Great Detective. Because this was the real me: Mr Bit-Part, loser and dimwit *par excellence.* My brain was numb, my vision fading, as I sank down into unconsciousness, slowly, painlessly, irresistibly, deliciously down…

32

After that, a long time after, came voices: many of them, some which I vaguely recognised, although I was unable to understand a word of what they said. There was movement too, doors opening and closing, shifting images of blurred figures, a kaleidoscope of dizzying colours.

I must have been out for a while. There were a few periods of some sort of consciousness, but they were brief and hazy. However, when I properly came to, I was in the familiar surroundings of Roz's spare bedroom. Memories began to trickle back: the chase across London; the woman who was Marla, then Kate and finally Georgia; the living room in her flat and my risible triumph as she gave her false confession. And then Kirstie beside me, passing me the too-strong coffee; Kirstie's last kiss and supreme betrayal...

As I floundered in the memories of my gullibility, feeling helpless and utterly useless, my sister came into the room. The sight of her, petite and smiling, my dear Roz, who'd brought me up and always looked out for me, made my tears well up, and I scrambled out of bed and hugged her fiercely. "Oh, Roz, I've been such a fool..."

Typically, she didn't contradict that. "Darling Glen, you have the knack of choosing the most unsuitable girls," she scolded lightly, and, as we held each other close, I realised that she was crying too.

Finally, she released me, passing a hand over her face to dash away those tears. There'd been a lot of those in the past few days!

"Get yourself showered and shaved," she ordered. "Perry's cooking you a late breakfast, then you and I are off to Dismal Desmond's. You've got a statement to make, which could outdo *War and Peace,* and there's a detective inspector coming from London to see us."

"But what's happened?" I demanded.

Roz took a deep breath and explained. Venetia had been so drunk, that she'd passed out in the taxi, and it had taken Roz, the driver and Hemmings the concierge to extricate her and get her in the lift and up to her flat. Brenda Ballenheim had been called into action to help Venetia to bed, while Roz had finally managed to call the police. However, she'd been confident that I'd have the situation firmly under control. *Hhmm...*

"As to what's happened," she went on, "apart from the police arriving in Longdale Mews to find Rupert Blount's body and you junked up to the eyeballs and dead to the world, I've no idea. That's why this inspector's coming to see us. Kirstie and the Kate/Marla woman knocked you senseless with a very potent sleeping draught and then scarpered. The doctor who was called to the scene felt that the best thing would be for you to sleep it off. You've done that big-time. It was Tuesday night when you went under, Thursday morning now. So, you'd better get a wiggle on – it's about time – and we can find out exactly what the state of play is."

As directed, I showered, put on fresh clothes and did full justice to Perry's fry-up. We chatted about this and that, but I felt that he was even more cheerful than usual; and believed he and Roz might have patched things up.

Roz drove me to the police house. Flora Burge greeted us warmly and showed us through to the sitting room, where the good sergeant awaited us. A slim, efficient-looking woman of forty-something stood as we came in. She introduced herself as DI Anne Darvill of the Metropolitan Police.

Once the formalities were over, and Flora had smilingly obliged us with un-doctored coffee and biscuits, DI Darvill took charge.

"Your sister's given Desmond a full account of everything that's happened," she said. "But there are a number of gaps to fill in. Firstly, you should know that Kirstie Ryde and Georgia Derry were arrested at Heathrow early yesterday morning. They've made a full confession. I get the feeling they're rather shocked by the horror of it all. Once they'd set it in motion, it would have been difficult to stop. And in the end, they were overwhelmed by a monster of their own making."

It had come about something like this. Years earlier, back in Selsby, Leo Hartman, still feeling some responsibility over Jamie Ryde's death, lent some financial support to Barbara and Kirstie Ryde. At school, Kirstie had shown a talent for acting and wanted to go to drama college. The fees were far out of her mother's reach, and Leo stepped in. His own daughter, Marla, had quarrelled with him, and he presumed she was living somewhere in London. Neither he nor Venetia saw anything of her. Kirstie became a surrogate daughter, despite Venetia's protests; although, given Leo's *penchant* for young women, that might not have been all. However, when Leo died of a sudden heart attack two years ago, Kirstie had expected to be left something in his will. But she received nothing.

Kirstie and Georgia Derry became friends through their work in the theatre: Kirstie an actress, Georgia a make-up artist. Kirstie stayed with Georgia whenever she was in London but returned to Selsby when resting, getting by on the money she earned from waitressing at the Frobisher Arms.

After Leo's death, Kirstie needed money. Georgia, too, was far from well-off. Kirstie had an idea. No-one had seen Leo and Venetia's daughter, Marla, for years, and Kirstie knew she'd never returned to Selsby while the Hartmans had lived there. Kirstie had had only contempt for Venetia. The woman had always been dismissive of her and, over the years, had become increasingly enslaved to alcohol. How might Venetia react if Marla suddenly reappeared in her life?

They decided to give it a try. Georgia had received a small legacy a year or so previously, and now was the time to put it to good use. They paid rent on the vacant flat above Georgia's in the name of Kate Blenkinsop, a freelance journalist hardly ever there, yet whose assignments were few and far between; that is to say, non-existent. The real Kate Blenkinsop, a former college friend of Georgia's, was safely in Australia, having emigrated there when she'd married a few years previously. The flat housed an array of 'Kate's' clothes, which could be called upon whenever Marla decided to pay her mother a visit.

"The invention of Kate was clever as well as timely," Darvill said. "They agreed they couldn't openly reinvent Marla Hartman in case someone who knew her happened upon the name. And for all they knew, Marla was still alive. It would be best if Kate/Marla was only known to Venetia as her daughter. Venetia led quite a secluded life with no more than a handful of acquaintances in and around London. And what Kirstie and Georgia couldn't know, when they devised the idea of Kate, was quite how useful she'd become."

Venetia welcomed her darling daughter with open arms. She settled money on her, which Marla always insisted upon in cash, bought her expensive jewellery and remained ignorant of the fact that, on her visits, Marla would 'borrow' a few pieces from her mother's overburdened jewellery box. If Georgia hadn't confessed to those thefts, Venetia would never have missed them.

"It was a decent scam," Darvill went on. "But they'd got to the point where they were unwilling to let it go. 'Marla' was fully accepted by Venetia as her long-lost daughter. Venetia had wealth flowing from every pore. Why not go for the whole lot? It would set them up for life. But when Pamela Segrave came into the mix, things began to get complicated."

Georgia couldn't believe it when Kirstie told her about the wacky ex-hippie, who'd recently come to live in Selsby. They were distant cousins! They'd met a while back in a solicitor's office, after Pamela's mother had died. Georgia had met up with Pamela on a couple of occasions thereafter, but the other woman had moved away and not left a forwarding address.

The disturbing thing about Pamela was that she'd known Marla and was in fact proudly wearing the locket the Hartmans had given their daughter on her eighteenth birthday. There'd obviously been bad blood between Pamela and Marla over the man whose photograph was in the locket. Pamela would rant on and on about it, and the danger was that she might know what had happened to Marla, or even where she was now living.

Kirstie and Georgia felt they had no alternative. Everything had gone so well up to now. As a child, Kirstie had known Marla and had shared everything she remembered about her. Venetia was convinced by the deception, and there seemed to be no limit on what they could get out of her. Pamela would have to go.

The idea was Kirstie's. Her uncle, Ned Braley, had always operated one step ahead of the law. Kirstie tempted him with the prospect of easy pickings from Pamela's bungalow, gave him the time and day to go there.

Kirstie was supposed to be working in theatre in London that day, understudying a supporting role. "She cried off that morning, pulled a sickie," DI Darvill said. "I checked back on it yesterday. The production company was a bit hazy, but someone finally turned up a record of it."

So, Kirstie travelled back to Selsby incognito, waited round by Pamela's bungalow and brained her when she came back from the pub. Then she concealed herself indoors. Ned broke in, started filling his capacious pockets and saw Pamela's body. He panicked and rushed out into the lane. Georgia, as Kate Blenkinsop, was waiting at the bend and deliberately ran him down. An alarmed and innocent motorist, she left the car and dashed up the lane to the phone box to alert police and ambulance.

The figure Roland Pettifer saw bending over Ned Braley's body was Kirstie. She was putting the murder weapon, the statuette, *into* his pocket, so that he'd be blamed for Pamela's death.

The distraught Kate Blenkinsop was kindly put up for the night by Morgan and Lorna Tambling, then interviewed for the *Bugle* next day by Roland Pettifer. In Kate/Marla guise, she cut a striking figure. They were to remember her.

"That Saturday afternoon, when Roland visited Kirstie's dressing-room after the matinée," DI Darvill went on, "was when it all started to go wrong. Georgia was in the room, making up as Marla prior to calling on Venetia, and Roland saw the girls together. He must have been immediately suspicious, and they realised it. Georgia quickly changed back into her normal clothes and followed him to the tube station, where you, Mr Preston, stepped in and thwarted her. She followed you both to Selsby, and this time was successful in pitching Roland under the wheels of Mrs Blakeman's car."

"Shirley said she thought she'd seen someone sneaking away," Roz put in.

"And I thought Roland had glimpsed someone outside, before he left the pub," I added. "So, he *was* pushed, Roz. Which absolves you of any blame."

"Absolutely," Darvill concurred. "And that brings us to Roland's dying words, Mr Preston."

"He said "Warn – Marla"," I answered. "My immediate thought was that he wanted me to warn Marla that she was in danger."

"But there was a slight pause between the two words?"

"Yes, there was. He was in shock, dying, struggling to force the words out."

"So, he might, for instance, have been trying to say, "Warn *her* – Marla." Which could have meant that he wanted to warn someone, probably Venetia, with whom he was friendly, that she was in danger from Marla. Venetia would have told him that her daughter had fairly recently come back into her life and, that afternoon, Roland would have understood that the woman he'd seen at the theatre bore a marked resemblance to Marla."

Things didn't get better for Kirstie and Georgia. Rupert Blount reappeared. Kirstie had heard about him all those years ago. He'd been chasing after Marla then, and still was. He'd carried out the Hannon Hall burglary around that time. He'd stayed at the Hall several times with his parents and soon got to know the layout. He'd made Marla a present of the Hannon necklace, when he'd gone to London in pursuit of her. But not long after that, he was imprisoned for trafficking and dealing and lost touch with Marla. The necklace, worth a hefty sum, had been discovered in Pamela's possession – one of the items Ned had picked up. So, she must have stolen it, along with the locket, from Marla.

Now Blount wanted to trace Marla. He was hard up and felt she owed him something. He came back to Selsby to see Morgan Tambling. Morgan had been a party to the Hannon Hall burglary and, if he didn't help him out, Blount would split on him. Morgan couldn't afford that. Despite what Georgia had tried telling me, the Frobisher Arms was a lucrative concern, thanks to the hard work he and Lorna had put in. Morgan had paid Blount some hush money to keep him at bay but was savvy enough to know that it wouldn't end there.

Morgan occasionally called on a lady friend, the landlady of the Parrot & Cage in Shoreditch. One time he was there, Georgia, who lived nearby, called in for something for lunch. She was visiting Venetia that afternoon and was dressed as Kate/Marla. Darvill thought she probably got a buzz from adopting the Kate/Marla persona, receiving a lot of attention she wouldn't have otherwise attracted. Morgan followed her and found out about the scam she and Kirstie were working. He agreed for them to continue, but there'd be a pay-off. He'd always fancied Kirstie and promised not to give them away, provided she was nice to him. To an extent, Kirstie, though reluctant, had to play up to him. A ladies' man, whose appeal was beginning to wane as he slipped into middle age, Morgan got a boost from his power over the two girls.

Meanwhile, Rupert Blount had his own agenda. He distrusted Morgan, was sure he was holding something back. On the evening of Venetia's soirée, Blount followed him to London, watched 'Marla' arrive at Cavanaugh Close and followed her back to Longdale Mews. He forced his way into her flat, and Georgia, who'd been warned by Kirstie that he was around, took the opportunity to despatch him.

Previously, it had been Georgia, complete with blazer and white fedora, aiming to put the blame on Blount, who'd shoved me on the escalator at Green Park. Kirstie had known what to expect and had insisted that she simply wanted it as a warning to put me off.

Morgan Tambling was next, stabbed by Georgia. It was a hasty attack, for Perry Blakeman was present and, to an extent, thwarted her. As soon as the girls realised that Morgan was likely to recover, they knew it was all up with them. They'd have to abandon the plan of Venetia meeting with a drunken accident and Marla inheriting the lot. The night of the meal at Radolfini's, their plan was to take the already incapacitated Venetia back to her flat, where Kirstie and Georgia would clear out as much as possible in the way of cash and valuables. They'd opened an offshore account in Kate Blenkinsop's name some months previously and cash deposits had started to stack up nicely.

They'd planned to leave the country the next day. In the upstairs flat, they'd left a key fob, belonging to Morgan and stolen by Kirstie, by the cupboard which had housed Blount's body. It would muddy the waters for the police and give the girls more time to make good their escape.

"It started as a reasonably sound idea," DI Darvill concluded. "But too many obstacles got in the way. Pettifer, Tambling, Blount, Pamela Segrave, and of course you, Mr Preston. It became too much for them to handle and inevitably ended in disaster."

33

Darvill then wanted to hear the story as it had unfolded from my point of view, beginning with my meeting with Roland Pettifer at Liverpool Street tube station. Afterwards, I sat with Sergeant Burge and condensed this into a statement, while Darvill and Roz chatted away in the sitting room, and Flora supplied more coffee.

Burge told me privately of his relief that Ned Braley, an out-and-out rogue for whom he'd had a soft spot and who'd kept a step ahead of him over many years, had at least been innocent of murder.

But he'd been shocked at how Kirstie Ryde had turned out. "Dare say I shouldn't be. I remember that father of hers when I first came to Selsby. He cleared out when she was no more than a babe in arms, and darned good riddance, I say. He was a scoundrel and no mistake, and that mean streak must've passed down to her. Such a pretty little lass – it's a crying shame."

I said nothing to Burge but felt the same. As we made our way back to the bungalow, Roz remarked upon it.

"The DI asked me to pass you a message. Apparently, when she was interviewed yesterday, Kirstie asked if you were okay – she seemed concerned about you."

I nodded grimly. Perhaps I'd been right: there *had* been something, some feeling. But it hadn't been enough and couldn't matter now. It was time to move on.

Even though she was driving, Roz laid a tender hand on my arm. I grinned wearily. "You were right," I said. "I do seem to pick them."

"You're a nice guy," Roz encouraged me. "Your nice girl will come along one day."

I shrugged. "Maybe. But one thing I'm glad about. You've got your nice guy back. Make sure you hang on to him now."

"Oh?" She seemed genuinely surprised. "How do you know that?"

I hadn't needed to be a great detective to do so. During my brief, waking periods the previous night, I'd been aware that there might be more than one person in the bed on the other side of the wall.

"The signs have been there," I replied enigmatically.

"Perry and I have had a long chat, and we both feel we should give it another try."

"Well, go for it," I advised her wholeheartedly. "You'll be good for each other."

Perry had the door open for us on our return, a broad smile on his face.

"I know what you're about to say," I greeted him. "And it's the best news I've had in a long while."

So, our meal that evening was by way of a double celebration: that Roz and Perry were back together, and that I was alive. It might take me some time to get Kirstie Ryde out of my system, but, reading between the lines, I believed she'd managed to dissuade Georgia, who'd been in a vicious mood, from putting me out of the way altogether.

Shirley Newbury joined us, and she was another one on Cloud Nine. This was the biggest story in the *Selsby Bugle's* hundred-and-ten-year history. She wanted to interview me and, even though I wasn't keen, I decided to go ahead. The publicity would do me no harm: the bit-part actor, who seemed to specialise in getting bumped off, almost going to glory in similar fashion in real life. Shirley wanted to dedicate the story to Roland's memory.

There was more good news, in that Morgan Tambling was likely to make a full recovery in due course. He'd denied any involvement in the actual burglary at Hannon Hall, though admitted that he'd discussed the idea with Rupert Blount. Since Blount was dead, nothing could be proved either way.

We believed that when Morgan returned to the Frobisher, he'd be much chastened. Lorna would come into her own and keep a close eye on him.

In view of what had happened, Barbara Ryde had brought forward her plans to move to her sister's in Cornwall, and Lorna had taken the opportunity to install Perry as head chef and a young married couple from the village to help in the bar, kitchen and restaurant. Roz and Shirley had promised to give Lorna every support. I was confident that they would.

I decided to head back to London a couple of days later: after all, three was a crowd. But what finally made up my mind was that, on the penultimate afternoon, I received a phone call from my recalcitrant agent, Eric Di Mario.

"Glenno, my boy! How's it hanging?"

My first impression was that Eric had been walloping the lunchtime claret. It was almost unheard of for *him* to phone *me.*

My response was cautious. "Not bad, Eric." *Just missed out on being murdered earlier in the week.* "What's this, then? Got some news for me?"

"Have I got some *news* for you? My sweet, darling boy, your Uncle Eric has only come up trumps again."

Again? "Oh, right."

"All that's happened, Glenno, is that I've negotiated you nothing less than a *title role.*"

"Hold up a minute, Eric. Did you just say the words 'title' and 'role'? And did you sort of run them together?"

"Precisely, old chap."

"A title role for me? Eric, you do realise you're speaking to Glen Preston? So – for *me?*"

"For you and none other, Glen. Perhaps you'd pop in and see me. How about tomorrow?"

"Well, okay. I'm back in London tomorrow. What time shall I call in? I can make it as early as you like?"

"Oh, no need to rush, my old chum. Let's say late morning. About eleven-thirtyish?"

Silly me. Of course, Eric would be exhausted after all the efforts made on my behalf. We agreed on eleven-thirty, and I returned to share the good news with Roz and Perry. I was speechless. *A title role?* Surely, he'd got me confused with someone else?

They assured me that couldn't possibly be the case – Eric and I had known each other for too long – and that a title role was no more than I deserved. Which was an excuse for more celebration.

The following morning, I was up with the lark. I intended catching an early train to London, because there was something I had to do before I met up with Eric.

Over dinner the previous evening, we'd talked a lot about what had happened, and Roz wondered what might have become of the real Marla Hartman?

We reached the conclusion that perhaps, after all, Marla was dead. Even if that wasn't the case, she'd dropped out of sight.

"Who knows?" Roz concluded. "Maybe something happened to make her change her ways, and she's happily married with a couple of squawking kids."

Wild and somewhat tipsy speculation followed. I didn't join in. Somewhere in my fuzzy brain, a distant bell was ringing. And later, I got to thinking, resulting in my early departure the following morning.

I took a fond farewell of my sister, promising that I'd be down again soon and inviting them for a day out in London at the earliest opportunity. Perry walked with me to the station, chatting merrily away about his plans for the Frobisher's restaurant. He was glad to be back with Roz, for he'd made the wrong call in going off to London and hadn't been sure if she'd want him back.

"My impression was that she did," I said. "Roz can be hasty sometimes. Her work hadn't been going well, and I think she'd come to realise that she'd been *too* hasty. I think you reappeared at the right moment, and you both need to make sure you stay together. You're good for each other, Perry, and I know you can make her happy."

"Roz? Happy?" He grinned. "That's a tall order."

Although she'd looked happy enough those last few days, certainly since Perry's brush with the law over the attack on Morgan. She'd fought his corner tigerishly.

"But you're the guy to do it," I said.

We shook hands, embraced, and I set off back to London.

Once there, I travelled across to Stepney and St Agnes Church. I called into the church office, gave my name and asked if it'd be possible to speak to Hannah Ainsley. I told the secretary I'd be in the café in the church's side wing.

It was still only mid-morning, and the café was almost empty. I took my cappuccino to a corner table and sat studying the beautiful stained-glass window of the Good Shepherd carrying his lost sheep, the colourful prayer cards and booklets on the little stall and the cheerful faces of the ladies behind the counter. All in all, a place to sit quietly and reflect; somewhere to think, pray, hope; and perhaps confess.

I stood as Hannah entered and came over to me, looking as weary and harassed as when I'd first met her. How much had happened since then!

She smiled as she reached me, and we shook hands, her grip firm and assured. I offered her a coffee, but she declined. As we sat, her eyes appraised me, seeking, perhaps fearing, my reason for being there.

"Mr Preston – Glen – this is a surprise. Did you find what you were looking for?"

"I think I'm very close," I replied.

Her gaze didn't leave my face. She'd retained her smile, but there was a hint of anxiety about it. "You're here again about Marla, aren't you?" Her voice was low, almost furtive.

"Yes, I am." I held her gaze momentarily, but she didn't flinch away. "Hannah – I'm sure you know. But Marla died, didn't she?"

Those last words broke the spell. Her gaze fell to the table, and she sat with her head bowed. She sighed, and then, as if having reached a decision, her face travelled up slowly, and her eyes looked steadily into mine.

"Yes, Glen," she said. "Marla died a while ago. And I have to say I'm glad that she's gone."

34

Summer 1980

Marla gazed at the photograph of the two of them together. She and Hal – the way she'd hoped it might have been for ever. What had she known of love before she'd met him? She'd been utterly self-centred, proud of her striking looks, contemptuous of those beneath her in the social scale.

Her mother had aided and abetted her. Venetia, she'd learned, had come from a poor background, working as a chorus girl (that had been the charitable version), until Leo Hartman had spotted her, become enslaved and whisked her away to better things.

Marla had been their only child, and Venetia besotted with her. Nothing was too good for her darling daughter. Marla was given everything money could buy, and Leo's wealth was a bottomless pit.

Not that her father had gone along with most of it. He'd tolerated Venetia's extravagances in the early days, but once it had become apparent that they were unlikely to have a second child, he decided he didn't want Marla to become vain or spoiled, both which, to be truthful, she already was. Leo's had been the voice of caution and reason. But Venetia was expert at flirting and wheedling and too often succeeded in getting her own way. Perhaps she hadn't meant to, but by her behaviour she managed to turn Marla against her father.

So, what had Marla known about love?

Only her mother's stifling version of it. Her father's had been distant and disapproving, which Marla, in her innocence, had never been able to equate with love.

She grew up in the 1960s, where love evolved into many different meanings, and where, with her stunning looks, she was never short of admirers.

But one quality, which Marla had inherited from her father, had been a measure of control. As she progressed through her late teens, she learned not to give herself away too easily. She knew what men wanted from her, and it amused her to string them along. Jamie Ryde, Morgan Tambling and Rupert Blount, among others, found out about that.

Until the day it all changed. The day she fell hopelessly in love.

Her parents had set her up in a flat in Chelsea, and she'd wanted for very little. Two other girls lived in the same building, girls of similar background and outlook, and the three of them would go together to discos, clubs, gigs and parties, where they'd quickly become the centre of attention.

She met him at a gig, had spotted him up on stage, dark-blond hair down to his shoulders, striped shirt ripped open to show off his burly chest, tight white flares. He was on lead guitar and could really play. The group called themselves *Daze of Sorrow*. He was brilliant, the drummer okay, but the girl on vocals, long, tangly hair and a red dress which brushed the floor, really didn't have it.

Between numbers, the guitarist caught Marla's eye. They seemed drawn to one another, and she knew she couldn't leave without at least knowing his name.

Her friends, Suzie and Cordelia, had noticed a group of guys around the bar at the back of the hall and thought they should get acquainted. "You coming, Marla?" "Yah, be there in a bit." She spoke casually, because *he* was holding her gaze, as she got up and wandered languidly after her friends. She wanted him to see where she was heading.

The group were into their last number, and Marla was hanging around near the bar. A creepy guy of at least forty had started to come on to her, his lustful eyes feasting on her legs and cleavage. "No, it's fine. I'll get my own," she insisted, trying to fend him off.

"Why not let me?"

She turned sharply. The creepy guy had gone, almost as if he'd dematerialised. The handsome guitarist stood beside her, looming over her, a big, white smile creasing his tanned face.

She smiled back effortlessly, sensing that her whole body had come alive. "Sure. Vodka and Coke, please."

"Make it two, Jack." There was a confidence about him, a presence, which had brought the barman over in an instant.

"I'm Hal. Hal Page. What's your name?"

"Marla."

"Not seen you here before. I'm sure I'd have noticed."

They were served their drinks and took them to a quiet corner.

"My first visit. I think my friends have abandoned me." She could just make out the tops of their heads among a press of admirers.

"Bound sure to be chicks, then, 'cause no fella in his right mind would abandon you. What d'you reckon to the group?"

"Guy on drums was okay. You were brilliant."

Hal pulled a face. "Long way to go. We're just getting it together. Pal of mine's going to join us. He's a decent bassist, and we need help with the vocals. We're having a jam tomorrow afternoon. There's a barn round the back they let us use."

"Can I come along and listen?"

"Yeah, why not? You'll brighten up the place no end."

She hoped they might go on somewhere, just the two of them, when the session finished. They really seemed to be hitting it off, and she couldn't remember having been sold on a guy so quickly. She was ready to throw caution to the winds. All Hal had to do was say the word.

But there was an obstacle in her path: the tangly-haired girl in the long red dress, the vocalist who couldn't sing.

She'd just shown up and wasn't looking friendly.

"Hal, let's split now. Jimmy's coming with us. Thought we'd shoot some H." She stared at Marla as if she'd just crawled out from under a stone. "Who's she?"

"Her name's Marla," Hal replied easily. "Wanna come along, babe?"

Marla's face split in one of her superior smiles. "Better not. Doubt if I'd be welcome."

The other girl's sneer told her she wouldn't be.

Hal grinned, alive to the situation. "Okay, Pam. Let's go." Unseen by her, he mouthed, "Two o'clock, tomorrow."

She nodded briefly, watched them leave. She'd be there, no way she'd pull out. When she arrived the next day, this guy Jem was with them, another dreamboat with looks and body to die for, and her first thought was, *"Hell, I could have them both…"* But she put that thought away the moment Hal looked at her.

Her heart melted; speech failed her. Having to sit before her legs gave out, she plumped down on an old bench.

"Marla – hi! Glad you could make it."

She couldn't speak, just smiled back winningly, and then he was standing over her, as if he'd conquered her and she was his prize (he had; she was), and Jem was looking on admiringly, perhaps enviously. Although she got the impression that he and Hal were good mates and wouldn't get in each other's way, because they never needed to.

She wasn't keen on Jimmy, the drummer. He looked spaced out, his eyes like saucers, appraising her greedily. But at least she didn't get a similar reaction from Pam.

Pam showed up late, the worse for wear, her clothes looking like she'd thrown them on, her unwashed hair all over the place.

"C'mon, Pam, we've got a lot to get through," Hal greeted her, a bit stiffly. "Don't think you've met Jem, by the way?"

Pam ignored Jem's cheerful greeting, her inimical gaze on Marla.

"What's *she* doing here?"

"Marla's just come along to listen."

Pam suggested roundly in a public-school voice exactly where Marla could go, once she was through with listening. She snatched the mic from its cradle. "Well, hadn't we better get on with it, then?"

The guys all shrugged and started into a number.

Marla could hardly keep from laughing. The music was okay, Hal making his guitar talk, while Jem added something on bass and was strong on backing vocals. But Pam was dire, at times too shrill or too feeble, and Jem's voice drowned hers out, she was unable to stay with him. Hal kept halting them in mid-number. They were supposed to be cutting a disc in a few days. He was trying hard not to lose it with Pam, and Marla guessed she was being deliberately obtuse, trying to get under his skin. Very soon, however, she flipped completely, flung down the mic and swore at them all. "How d'you expect me to concentrate with that bitch sitting there smirking?" She stormed off, bequeathing Marla a look of pure hatred as she went.

"Well, that screws us." Jimmy battered his sticks on the cymbals in frustration.

"It may not." Jem was calm, reasonable. A look passed between him and Hal, and he turned to Marla. "Don't sing, do you, babe?"

"Gotta be better 'n Pam, even if she just farts the words," Jimmy mumbled.

Marla was already on her feet. "I'll give it a try." She'd been in a girl group, that last term at school. She reckoned she hadn't done too badly, even though the others had been awful.

She'd been bopping along to the beat and had quickly picked up the words. Hal passed her the mic. "See how it goes," he whispered and, as she took hold of it, their hands touched briefly, and it felt like an electric shock shivering through her body. She'd do this for him, for them, make it unforgettable. The words couldn't have been more fitting.

Yours is the one,

The only face I see.

So, bring it home,

Just bring it home to me.

And see just who I am,

And why I'm wanting you

To make my every wish,

My every dream come true…

"That's the stuff," Jem enthused, after they'd run through it twice. "You're in, babe."

"Something else, if you ask me." But she knew Hal wasn't referring to her voice, which was neither bad nor great. Knew he meant her.

She took him back to her pad later, where they made love. Dear God, she was his, body and soul, and she'd never experienced such wanting, such total abandonment or complete satisfaction, such bliss.

*

As she sat, gazing wistfully at his photograph, Marla knew that that day and the heady weeks which followed, had been for her the very essence of what love was: its height, its topmost peak. Because after that, life kicked in.

There'd been the drugs, of course. Those endless parties, where crack and H were passed around like candy. They all did it. No-one was exempt. There were those like Jem, who'd go with the flow but draw the line at the stuff taking over his life. Those like Pam, desperate to be included, to be wanted, soon getting to the stage where they couldn't help themselves.

Those like Hal.

Marla went with it for too long. She'd done drugs since school, only the soft stuff, until she'd met Roop. He introduced her to LSD and coke, but she was wary enough to know that it was his underhand way of weakening her defences, so that he could get her into bed. So, she made sure she only used it when *she* wanted, usually when he wasn't around.

Once *Daze of Sorrow* had folded, and Jem had gone his own way, Hal seemed to lose some of his impetus. But she chivvied him along. That first time he came out of rehab, she insisted on a change of scene. Pam was still around – hell, when was she never around? She was living in some hippie commune now, an arty-farty bunch into their wacky paintings, sculpture and jewellery.

Pam had attacked her once when they'd been rehearsing for *Daze*. She'd been still hanging out with them, even though Hal had told her in no uncertain terms that he and Marla were an item. The guys had gone outside the barn for a joint, and Pam had crept up behind Marla, tried to strangle her. Marla had managed to sink her teeth into Pam's hand, making her cry out and release her. She'd twisted round and grappled with Pam, both girls shrieking, and Pam the stronger, fuelled by her hatred. Fortunately, the guys had rushed back in, Jem and Hal pulling them off one another, Jimmy chuckling away, enjoying the spectacle of two wildcats spitting and snarling.

Pam flounced off then, but there were other times when she'd suddenly appear, accusing Marla of snatching away *her* Hal, calling her every name under the sun. Wherever Marla went, there was always the chance that Pam wasn't far away.

The change of scene happened. Some musician Hal had known back in the sixties was heading to Holland to start up there and needed a decent lead guitarist. They went with him. *Electric Airplane* was born, and she rejoiced that

Hal had got his mojo back, was playing his heart out again, all for her, only for her. She couldn't begin to imagine life without him.

They were good years in Holland but, as they passed, the old demons returned. Marla had money of her own and, thus far, it had seen them through the bad times. She'd lost touch with her parents. That last quarrel with her father had been bitter, and she'd turned her back on him; realised, too, that she'd long outgrown her mother's brand of cloying, self-reflecting love.

Hal got sick. A rogue batch of cocaine almost killed him. She'd gradually come off the stuff because she'd seen what it was doing to him. She was still and always utterly in love with him, tried time and again to persuade him to take her advice, to fight against temptation, but there was always something, some enemy within, which won over him. *Electric Airplane* folded and, once Hal was well enough, they returned to London.

But he became too ill to work. She used the rest of her money to rent a small flat in Stepney, nothing to what they'd been accustomed to, but all they could afford. The years had taught her resilience. She called herself Marla Page now, Hal's common-law wife, and she worked, something she'd never properly done in her life. The nearby church had opened a café, and she got herself a job there for a few hours a week and cleaned for a couple of the vicar's housebound parishioners, scraping together enough for her and Hal to survive.

Except that Hal didn't survive.

He was too dependent on the stuff, found ways, friends who thought they were doing him a favour, keeping him supplied while Marla was out working, slaving, pouring out her very self for him. Hal overdosed, and the doctors couldn't save him.

Finally, in that cramped little flat, when he'd gone and she was drowning in her grief, who should come to her, but Pam.

The ultimate, overwhelming insult.

Pam had changed, but only in that she'd nearly kicked the habit, after long years of addiction. Her hatred remained. Implacable.

"I've seen you working in the church café. Some good it's done you. He was mine. You took him away. Now he's lost to you too. You know now what it is to grieve, and I'm glad, you bitch, glad you're suffering, hope it *kills* you."

Marla didn't see the blow coming. Pam clouted her across the face with all the force of her hatred, flinging her across the room to collide with the wall. She felt her senses fading, conscious of Pam's blurred figure standing over her, her hand reaching down to snatch the cherished locket from her neck, the locket which had held Hal's photograph for so long, so that he might always be next to her heart.

When Marla, bruised, dazed, her body sore and head ringing, finally regained consciousness, she found Pam gone. A drawer hung open. Pam had taken more of her jewellery. She'd done that before, stealing some necklace Roop had once given her, *'a token of my undying devotion',* which she'd never worn, never even looked at.

As she sat, crumpled, by the wall, Pam's parting words rang in her ears. They would haunt her forever. "You evil whore! I *hate* you. You'll never be safe from me. *You killed him.* He was mine, *is* mine. I'll be back, bitch. And when I've tormented you enough, I'll *kill* you."

She felt cold all over. Staggering through to the bedroom, she flung herself across the bed and wept, wept, until she was completely dry of tears, utterly empty of grief.

Of everything: life, hope. Was it possible to be at a lower ebb?

Finally, hardly knowing what motivated her, Marla got to her feet. *"You'll never be safe from me. I'll kill you, kill you…"*

She was at the end of her tether, knowing she couldn't face much more of Pam's senseless persecution.

Knowing there was only one course of action open to her now…

35

August 1986

Hannah Ainsley sat in silence for a while, wearied even further, I suspected, by her narrative and what it had cost her. Without looking up, she said softly, "How did you know?"

"I didn't," I said. "But here, St Agnes, was the last recollection of Marla. When I came here before, you remembered her and Pamela and Hal. You spoke of them with such assurance. Yet, when I was thinking things over only yesterday, I remembered Fliss Potts talking about how well you organised the Craft Fairs and referring to you as the *new* curate's wife. I didn't think you could have been here that long. But when we spoke before, you recalled Hal, who died six years ago. And again, only yesterday, my sister was speculating over what might have happened to Marla, and the possibility that she might have dropped out of sight and be happily married."

"Dear Fliss." Hannah looked up and then smiled warmly, a warmth which seemed to bathe her whole face in light, enabling me to glimpse, behind the weariness and everyday clothes, a startling, yet understated beauty. "Bless her. Tim's been curate here for three years: in many people's eyes, he'd still be new."

"And Tim knows that you were Marla?"

"Yes, he does. We have no secrets – none. Your previous visit rocked me, Glen. That someone was here asking questions about the woman I'd been. I felt caught out, wondered if I'd given too much away. It doesn't really surprise me that you've come back."

"I'm only back to bring closure, Hannah. A line can be drawn under Marla's story. What you've told me will go no further."

She reached across the table, her hand closing over mine. "Thank you, Glen. I'm grateful." She sat back in her chair. I sensed she'd lost some of her tension, as she gazed, smiling wistfully, at a point several years beyond me.

"When Pam stormed out, I was cold all over with dread. All my money had gone, and even then, I couldn't bear the thought of going back to my parents, cap in hand. It would have been so easy, and before I knew it, I'd have slipped back into the old ways." Hannah shook her head, and her eyes met mine. "I couldn't do it. Life had been kind, too kind, lavishing so much on me. I was old enough and experienced enough to understand that it couldn't last forever. This was now the flip side to what I'd had and been.

"I paid up the rent, packed my few belongings and left. I changed my name by deed poll, moved across London, changed my appearance, so that I could distance myself from Pam in every way. I rented a tiny flat, tinier than the one I'd just vacated; and I worked, worked to get by and to forget.

"Marla had gone forever. Hal's love for me and mine for him had begun the change, but his death chastened me. I tried to dismiss the feeling, but after about a year, I sensed that I was being drawn back here, to Stepney, to St Agnes. When I'd lived here before, we'd been part of a whole community of down-and-outs, addicts and recovering addicts, in need of care and needing to be offered the chance to get their lives back on track.

"Hubert Melford, the vicar who'd been here when I'd worked in the café, was amazingly kind. He found me lodgings and a cleaning job, and I helped in the soup kitchen. I hadn't had much contact with him before, but even so, he didn't recognise me. Neither did Pam. I saw her once, about four years ago, at a Craft Fair, when I was helping on the refreshment stall. Panic swept over me. I hardly contained the urge to run away. But she didn't recognise me either. I served her with a cup of tea, struggling to prevent my hand from shaking. She looked right through me: she was worlds away. I noticed she was wearing the locket, which she'd stolen from me. I was resigned to letting her keep it, just relieved when she walked away. I didn't need it anyway: Hal lived on in my heart, in the wonderful memories of our good years together.

"Then, one day, just about three years ago, Tim Ainsley arrived here as curate. He's such a gentle man, so alive to the needs of others. We sat and talked and hit it off immediately. He'd lost his wife in a road accident, and I told him about Hal, told him everything, leaving nothing out. I thought he might want to distance himself from me, but instead, we grew closer. We married eighteen months ago.

"I read in the paper of my father's death two years ago. I went along to his funeral, stayed well back, not that anyone would have recognised me. I'd been mean to him, when all he'd wanted had been for me to lead a steady and responsible life. My mother was there, of course, but she never realised who I was. But then, I was very different, in appearance and attitude, from the Marla she'd known. Glen, you must tell me: why were you looking for the woman I used to be?"

I gave her the whole story and sensed that she was moved by it, saw the beginnings of tears in her eyes, when I explained that her mother's life had been in danger.

"I should never have neglected her," Hannah said. "I may not have needed her; but she needed me."

"She'll need you now," I replied. "I'm sure the Ballenheims are good neighbours but, with Roland gone, she'll be very lonely."

"And Kirstie Ryde," she sighed. "Little Kirstie. You wouldn't believe how she looked up to me, Glen, how she wanted to be like me. Oh, dear God, I must visit her. She'll need a friend too. Do you think she and the other girl regret what they did?"

"It all got out of control, Hannah. I didn't know Georgia well, but I can't believe Kirstie would have wanted it to go to the lengths it did."

She pushed back her chair, and I got to my feet feeling that we'd gone as far as we could. Hannah held out a hand: there was a sense of purpose about her, as she prepared to meet the new and complex challenges of Venetia and Kirstie. I wished her the very best, made it clear I shouldn't be back again.

Hannah walked out to the street with me, and we said goodbye. To my surprise, she embraced me, brushed her lips against my cheek.

"Thank you, Glen."

I was puzzled. "But all I've done is dig up your past and -?"

"You've shown me who I need to be."

"But you needed no help from me," I replied.

As we parted, she turned to greet a man approaching from the opposite direction. From the clerical collar, from their warm greeting, I could tell he was her husband. They were chatting away busily, linking hands, as they made their way back to the church. I walked on, glad that Marla had found love and purpose, and had turned her life around.

*

I made my way across London to Eric Di Mario's office, up a steep flight of stairs above a Soho betting shop. As I knocked and entered, Eric unfurled himself from behind several stacks of playbills. I felt I'd just disturbed his hibernation.

"Glenno, my boy!" He came around the desk, dressed in an offensive green suit with a mustard-coloured check, his horsey teeth gleaming effusively. "What a pleasure it is to see your handsome face. But sit down, sit down. Coffee?"

I declined. He might have drunk it by the gallon, but I found it utterly vile.

"I have the paperwork right here, Glen. All you have to do, my lovely boy, is sign on the dotted line, and the part is yours."

I removed a pile of long-defunct theatre programmes before settling on a chair. "Er, I'd like a few details before putting pen to paper, Eric."

"Delighted, Glen. *De*-lighted." Eric proceeded to give the relevant information. This was a TV drama, to be shown on an independent channel. He named a producer and director, both whom I'd worked with before, and a leading lady, whom I'd met and found charming. All this seemed to pass muster, but I still couldn't believe it. There had to be a catch somewhere.

"Eric." I tried to keep the elation out of my voice. "Can I just get this straight? A TV drama?"

"Correct."

"And I'm in it – in the title role?"

"Spot on, darling boy."

"Me? Glen Preston? Not getting me confused with someone else?"

"Glen Preston's the name on the contract in front of me."

"What's the show called?"

"Eh? Oh, *'The Man Who Ran and Ran'*."

"And I'm this running man?" The elation was starting to evaporate, although Eric was beaming from ear to ear.

"Absolutely."

"And from whom am I running?"

"Oh, a mysterious killer, who's out to get you."

This was beginning to sound as if I'd been here before. "And where am I running to? Into the arms of a beautiful woman?" (The leading lady would be nice).

As if.

Eric was suddenly looking uncomfortable. "Er – well, no-o. Um, you get shot in the back, and then the opening title sequence rolls."

"Ah."

"But…"

"Yes?"

"You may appear later on in one or two flashbacks."

"Oh, really? One? Or two?"

"Um, we-ell, the writer's not *quite* sure at present."

In other words, he'd write them in, and they'd be edited out.

Déja vu.

Eric looked hurt. I took pity on him, as always. I signed the contract. Bottom line was, I had some work again. Eric promised to have something else lined up once I'd finished getting shot in the back again. Another tour, perhaps? Well, why not? I couldn't afford to rule anything out. We shook hands, and I told him to keep trying.

Because he was always trying.

However, as I left, I felt a bit different. Not quite so ordinary; not quite so useless. Life wasn't bad.

Roz and Perry were back together: I thought there was a good chance they'd stay that way.

Perry in a full-time job. Morgan's impending recovery.

Marla's redemption.

And Glen Preston in a title role? Well, it was a beginning…

Michael Limmer is the author of five mystery thrillers, of which *Marla* is the latest. All are available from Amazon. He is also a short story writer of both mystery and Christian fiction. All profits and royalties from the sales of his work are shared between three Christian charities.

If you've enjoyed this book, please visit Mike's website at *mikesmysteries.co.uk*

PAST DECEIVING

Aidan Verney is recuperating in a small Devonshire village. When two suspicious deaths occur, he finds himself drawn into a mystery, the answer to which lies far back in the past, and menaced by an unscrupulous killer who's very much in the present…

TIME KNOWS NO PITY

Down the helter-skelter of the years, Luke Stone would always carry with him that last glimpse of her pale face, so breathtakingly beautiful, so incontrovertibly dead…

Both titles available from Amazon as paperback and e-book.

Printed in Great Britain
by Amazon

16530515R00119